G'DAY TO DIE

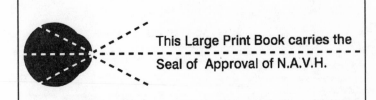

A PASSPORT TO PERIL MYSTERY

G'DAY TO DIE

MADDY HUNTER

WHEELER PUBLISHING

An imprint of Thomson Gale, a part of The Thomson Corporation

THOMSON
————✳————™
GALE

Detroit • New York • San Francisco • New Haven, Conn. • Waterville, Maine • London

THOMSON
✦ ™
GALE

LIBRARY OF CONGRESS CATALOGING-IN-PUBLICATION DATA

Hunter, Maddy.
　　G'day to die : a passport to peril mystery / by Maddy Hunter.
　　　p. cm. — (Wheeler Publishing large print cozy mystery)
　　ISBN-13: 978-1-59722-437-6 (softcover : alk. paper)
　　ISBN-10: 1-59722-437-5 (softcover : alk. paper)
　　1. Tour guides (Persons) — Fiction. 2. Older people — Iowa — Fiction. 3. Tourists — Fiction. 4. Women biologists — Crimes against — Fiction. 5. Australia — Fiction. 6. Large type books. I. Title.
PS3608.U5944G33 2007
813'.6—dc22　　　　　　　　　　　　　　　　　　2006037326

Published in 2007 by arrangement with Pocket Books, a division of Simon & Schuster, Inc.

Printed in the United States of America on permanent paper
10 9 8 7 6 5 4 3 2 1

To Aunt Kelly —
Who has always been there for me
when I've needed her most.
This book couldn't have been written
without you, Auntie!
Love you —

mmh

CHAPTER 1

If you were to ask your average American to locate the West Coast on a map, he'd rap a knuckle on California. If you were to ask your average Australian the same question, he'd slap his hand over the lower right hand corner of his country to indicate Victoria — a state whose *southern* border flanks the sea, but whose landlocked western border is a whopping fifteen hundred miles away from Australia's *actual* west coast. Which, comparatively speaking, makes it the geographical equivalent of Iowa.

There's a simple explanation for this anomaly.

It's Australia. It's complicated.

We'd spent our first full day Down Under motoring along Victoria's Great Ocean Road, a one-hundred-sixty mile, two-lane, roller coaster of a highway with panoramic views of the Southern Ocean's golden beaches, pounding surf and wind-tortured bluffs. In the late afternoon we'd arrived at Port Campbell National Park so we could ooh and ahh over the chimney stacks of rock that rise from the sea like gigantic lumps of coal. Our travel brochure refers to these craggy monoliths as, "The Twelve Apostles," and they were nothing short of spectacular. With the fearsome Southern Ocean gnawing at their base and the sun gilding them with blinding light, they were the most dazzling natural wonder I'd seen in my fifteen month stint as a tour escort.

"What a gyp," Bernice Zwerg grated in her ex-smoker's voice. She crab-walked over to me as we gathered inside the protective shelter of the visitor center, waiting to re-board our tour bus.

"Why is it a gyp?" I wasn't surprised by Bernice's negative reaction to one of Australia's most breathtaking landmarks. Bernice hated everything.

She held up her travel brochure and squinted at me down the length of her blue-zinc-oxide-covered nose. It was January, the height of summer in Australia, so all the seniors in my group were taking measures to prevent sunburn. Bernice's nose matched her sandals today, a striking example of how fashion savvy she'd become since her bunion surgery.

"Twelve Apostles? Did anyone bother to count them? There's only eight. I paid to see twelve, so I'm looking into my future and seeing — refund."

"Maybe the Aussies have a different numbering system," offered Helen Teig as she dragged her three-hundred-pound frame toward us. She used her travel brochure to fan her face, which had turned candy-apple red in the hundred-degree heat and body-battering wind. "Maybe 'twelve' to them is 'eight' to us."

Bernice rolled her eyes. "That's the dumbest thing I ever heard. Hey, you." She thwacked the arm of a ruggedly good-looking tour guest whose pale green bush outfit and wide-brimmed Akubra hat hinted that he was either a homegrown Aussie or a seasoned *Travelsmith* shopper. His name tag identified him as Heath Acres. She flashed three fingers before his face. "How many fingers am I holding up?"

"Wot's she want to know?" shrieked the grizzled gnome of a woman who clung to his arm.

"She wants to know how mini fingahs she's holding up," he said in a vowel-altering

Crocodile Dundee twang that labeled him as a local.

"Why? Can't she count?" The little woman fixed Bernice with an impatient look. "Three fingers. Wot are you? Stupid?" The woman's hair was a wild, windblown cotton ball. Her eyes were pinpricks of brilliant blue in a face so deeply seamed with wrinkles that she looked as if she'd spent the last thousand years smoking Marlboros in the desert. I suppressed an uneasy shudder as I studied her face. Oh, my God. I was on a two-week tour of Australia with the world's oldest living human.

"Excuse me. There used to be twelve," said a tall, chestnut-haired, middle-aged man in neatly pressed walking shorts and sandals. "Unfortunately, time hasn't treated them kindly. Four of them have collapsed into the sea, and there's another that looks to be on the verge." He punched a button on the fancy digital camera that hung around his neck and angled the display screen toward us, poking the screen with his forefinger. "This one here. Did you notice? The base has been all but eroded away. In another few years there may only be seven."

The Magnificent Seven," said Helen, hand splayed over her ample bosom. "I loved that movie. Yul Brynner was so . . . so . . ."

"Bald," snapped the thousand-year-old woman.

"As a bowling ball," agreed Helen. "Yul was a real trendsetter when it came to hairstyles."

"Those are some great pictures," Bernice allowed as she hovered over the man's camera. "I've got a digital camera. How come my shots don't look like yours?"

Whoa! Had an actual compliment just escaped Bernice's mouth? Grab your bobsleds; hell had officially frozen over.

"I'd better be a halfway-decent photographer," the man said, laughing. "It's how I make my living. Guy Madelyn." He gave her a smile that animated his face. "Weddings are my specialty, so if you're ever in the market for a high-priced wedding photographer, I'm your guy. Pun intended."

Bernice peered up at him, doe-eyed. She gave her name tag a demure touch and her stubby eyelashes a seductive flutter. "I'm Bernice. Did I mention I'm a widow?"

She was twice his age and half his height, with a dowager's hump that rivaled Ayers Rock. Oh, yeah. That was gonna fly.

"I got pictures!" Nana shuffled toward me in her size five sneakers. She was wearing a duckbill visor, white capri pants, and a shell pink T-shirt embroidered with flowers, songbirds, and the words, IOWA'S NO. 1 GRAMMA. My brother Steve's family had splurged last Christmas and bought her one in every color, which had aroused a bit of envy among her friends. T-shirts bearing the words *Best, Greatest,* or *No. 1* were all the rage at the senior center.

"You wanna see, dear?" She handed me a fistful of Polaroids, narrating as I flipped through them. "That's the wooden walkway leadin' to the lookout points. And there's them scrubby bushes growin' beside it. Don't know how that pink flower ever managed to sprout up in the middle of all them brambles, but it sure is pretty. That's Dick Stolee after the wind blew his baseball cap off his head." She lowered her voice to a whisper. "I was waitin' to shoot the expression on his face when his toupee flew off, but it just sat there. It was pretty disappointin'. He must be springin' for better glue than what he was usin' in Switzerland."

Guy Madelyn craned his neck to peek at Nana's shots. "Have you tried a digital camera? I'm sold on mine."

"Already got one," Nana said, "but it's too much fuss. Pricey batteries. Pricey memory cartridges. Pricey photo paper. Monkeyin' with every picture you download. So I'm back to my Polaroid. Pixels might be the in thing, but I'll take instant gratification any day."

I flipped to a photo of an isolated limestone tower.

"Can you guess which apostle that is, dear? I think it's a real good likeness."

Bernice burst into laughter. "The rocks don't have names, Marion. Someone called them the Twelve Apostles as a marketing gimmick."

"That's St. Peter," Nana continued, "and the puny one in the next shot is Judas. You can tell 'cause it looks more sneaky than them others."

"Which one's Dopey?" asked eighty-nine-year-old Osmond Chelsvig, hobbling over to us on the bone white spindles that were his legs.

Osmond's inability to distinguish dwarfs from apostles wasn't surprising, considering he hailed from a long line of agnostics.

"Excuse me." Guy Madelyn was suddenly at Nana's elbow. "Would you mind if I take a closer look at your photos? You seem to have captured some unique angles that I missed entirely."

"No kiddin'?" She handed the stack over, smiling broadly as he examined every snapshot. "I didn't think they was so special, but the light here's real bright, so it makes everything look good."

"You're being modest. The Australian light isn't what makes your shots so outstanding. It's your composition. Your contrast. Look at this shot." He flashed it at the handful of guests circled around us. "You've turned an ordinary pink flower into something extraordinary. And on a Polaroid camera, no less. You have an incredible eye." He lowered his gaze to her name tag. "Marion Sippel, eh? I'm not familiar with your name or your work, but tell me I'm right in assuming you're a professional."

Nana gave a little suck on her dentures. "I do have some professional trainin'."

"I knew it. Where did you study? The Royal College of Art? The Brooks Institute?"

"Windsor City Senior Center. They run a two-hour minicourse last November. It was real in depth."

He let out a belly laugh. "You took pictures like *this* with only two hours of training?"

"It was s'posed to be four, but we run into a schedulin' conflict with the low-vision group's Christmas cookie and pickled herrin' exchange."

He shook his head, awe in his voice. "Mrs. Sippel, if you'll allow me an unbiased opinion, these photos are nothing short of Ansel Adams caliber. I'm speechless."

"Lemme see those," said Bernice, snatching the stack from his hand.

"Me, too," said Helen Teig, grabbing a fistful from Bernice.

"Careful!" Guy shouted as Nana's photos made the circuit, passing from hand to hand. "Don't get your fingerprints on them. Have a quick look, then give them back."

Amid the buzz of enthusiasm, he turned back to Nana. "Have you ever thought of turning professional, Mrs. Sippel? Hollywood glitterati are willing to pay ridiculous amounts for wedding photos these days, and the photographer they're clamoring for is me. But I'm having trouble going solo. Too many remarriages to keep up with. I've been looking to hire another photographer, but I haven't found anyone suitable — until today. Are you available? I'd start you out as an apprentice, but with your talent, I could probably guarantee you a six-figure salary."

A hush descended over the crowd. Limbs froze. Mouths fell open.

Bernice hit a button on her digital camera and shoved it in Guy's face. "I take some pretty good pictures myself. See here? What do you think of that contrast? And look at

this one. Have you ever seen better composition?"

"My Dick takes better pictures than that,"
Helen claimed. "DICK! WHERE ARE
YOU? GET OVER HERE!"

"I've taken some mighty fine pictures,"
said Osmond, elbowing Bernice out of the
way. He angled his camcorder display screen
in front of Guy. "My scenery's moving, but
if you see anything you like, I'd be happy to
freeze-frame it for you."

"This is Mushroom!" cried Margi Swanson, waving a snapshot of her cat in the air.
"I took it myself. You think I have potential?"

"Get out the way!" snarled the thousand-
year-old woman as she pushed toward Guy.
"I've got a photo for you."

I stood on tiptoes to sneak a peek at the
sepia-toned picture she handed him. The
print might once have been glossy, but time
and touch had dog-eared the corners and
dulled the finish so much that all I could
see was an irregular pattern of creases cob-
webbing an image that was no longer clear.

Guy studied it for a long moment in the
manner of one accustomed to handling
other people's photographic treasures. "A
lovely picture," he said kindly. "But if you
want to preserve it, I'd suggest a frame

rather than a wallet. Or perhaps a photo-restoration process. They'd have this looking good as new in no time."

"Come along, luvy," said the young man in the bush outfit, tugging on the crone's arm. He retrieved the print from Guy and gave him an appreciative wink. "Photo of her mum. You know how that goes, mate. She shows it to everyone."

"No problem. Would everyone please start handing Mrs. Sippel's photos back? I don't want to lose track of any."

Bodies shifted. Elbows flew. I got jostled left and right and suddenly found myself ejected from the crowd like a stray pinball. I skidded to a stop on my new ankle-strap wedges and looked back at the melee. Geesch! Who'd have guessed that one teensy compliment could start such a feeding frenzy?

"Emily!"

I looked across the room to find a man beckoning to me. But this was no ordinary man. This was Etienne Miceli, the Swiss police inspector I'd fantasized about marrying.

"Come join us!" shouted his companion.

And this was no any ordinary companion. This was Duncan Lazarus, the doggedly persistent tour director who fantasized

17

about marrying *me.* The two men had become "buds" since they'd met two months ago and seemed to be enjoying the kind of intense male friendship that's so ballyhooed among Marines, fraternity brothers, and belching-contest finalists.

"Be there in a sec," I shouted back, still unnerved by the prospect of juggling both of them for the next fourteen days. But this had been their idea. They insisted on going head to head on a level playing field, like players in a *Survivor* challenge, and no argument on my part could change their minds. So here they were, vying for me as if I were the lone bucket of chicken wings on an island whose only other food source was sand flies. This pretty much confirmed something I'd been unwilling to admit until now.

I hated reality TV.

As I marshaled my courage to join my two suitors, the crowd encircling Guy spat out another guest who came hurtling straight toward me. "Eh!" I cried, sidestepping her before her sturdy Birkenstocks creamed my open-toed wedges.

"Oops! Sorry." She paused for breath, shivering as she stared back at the mob. "I didn't mean to get caught in the middle of that." She patted down her oversized blouse and hiking shorts as if taking inventory, before flashing me a smile. "I've never seen people get so maniacal over photographs. I specialize in chopping off heads, so I don't even own a camera. I learned long ago that postcards are the way to go. I'm Claire Bellows, and you're obviously not part of the Aussie Adventures tour since you're not wearing a name tag."

I returned her smile. "Emily Andrew. I'm part of the tour, I just don't do name tags."

"I like that idea." She removed her ID and stuffed it into her breast pocket before wiping beads of perspiration from her brow. "We're not schoolkids, right? I hate name tags, and I'll be stuck wearing one for a whole week after the tour is over."

"Conference?"

"Yeah. Scientific meeting in Melbourne. How 'bout you?"

"I'm on the job as we speak. Official escort for a group of Iowa seniors who are in the middle of that mob over there."

"So you're not alone?" Claire Bellows reminded me a little of Rosie O'Donnell — dark-haired and heavy-legged, with a directness that oozed confidence. "I always travel alone. When you're by yourself, other tourists feel sorry for you, so they adopt you.

19

It's a great way to meet new people. If I keep at it, I figure I'm bound to run into Mr. Right one of these days. Are you married?"

"I used to be." I let out a sigh. "It's a long story."

"I've never been married. I'm thirty-seven years old, on a career track that has my head pressed against the original glass ceiling, and unless I can reinvent the wheel and wow my company's CEO, that's where I'll be stuck until I'm ready to hang up my lab coat. So I've officially entered the marriage market." She wiggled ten brightly polished nails. "I even got a manicure to kick off the event. First one in my life. I want it all — husband, two-point-three kids, dog, gas-guzzling SUV. I hit the snooze button on my biological clock when I started work and the alarm is about to go off, so I'm pulling out all the stops. Guaranteed, I'll be walking down the aisle in the next few months." She nodded emphatically and glanced around the room as if scouting out likely prospects. "Do you have time to date much?"

"Um . . . dating is a problem."

She opened her collar wider, fanning herself with the placket. "Well, don't be surprised by what you find when you get back into the dating scene. If you don't have good instincts, you're going to end up disappointed." She bobbed her head toward Etienne and Duncan. "You see those two hunks over there by the window? Case in point. The two best-looking men on the tour, and they're taken."

My neck grew warm with self-conscious guilt, but in my own defense, *this wasn't my fault!* I wasn't flaunting them like trophies. I hadn't even invited them to join me on the tour! What was I supposed to do? Send one of them home? They hadn't even bothered to buy cancellation insurance!

Claire let out an anguished moan. "It never fails. The gorgeous guys are always gay."

I jerked my head around to stare at her. "What?"

A gust of wind whistled through the room as our guide banged through the main entrance, his navy blue uniform putting him in danger of being mistaken for a United States Postal Service worker. His name was Henry, and in addition to narrating our travelogue, he drove the bus, prepared and served midmorning tea and cakes, directed us to the restrooms, counted heads, snapped guest photos, maintained our vehicle, treated minor injuries, exchanged currency, and could belt out a rendition of "Waltzing Matilda" that made your teeth vibrate. I was dying to see what he'd do for an encore.

"If I can trouble you for your attintion!" he called out. "I apologize to those of you waiting to board the Aussie Advintures bus, but one of our tires has blown, so I'm waiting on a mechanic from Port Campbell for assistance. No worries, though; we'll only be delayed an hour or two. Sorry for the inconvenience."

Groans. Hissing. "What are we supposed to do for two hours?" a disgruntled guest yelled.

"Introduce yoursilf to your mates!" Henry suggested. "You're in this for two weeks togither. Give it a go."

Claire gave my arm a squeeze. "I'm a little stiff, so I'm going outside to walk off the kinks and check out a minor curiosity. See you on the bus."

"But wait —" I sputtered as she broke for the door, followed by a slew of other guests. I had to set her straight about Etienne and Duncan before her imaginings became grist for the rumor mill. If there was one thing I'd learned in Ireland, it was to nip a vicious rumor in the bud before it had a chance to blossom.

Battening my hair down with a bandanna, I signaled Etienne and Duncan that I had to leave, then exited the building, bracing myself against the brutal force of the wind.

The sky was electric blue, the sun so hot that it rippled the air. I shivered at the hostile acres of briars and brush that stubbled the cliff top, then stepped onto the slatted walkway that knifed through them, noting the frequent signs that cautioned visitors to PLEASE REMAIN ON THE WALK-WAY. Oh, sure. Like there was someone on the planet who'd willingly stray *off* it?

I spied Claire and the other guests a city block away, hustling full speed ahead in spite of the heat and head wind. I couldn't chase her down in my five-inch stacked heels, so I trudged behind for an exhausting five minutes, cursing when I reached the brow of the cliff, where the walkway split into a T.

I squinted east and west, wondering which way she and everyone else had gone. Nuts! This called for serious deductive reasoning. *Eenie, meenie, meinie, moe . . .*

Interrupted by the sudden clatter of footsteps behind me, I turned to find Guy Madelyn hiking my way. "The wind's a pain," he called out, his shirttails flapping around him, "but at least it keeps the flies from tunneling up your nose." He paused beside me and nodded seaward. "Did you know that if you leaped off this cliff and started swimming south, you wouldn't run into another landmass until you reached Antarctica?"

"Assuming you leaped at high tide."

He raised his forefinger in a "Eureka!" kind of gesture. "Timing is everything. I'm sorry, I didn't catch your name in the visitor's center."

"Emily Andrew. You want to hire my grandmother as your new crack photographer."

"Mrs. Sippel is your grandmother? She has some fine photographic genes. Did she pass them on to you?"

"I got the shoe and makeup genes." I regarded him soberly as he opened the lens of his camera. "Were you serious about wanting to hire Nana?"

"I'll say! And I'd like to sign her up before the competition finds out about her." He scanned the horizon through his viewfinder before motioning me toward the guardrail. "Could I get a shot of you with the great Southern Ocean as a backdrop? I don't charge for my services when I'm on holiday."

Was I about to be discovered? Oh, wow. I

might not have made it as an actress, but could Guy Madelyn transform me into a cover model?

I struck a pose against the guardrail and emoted like a *Sports Illustrated* swimsuit model. Sexy. Sultry. Windblown.

"Can you open your eyes?"

I tried again. Sexy. Surprised. Windblown.

"Maybe we should try this from one of the lookout points. We're getting too much light here."

Which I interpreted to mean, it was a good thing I was otherwise employed, because I had no future as a cover model.

"So you're not here to shoot a wedding?" I asked as I walked double time to keep up with his long strides.

"Family reunion. It seems the Madelyn side of my family played as important a role in Australian history as the *Mayflower* passengers played in American history, so when my wife and kids fly out from Vancouver in a couple of weeks, we're planning to meet all the Aussie relatives for the first time. The kids are really fired up, which is remarkable since they're at the age where nothing impresses them. But I think they're finding the idea of celebrity status for a few days 'way cool.'"

"Because they're related to a famous photographer?"

He laughed. "Because the town is planning to honor us with an award to recognize the contribution my ancestors made toward populating this part of Victoria. We've dubbed it the Breeder's Cup. The kids figure we'll be the only family in British Columbia with a commemorative plaque for inveterate shagging, so that gives them bragging rights. Kids, eh?"

Noticing a discarded candy wrapper littering the wayside, I ducked beneath the guardrail to pick it up, frowning when I realized what I was holding. "This is one of Nana's photos. What's it doing out here?" It was bent, and a little scratched, but in good shape otherwise. I showed it to Guy, who threw a curious look around us.

"I was positive all your grandmother's photos found their way back to her. People can be so damned careless. I hope this is the only one she's missing."

"Dumb luck that I found it." I slipped it into my shoulder bag for safekeeping. "So, where did your ancestors emigrate from? England?" I knew everyone in Australia was an import, except for the Aborigines, who'd been roaming the continent for either four centuries or sixty thousand years, depend-

26

ing upon which scholarly study you wanted to believe. Yup. The scientific community had really nailed that one.

"Portsmouth. They set sail in the early eighteen hundreds on a ship called the *Meridia,* and fifteen thousand miles later wrecked on a submerged reef along this very coast. My relatives were among the lucky few who survived." He bobbed his head toward the open sea. "Look at all that water. If you took it away, do you know what you'd find? Sunken vessels. Over twelve hundred of them. More than anywhere else on earth. This whole place is a graveyard, which hammers home a very salient point."

"What's that?"

"Air travel is a wonderful thing."

We followed the walkway through a stand of trees that were as stunted and gnarled as Halloween ghouls, then descended a short flight of stairs to a lower level with sweeping views of the deeply scalloped coastline and the thundering —

Guy suddenly ducked beneath the guard-rail and charged through the underbrush, heading straight for the cliff's edge. Eh! Were Iowans the only people who ever observed the rules?

"What are you doing?" I screamed after

him. "Didn't you read the signs? You're supposed to stay on the walkway!"

He dropped to his knees twenty feet away
and rolled something over.

Oh, God. It was a body.

CHAPTER 2

"What do you s'pose she was lookin' for?" asked Nana, her nose pressed to the visitor center window.

"A husband," I said as we watched two officials load a body bag into the rear of a van labeled — CORONER — CITY OF WARRNAMBOOL.

I'd run back to the visitor center after Guy made his discovery and tracked down Henry, who'd punched a number into his cell phone before dashing off with his medical kit. When emergency vehicles started screaming into the parking lot, I gave the police and paramedics directions to the site, then joined the other guests in the climate-controlled visitor center to await the outcome. With speculation about the nature of Claire Bellows's injury running rampant, Osmond Chelsvig conducted an independent poll of our Iowa contingent and announced the results with the same giddy excitement that overtook him during off-year school board elections.

"Broken leg gets six votes. Diabetic coma gets one vote. Head trauma gets two votes. Ingrown toenail gets one vote. And, 'She's faking it to draw attention to herself' gets one vote."

We all threw disgusted looks at Bernice, who crossed her arms defensively. "You can't prove that was me. That's the beauty of secret ballots."

When the coroner's van pulled into the parking lot an hour later, I realized that all of us had been wrong. Claire Bellows was more than injured.

Claire Bellows was dead.

"She might have succumbed to heat-stroke," suggested Tilly Hovick, who leaned heavily on her walking stick as she observed the activity in the parking lot. "I believe that in extreme circumstances, heatstroke can cause death. If she was sensitive to the sun, she should have had an umbrella, though in this wind, an umbrella would be about as practical as flip-flops in the Arctic."

"I bet she died of thirst," said Lucille Rassmuson, whose fluorescent pink muu-muu made her look like a pitcher of cherry Kool-Aid. "I thought I was going to die of thirst myself when I was out in that heat."

"People don't die from thirst," Margi Swanson corrected helpfully. "They die from dehydration. We've treated a few cases at the clinic. Would you like me to explain the physiology to you?"

"NO!" a chorus of voices sang out.

"I'll till you what killed her," rasped an unfamiliar voice in an Australian drawl. "Nature." With his accent, it came out, "Naycha."

He strode into our midst with testosterone-laced swagger, hooking his thumbs into his belt loops as he squinted at each of us. He was wearing a tank top, shorts, thick socks, and boots that looked as if they'd kicked around a construction site for decades. His face was the color of tree bark, seamed and unshaven, and on a leather string around his neck hung a tooth the size of my baby finger. Probably one of his own. His name tag read, JAKE SILVER-THORN.

"My giss is taipan," he said around the toothpick that was wedged in the corner of his mouth. "Didliest snake on earth. There's only one good thing about being bitten by a taipan."

"Would that be that there's an antitoxin available at local pharmacies?" asked Tilly.

"You die quick. Though some say, not

quick enough."

It suddenly grew so quiet, I could hear sweat popping out on everyone's upper lip. "How quick?" asked seventy-six-year-old Alice Tjarks in a voice much more tentative than the one she used to announce the daily farm reports on KORN radio.

"Two minutes. Four, tops. The most agonizing four minutes you'll ever spind."

I stared down at my open-toed wedges with the ankle straps and wondered if I should reconsider my footwear options.

"The taipan's a northern vipah," Jake went on in his growlly voice. "But there's three million square miles of imptiness around us, most of it unexplored, so no one really knows what's out there. Taipan's niveh been spotted in Victoria, but that doesn't mean it's not here." His toothpick bobbed as he stretched his mouth into a knowing grin. "Or maybe it was a ridback that bit her."

"What's a redback?" asked Margi.

He made a tarantula of his hand and wiggled it in the air like a hand puppet. "An eight-ligged killing machine."

Nervous twitters. Gasps. Dick Teig burped.

"Your ridback isn't the worst of its kind. One nip by a Sydney funnel wib and you're looking at instantaneous dith, but a ridback toys with you a bit. If he gives you a nip, you can look forward to a few minutes of frinzied twitching before you discharge every fluid in your body and die a grisly death."

Snakebite? Spider bite? *Uff da.* Dying from thirst was looking better by the minute.

Tilly waggled her cane in the air. "Is the redback indigenous to this part of Victoria?"

"The buggeh breeds especially will in Victoria." He looked down at his feet and cracked a smile. "Why do you think I wear boots?"

"Is Imily Andrew here?" a man called from the doorway.

Recognizing him as one of the officials from the coroner's office, I hurried over to him. "I'm Emily."

He was a well-built guy around my age who had a Mel Gibson thing going with his looks, which made me wonder if all Australian males were six feet tall and gorgeous. He nodded politely and flashed his ID badge. "Peter Blunt. Warrnambool Coroner's Office. I apologize for the interruption, but I need to ask you a few quistions. I promise it won't take long." He opened a pocket-size spiral notebook and readied a ballpoint. "You were with Mr. Madelyn when he discovered the body?"

I nodded. "I stopped to admire the scenery near one of the lookout points and was stunned when Guy took off into the underbrush, ignoring all the posted signs. I didn't see the body until he fell to his knees, and that's when I ran back here for help. I'm afraid my participation ends there."

"Did you know Ms. Bellows?"

"I spoke to her for a few minutes before she left the visitor center, but that was the first and last time. The tour only began yesterday, so none of us have had much of a chance to chat yet."

"Was she complaining of any ailments? Dizziness? Pain?"

"She said she was a little stiff. And she looked pretty hot."

"Thirty-eight degrees Cilsius will do that to you. We're having an unusual bad spill of heat. A sorry wilcome for you, isn't it? Have you any idea why she might have lift the boardwalk?"

"She told me she wanted to check out a minor curiosity while the bus was being repaired."

"Did she say what?"

"I didn't ask, and she didn't say."

"That's the thing about the Shipwrick

Coast," he said matter-of-factly. "It's such an awesome sight that tourists niveh tire of exploring it. There's some blokes who won't rist until they see every wind shift and tidal change. Tourists use up more film here than anywhere ilse in Victoria." He flipped his notebook shut. "Thanks for your hilp, Ms. Andrew."

"No more questions?"

"That's it."

"So you don't think foul play was involved?"

He eyed me curiously. "We didn't find any evidince to indicate a crime had been committed."

"Oh, thank God!" I grabbed his forearm and squeezed gratefully. "You don't know how happy I am to hear that." Given the number of bodies I'd stumbled upon on my last four trips abroad, I was relieved that Claire's death didn't smack of homicide, but the fact that her dreams of a husband, children, and a gas-guzzling SUV would never be fulfilled left me oddly dispirited. "So, what happens now?"

"Postmortem. She might have had a preexisting condition that contributed to her dith, so that's what we'll be looking for. Hilthy adults don't collapse and die for no reason."

I sidled a look at Jake Silverthorn and lowered my voice as if I were sharing an original thought. "Do you suppose she might have been bitten by, say, a poisonous snake or spider?"

Peter bowed his head close to mine, and said in a knowing undertone, "You've rid the book, haven't you?"

"Book?"

"The Big Golden Book of Reptiles, Insects, and Marine Life that Can Kill You in Australia."

I stared at him, deadpan. "There's a whole book?"

"It used to be an encyclopedia, but they condinsed it into an abridged coffee table edition with great color illustrations. It only lists the didliest buggehs, so you don't have to waste time looking at the ones that give you more than an hour to live."

A whole hour. Imagine. You'd have time for a pedicure before you kicked off.

"But if you ask me, the thrit is way over-blown. The last time I saw a report of someone dying from a snake or spider bite was an eon ago."

"How much of an eon?" I asked. "Ten years? Twenty?"

"Two weeks. But I'm talking about the whole country."

"Thanks for your patience!" Henry's voice

reverberated through the room. "Our bus is back in working order so I'd appreciate your boarding as soon as possible. I'm hoping to make up time on our way back, so instid of stopping for dinner en route, I'll order boxed lunches and lit you eat on the bus. That way you'll still be on time for our 'Meet and Greet' back at the hotel. So sorry for the inconvenience, mates. Really."

As the room began to empty, Peter urged me out the door. "Would you mind walking to the van with me so I can give you a business card? If you recall anything in the nixt few days that might be of use in our invistigation, ring me up."

He removed a card from the vehicle's glove compartment and scribbled something on the back. "This is my cill number, in case you need to reach me at home. You niveh know when those memories are going to kick in." He handed me the card, smiling with straightforward interest. "I don't suppose your tour group has accommodations anywhere around Warrnambool."

My voice dripped apology. "I'm afraid we're staying in Melbourne."

"My loss. I could have shown you sights along the Great Ocean Road that the guidebooks haven't even found."

"Riddy when you are, Peter," the other official said as he climbed into the passenger's side of the van.

I waited until they drove away, then crossed to the parking lot where our bus was being given a final once-over by the Port Campbell mechanic and a male audience high on testosterone.

Men were so predictable. A guy might not know a jackhammer from M.C. Hammer, but if he hears the far-off buzz of a drill or saw, he'll be out the door, tracking down the sound like a mountain man tracking bear. Once he locates the source, he bonds with the other guys who show up with ritual grunting, scratching, drinking, and standing around being useless. A lot of people think it's team sports that form the cornerstone of male relationships, but it's not.

It's power tools.

I found Etienne and Duncan on the shaded side of the bus, watching sweaty, windblown tour guests climb aboard — Etienne with his black hair, Windex blue eyes, and one percent body fat, and Duncan with his football player's physique, too-long blond hair, and dark brown eyes. I never failed to be struck by how opposite they were, and not just in looks. "How can you stand out here in the heat?" I swiped away the moisture that was drizzling down my temples. "Aren't you dying?"

"Bella." Etienne lifted my hand to his mouth and kissed my fingers. Duncan gave my hair a playful ruffle.

"Hiya, pretty. You're right. It's hell out here, but the mechanic had a pneumatic wrench that was poetry in motion, so we had to check it out, didn't we, Miceli?"

Etienne spun me around into his arms and whispered seductively against my earlobe, "It's made of titanium and can withstand a thousand foot-pounds more torque than your average pneumatic wrench. It's the bomb."

I grinned. "Do you know what that means?"

"I believe it means the essence of perfection." His voice rang with boyish enthusiasm. "I have a new American slang dictionary."

"How does a police inspector learn about foot-pounds of torque?"

"It's not something I learned," he whispered against my neck. "It's part of the programming software that goes with the Y chromosome."

"Hey, Em," Duncan interrupted, "is that a bug on your foot?"

"BUG?" I shot out of Etienne's arms. "Where? Which foot?" I thrashed around and swatted blindly, pausing after a few panicky moments to look down. "Is it gone?"

Duncan gave me a serious once-over. "Yup. Looks like you got it." He braced an elbow on Etienne's shoulder. "What do you say, Miceli? Time to climb aboard?" He gave me a flirtatious wink, the twinkle in his eye making me wonder if there'd been a bug there in the first place. I looked suspiciously from one to the other. Fast friends, were they?

I fixed Etienne with a questioning look. "I'm surprised you didn't flash your credentials at the coroner so you could get in on the investigation."

A moment's uncertainty flickered in his eyes before he remembered to smile. "They seemed to have things well in hand. No sense making a nuisance of myself."

But he always wanted to be in on the action. What was up with that?

"Twenty-nine, thirty, thirty-one," said Henry as he included the three of us in his head count. "That leaves eleven gists missing." He glanced around the parking lot. "Always a few stragglers who muck up the works."

I imagined it was only coincidence that my Iowa contingent had exactly eleven members, but they couldn't possibly be the culprits. Without exception they were always first for everything — to arrive at breakfast, to be out the door, to board the bus so they could claim the good seats by the restroom. They might be old, but in any given foot-race, they always smoked the competition.

I scanned the windows at the rear of the bus to do a quick head count, aghast when I saw there *were* no heads, only rows of empty seats.

EH! They *were* the culprits! Oh, my God. Where were they?

I gave Henry's arm a frantic tug. "It's my group that's missing. This is *so* unlike them. They're never late. Ever. Something terrible must have happened to them."

He unholstered his cell phone. "No worries. I'll call emergency services again if you like."

Etienne grabbed my wrist and aimed me toward the visitor's center, motioning with his hand. "Is that one of your group in the window?"

I strained to see what he was pointing at. It was fluorescent pink and filled the entire window, which meant it had to be Lucille Rassmuson. Oh, thank God. "Hold off on the phone call," I instructed Henry. "I see them. I'll be right back."

I rushed into the visitor's center to find all eleven of them cowering by the window, bunched up like grapes. "Are you guys okay? Is someone hurt? *What* are you doing in here? The bus is about to leave!" And then I said something to them that no other person in the annals of history has ever said to a group of Iowans. "You're late. Do you hear me? L-A-T-E. Late!"

They stared back at me like zombies. Good Lord, what was wrong with them? "Guys?"

"Did you know that of the ten deadliest snakes in the world, all ten are Australian?" said Dick Teig in a strained whisper.

"And there's a seashell here that can kill you if the creature inside chomps down on you?" said Grace Stolee.

"And there's a rock with thorny spikes that can pierce shoe leather and shoot you full of enough toxin to turn your innards to creme brulée?" added Dick Stolee.

"It's not a rock," said Bernice. "It's a fish that looks like a rock."

"Oh, yeah?" Dick sputtered. "Well, I think *you* look like a rock."

"And there's a saltwater crocodile that can leap twenty feet out of the water and eat you in *one* ferocious bite," fretted Lucille, though in her case, it might be *two.*

"And there's a big bird in the rain forest that can split you open with one swipe of its claw," Osmond croaked. "It's like a can opener with wings."

Since no one was waving around *The Big Golden Book of Reptiles, Insects, and Marine Life that Can Kill You in Australia,* I figured all this sudden knowledge had originated in one place.

Nana regarded me anxiously. "Emily, dear, did you know there's more things that can kill you in Australia than anywhere else on earth? That fella what looks like the crocodile hunter was nice enough to give us the scoop."

Note to self: *Kill Jake Silverthorn.*

"Okay, gang," I said in the most soothing voice I could muster. "I think you might be overreacting a teensy bit."

"Tell that to the girl who keeled over out there in the underbrush," argued Dick Teig, his gaze riveted on the floor in an obvious search for killer insects with dinner plans.

"None of us would have signed up for this trip if Emily had told us how dangerous this place was," complained Bernice. "It's all her fault. No one wants to be insect bait for

43

the next two weeks. I say we go home. And we better get refunds!"

"Show of hands for how many people want to go home," asked Osmond.

"EEE-YAH!" yelled Dick Teig, stomping his foot on the floor so hard, the windows rattled. "Die, you cussed bug."

Dick Stolee sidled up to him. "What'd you kill?"

Dick lifted his sandal. "Dust bunny."

Dick Stolee nodded. "Looks like a poison one."

Section two, subparagraph three of my official *Escort's Manual* states that the savvy tour escort "will do everything in her power to place her guests' minds at ease so they can fully enjoy every moment of their tour experience." Unfortunately, subparagraph three offered no suggestions about how to do that, so I was going to have to ad lib my butt off.

"Listen to me, everyone: the only thing you're in mortal danger of is missing the bus. We're not walking on a beach, so you can't be attacked by seashells. We're not wading in the ocean, so you can't be stung by rocks. We're not visiting the Great Barrier Reef, so you can't be devoured by crocodiles. We're not exploring the rain forest, so you can't be ripped open by birds."

Alice Tjarks shot her hand into the air. "Excuse me, Emily, but what's left to see if you're not taking us to visit any of the exciting touristy stuff?"

"Yeah," sniped Helen Teig. "We expect to get our money's worth!"

"We didn't fly all the way over here to do everything on the cheap!" Dick Stolee protested.

Gee, that worked well. "You *will* get your money's worth. It's a big country. There's plenty left to see. But you won't see any of it unless you get on the bus."

Foot shuffling. Sighs. Indecisive looks. "What about snakes?" Margi called out.

"You only have to walk a short distance to the bus, and it's on pavement, so just watch where you're going. Australian snakes prefer to slither in the grass anyway." At least, I hoped they did.

"Does anyone have a weapon in case Emily is feeding us a line of bull?" asked Dick Stolee.

"Tilly has one," Bernice piped up. "Let her go in front. If she sees a snake, she can beat the crap out of it with her cane while the rest of us hightail it to the bus."

Nods. Smiles. Grunts of approval. In the

next half second Tilly got body-passed from the back to the front, and everyone bunched up in line behind her.

"Are you okay with this setup, Tilly?" I asked skeptically.

She stood pencil straight in her madras skirt and visor, looking stern and professorial. "I've faced giant dung beetles in Africa and black flies in Maine. I should be able to handle this." She rapped her walking stick on the floor. "Come along, people! Look lively, or you'll be using your opposable thumbs to get back to Melbourne."

They scuffed across the floor in a solid clump, as if they'd been Super-Glued. "Hey, we still have a vote pending about whether we're going home. Can I see a show of hands?" Osmond yelled, as they squeezed through the door.

I whipped out my camera and got off a shot, grinning, as they shuffled across the pavement in caterpillar formation. I could see the caption under the photo in my travel newsletter: TOGETHERNESS, AUSTRALIAN STYLE. I snapped another for good measure, suddenly reminded of what Peter Blunt had said.

He'd implied that tourists use up all their film shooting pictures of the Shipwreck Coast. But Claire told me she always cut off

46

the heads of her subjects, so she didn't even own a camera. So if she hadn't gone back out into the heat to take pictures, why *had* she gone out?

CHAPTER 3

I took an instant liking to Melbourne with its grandiose Victorian buildings, modern high-rises, and colorful electric trams. Back in the 1850s some guy with a lot of vision drew a blueprint for the city, so streets are laid out in an orderly grid that has "Iowa Highway System" written all over it. Even people without maps can't get lost.

Unlike Iowa, however, Melbourne leans toward the eclectic. For instance, our hotel was located on a quiet side street around the corner from an imposing stone government building, a five-star Pan-Asian restaurant, and a boutique with a tasteful display of whips, chains, and leather bras studded with metal spikes. Iowans are more discreet about specialty boutiques like this. They prefer them to be located in places that are more off the beaten path. Like . . . LA.

We'd made it back from Port Campbell with an hour to spare before our "Meet and

Greet," so after showering and restyling my hair, I zipped myself into a strapless black number with a peekaboo cutout in the back, slipped into stiletto slides, grabbed my shoulder bag, and rode the elevator to the lounge on the top floor.

The glass-enclosed room afforded dazzling bird's-eye views of Melbourne's darkening skyline and city lights. Henry sloshed punch into glasses at a buffet table, whistling slightly off-key to a tune that was being piped in over the stereo system. "Boogie Woogie Bugle Boy"? Hmm. Was it odd that we were in Australia's cultural epicenter, listening to America's greatest hits of World War II?

I took quick visual inventory, surprised when I found none of my crew in the conversational groupings scattered throughout the room. I tried to ignore a frisson of worry. Five minutes 'til showtime; they should be here by now. I hoped they weren't all cowering in their rooms, too scared to go out, or . . . or stockpiling bug killer. That stuff could blow like a grenade if exposed to extreme heat, and not to put too fine a point on it, but it was poison!

"Are you Emily?" asked a man who spoke with a hint of a foreign accent. "Conrad Carver," he said, shaking my hand. "I heard your name being called out at the Port Campbell visitor center. Did the coroner give you any idea what might have happened to the Bellows woman?"

I suspected the reason Conrad Carver looked familiar was because he had Albert Einstein's hair and mustache. He was short and slightly built, with a unibrow that looked like a happy victim of Miracle-Gro. "He couldn't tell me a thing, other than he'd be performing a postmortem."

"It's a terrible way to begin a holiday."

"I'll say." Especially for Claire. "Are you traveling by yourself, Conrad?"

"No, no. My wife is with me. If you want to know the truth, this is our anniversary trip." He smiled modestly. "Fifty years tomorrow."

"Congratulations!" I clapped him on the shoulder. "That's a great accomplishment, especially in this day and age." I couldn't place the accent. German? Russian?

"You must give all the credit to my wife for putting up with me all these years. The long work hours. The extended travel. The phone calls telling her I'd have to miss the children's birthdays, again."

"What kind of work did you do?"

"I was senior paleobotanist for the Smithsonian Institution, and in my spare time I wrote botany textbooks for universities."

Guy Madelyn motioned to us with his camera. "Do you mind? I'd like to get shots of everyone."

"Why don't you take one of Conrad with his wife?" I suggested, stepping out of the way. "An anniversary photo. Where's your wife, Conrad?"

"Maybe later with my wife," he said, hooking an eager arm around my waist and yanking me close. "Say, cheese."

Guy pressed the shutter.

Etienne strode toward us, giving me a long, lingering look up and down. "Love the dress, what there is of it."

"Is this your wife?" Conrad asked, quickly dropping his arm.

Etienne flashed a slow smile. "She could be. All she has to do is say something other than, 'I need time to think about it.' "

Conrad looked me in the eye. "A handsome young man asks for your hand, and you don't say yes?"

"I brought you some punch, Em," Duncan interrupted, cutting in front of Etienne to hand me a glass. "The dress rocks. What's it made of? Spandex?" He planted a kiss on my bare shoulder, then lowered his hand to the peekaboo cutout at the small of my back, grazing his fingertips over the triangle of exposed skin. "Nice."

Guy stepped forward and introduced himself to Etienne and Duncan with enthusiastic handshakes. "Could I drag you gentlemen over by the window so I can get a few photos of you against the lights of the Melbourne skyline?" He studied both of them with narrowed gaze. "Interesting bone structure. I bet . . . Never mind. We'll see how it turns out. Do you mind?"

"Happy to be accommodating," said Duncan.

Etienne hesitated before nodding agreement. He threw me a meaningful look. "Don't move, *bella*. I'll be right back."

Conrad wagged a crooked forefinger at me. "I know now why you haven't said yes to the dark-haired man. The light-haired man is also in love with you. Every woman wants to be beautiful, but for the ones who are, it must sometimes feel like a curse."

Ooo, I liked this guy!

"Which one will you choose?"

I sighed my frustration. "Here's the thing, Conrad: last November I conducted a test that was supposed to resolve all my doubts about which man was the one for me, and it failed miserably."

"Both gentlemen flunked?"

"They both passed! It proved they're both

kind, generous, wonderful people, so I'm back to dithering again. And I hate to dither, but this decision is going to affect the rest of my life, so I have to be sure."

Conrad appeared fascinated. "I've never conducted a scientific test that involved human participation. What was the most difficult problem you faced?"

"Eating all the maraschino cherries they both piled onto my ice cream sundae. I get a stomachache just thinking about it."

As the background music changed to a rollicking rendition of "When Johnny Comes Marching Home," I saw my group straggle into the lounge as if their energy gauges were all registering "Empty." They checked their watches in one collective motion, then literally sagged against each other, sucking in air. Nana gave me a limp-wristed wave before finding a chair and falling into it.

"Conrad, how would you like to meet my grandmother?" Grabbing his arm, I waltzed him across the floor, stopping in front of Nana's chair. "Please tell me you haven't made the rounds of all the nearby convenience stores to clean them out of household pesticide."

She peered at me as if I'd just caught her switching my mother's soup cans out of alphabetical order.

"Nana! If those spray cans explode, they can become biological weapons!"

She snapped her fingers to get the group's attention. "Did anyone buy Raid?"

"Shoot," said Dick Teig. "How come I didn't think of that?"

"Make a list," yelled Osmond.

"Sorry, dear. None of us thought a that. It's a real good idea though."

I eyed her suspiciously. "So what have all of you been doing that's gotten you so tuckered out?"

"We done a little shoppin'." She cupped her hand over her mouth. "And you know how tirin' it is when the fellas are along and you gotta put up with their poutin', whinin', and grouchies. Your grampa only got grouchy one time when I took 'im shoppin', then it never happened again."

"What did you do? Drug him?"

"Nope. I left him home. Worked real good. Who's this you got with you, dear?"

I presented Conrad front and center. "Nana, everyone, this is Conrad Carver, who will be married fifty happy years tomorrow. How about that?"

Conrad looked a little embarrassed when spontaneous applause erupted. Sketching a little bow, he held up his hand for quiet.

"To be completely truthful, not all the years were happy, but we made it through the bad ones, so here we are."

"He looks like someone," Grace Stolee claimed. "Who does he look like?"

"He sounds like Count Dracula," said Bernice. "Where are you from? Transylvania?"

He gave Bernice a hard look. "Poland."

"Then how come your name isn't a foot long and end in 'ski'?"

He lifted his chin proudly. "I was orphaned in Hitler's war and adopted by an American GI, so my name doesn't end in 'ski'; it ends in 'ver'. Carver."

"But your name ended in 'ski' before, right?"

He fired a look at Bernice that, in the movie version, would have detonated her hearing aid and caused her head to explode. "Listen closely, please. My name is Carver."

"Wilcome, Australian Advinture travelers!" Henry leaped onto a low table that gave him a great overview of the room. "There's punch for you here, and the kitchen is sinding up a few nibbles for you to snack on."

We were suddenly invaded by a small army of waiters pushing food trolleys laden with oversized trays. "This is what we call 'bush gourmet'," Henry said expansively, "so gird your taste buds." One of the waiters handed him a small menu that he quickly perused. "You're in for a treat, mates. Chef Viggo has prepared smoked emu, crocodile macadamia brochettes with bush tomato chutney, bunya nuts, lemon-aspen lemoncurd, prawns fried in coconut with curried mayonnaise, handmade agnolotti filled with yabbie mousseline, baby wattle seed blini topped with cress, and baby Barramundi fish wrapped in paperbark tree sleeves and served with Kakadu plum sauce."

A ground swell of "Mmmms" traveled around the room, fading when it reached my group, who were staring at each other in gastronomic horror. "What kind of sauce did he say?" asked Osmond, desperately readjusting his hearing aids.

"There are two tricks to a succissful tour experience," Henry continued, brandishing two fingers in the air. "The first is to learn everyone's name, and the sicond is to talk to everyone. That's why you're here, mates. To be frindly. I also need you to fill out midical history forms, so I'll leave thim on a table by the door and you can hand thim back to me in the morning. So what do you say we git started? Eat. Drink. Mingle."

In the background Burl Ives serenaded us with "Mares Eat Oats," causing me to wonder if this was a subliminal call to the feed trough or a top-ten hit from Melbourne's Pop Chart list. I located the stack of medical forms by the door and beat back a sudden wave of grief. Maybe if we'd filled out the forms before the trip started, it might have given Peter Blunt some insight into Claire's death, or at least provided a starting point. I knew Peter didn't suspect foul play, but I wouldn't rest easily until we heard the results of the autopsy.

Conrad tapped my arm. "Would you like to meet my wife?"

"I'd love to meet your wife. And I'll even go one better. I'll introduce her to the whole Iowa gang. Where is she?"

"Over there by Mr. Madelyn. She appears to be in line to have her photograph taken. Let me run over there and bring her back."

I checked out the queue that had formed behind Guy and did a quick double take when I spied Etienne and Duncan posing with a top-heavy brunette in Daisy Duke short shorts and snakeskin boots who was gyrating against them like a Vegas showgirl. "Great moves," Guy encouraged, "but maybe you could just prop yourself against the men for a few seconds so I can get a still shot. Think, Greek temple. You're a vestal virgin and the men are gods."

She splayed herself against them, lips puckered and eyes at half-mast, looking hot and seductive. I rolled my eyes. This could take all night. She was never going to get the hang of the virgin thing.

Bernice came up behind me. "Who's the sexpot?"

"You got me."

"Looks like your two Romeos are finding out for you. It's the testosterone. Men don't know how to handle it. Give 'em an eyeful of bosom and booty, and they all turn into cave men. There's probably some fancy anthropological name for it." She grabbed Tilly and gestured toward the trio. "You're the professor. You see what's going on over there? What do you call that?"

"Group photo."

I would have chuckled if I hadn't been distracted by Jake Silverthorn's arrival on the scene. He stood just outside camera range, arms crossed, features tight, toothpick twitching in the corner of his mouth. He gave the brunette a "get over here now!" head bob. She stuck her tongue out at him and mugged for the camera.

"Lola," he said in a menacing tone.

"Git lost! Can't you see I'm busy with

some real gintlemen?"

"Don't make me come over there."

"Ooo. I'm scared."

Nana snapped a close-up of Bernice, Tilly, and me. "I'm gettin' photos of everyone on the tour."

"Don't give me that," Bernice said in an accusatory tone. "You're grandstanding. You just want to show off for the famous photographer."

"Listen here, Bernice Zwerg, if you knew me a little better, you'd know the reason I'm doin' this is on account a Emily."

Me? I stared down at Nana. "Why are you taking photos for me?"

She lowered her voice. "Mug shots, dear. In case it turns out that Bellows woman was done in by someone on the tour, I wanna have your suspects all lined up for you. Like what we done in Hawaii. I'm makin' one a them preemptive moves."

"Then why are you taking pictures of *us*?" Bernice asked, snorting. "Our group was in the visitor center when she died."

"I'm not gonna have no one accusin' me a discrimination." She held on to a corner of the photo as it developed. "One down."

"Oh! That reminds me." I presented my punch glass to Bernice. "Would you mind holding that for a sec?" Major exploration of my shoulder bag required two hands. I fished around until I found what I was looking for, then handed it to Nana. "Does that look familiar?"

"Well, would you lookit that." She stared at the Polaroid, puffing her cheeks out in confusion. "It's my pretty pink flower in the brambles. But what are you doin' with it, Emily? I thought I had it with me."

"I found it back at Port Campbell, lying on the ground by the walkway on the cliff. Do you have any idea how it got there?"

"I don't rightly know, dear. I s'pose somebody could a walked off with it when my pictures was makin' the rounds, but why would anyone want a picture a my wild-flower?"

Bernice shoved my glass back at me and eyed Nana's photo. "Good question. It's not even centered."

"Here's the missus," said Conrad, escorting a white-haired lady with heavily rouged cheeks toward us. "This is Ellie," he said proudly, beaming as we went through all the introductions.

"You mind me gettin' a photo a you two?" Nana dropped her photos on a nearby table and waved Conrad and his wife together.

"Is there a photography contest going

on?" Conrad asked, a little perplexed. "Why is everyone taking so many pictures?"

"Scrapbookin'," Nana said. "It's the latest craze. Big smiles now." *Bzzzzt.* She set the ejected print on the table, then motioned Conrad and Ellie to join her. "It'll be a real picture in no time at all. You wanna watch it develop? It can get pretty excitin' at the end."

Osmond arrived with a plate of goodies. "Would anyone like to try one of the crocodile macadamia brochettes? I got extra. They taste pretty good."

Bernice bit into one just as Burl Ives surrendered the air waves to a trio of female vocalists who started belting out the ever-popular, "How Much Is That Doggie in the Window." Oh, God.

Bernice's face screwed up in immediate revulsion. "Yuck! What's wrong with your taste buds, Osmond? This tastes like burned tailpipe."

"Give it back then." He plucked it out of her hand and tossed it back on the plate. "You're a pain in the neck, Bernice. You don't like the appetizers; you don't like the heat; you don't like the scenery; you don't like your room; you don't like to part with your money; you don't like people. Can you name one thing you *do* like?"

Stunned into silence by Osmond's rampage, she pursed her lips and cocked her head toward the speaker system, saying in a small voice, "I like the music."

"This is extraordinary," Conrad exclaimed as he bent over Nana's photos.

"What'd I tell you?" Nana said. "Watchin' them pixels come together makes your heart race, don't it?"

"I'm not talking about the photo you just shot." He lifted a print off the table. "I'm talking about *this.* Do you know what this is?"

"A flower."

"Do you remember where you took it?"

"I shot it back at them Twelve Apostles this afternoon. Along that cliff walk."

Conrad's voice trembled with excitement. "Marion, do you know what you've stumbled upon?"

I caught Conrad's eye. "What did she find? A rare primrose or something?"

He was struggling not to hyperventilate. "The flower is as common as a beach pebble. But do you see this plant growing beside it?" He stabbed his forefinger at the wild greenery in the background. "It's extinct!"

"No kiddin'?" Nana regarded the photo

with her usual calm. "I betcha someone just forgot where to look for it. My Sam was always misplacin' stuff. 'Specially batteries. After he died, we found enough nine-volt coppertops in his electric socks drawer to keep the Energizer Bunny goin' 'til his fur falls out."

Conrad gasped for air. "It's been extinct for over a hundred *million* years."

Chapter 4

Nana's jaw dropped halfway to her waist. If she hadn't been wearing denture cream with extra hold, her uppers would have been history. She gave Conrad's shoulder a playful thwack. "You're pullin' my leg."

"It's the truth! This plant belongs to a family of angiosperms that no one has seen for a millennia. Do you know what this means?"

"Eyesight's improved through the years?"

"It means, it's back! This plant might have properties that could unlock the great puzzles of medical science — cures for cancer, heart disease, obesity. It could be a fountain of youth for the elderly. An elixir for the infirm. A cure for male pattern baldness!"

"Do you suppose it could do anything for irregularity?" asked Margi. "That's a real common complaint at the clinic."

Bernice studied the photo over Conrad's

shoulder. "If you're expecting it to do all that, you're gonna need more than one crummy plant."

"Are you absolutely sure about this?" Tilly asked. "How does a plant that's been extinct for hundreds of thousands of years suddenly turn up at a local tourist site?"

"It's very simple," Conrad enthused. "Plants that thrived when the earth was one solid landmass couldn't survive the climatic changes when the continents split apart, so they died out. But on this continent, the climatic changes were less dramatic. The plants that died everywhere else not only survived here, they flourished. Australia boasts over twenty-five thousand species of plants. Think of it!"

Our thinking was accompanied by clueless staring and silence. "Is twenty-five thousand a lot?" I finally inquired. Hey, somebody had to ask the tough questions.

"As a comparison, Britain is home to only sixteen hundred species. Australia is a stew of botanical surprises. No one knows what's in the jungles because they're too dense to explore; no one knows what's in the interior because it's too hostile to survey; and the country has neither the financial resources nor the manpower to remedy the situation. Believe it or not, there are still eight thousand unnamed species of plants in government labs waiting to be classified." He crushed the photo to his chest, delight jacking his eyebrows to his hairline. "I'm beside myself. This type of angiosperm has never been known to exist this far south!"

I knew exactly how thrilled Conrad must be to have an extinct species reappear. I'd felt the same heart-pounding excitement when Clinique reintroduced a lipstick shade they'd discontinued years ago. "Should we be telling someone about this? A natural history museum? A university? Some government agency?"

"I'll call the University of Melbourne right away," Conrad said. "If their School of Botany can't help me, they should be able to direct me to someone who can."

"It's after hours, dear," Ellie reminded him. "They won't be answering their phones."

"They won't?" He checked his wristwatch, looking surprised at the hour. "But they have to answer. This is an emergency. It won't wait until morning." He wrung his hands in panic. "What am I supposed to do now?"

"I seen a couple a guest computers in the front lobby," Nana spoke up. "If I was you, I'd log on to the university's website, find the faculty directory, and phone one a them botany professors at home. That'd probably work."

He studied Nana for a heartbeat. "Here's your photo. I'll be right back." He took off for the elevator.

Ellie patted Nana's arm. "Bless you, dear. Even though he belongs to that organization for people with genius IQs, simple problems often stump him. Our life together would have been much easier if he'd been a moron." With a long-suffering sigh, she scurried after him, returning a short time later with a beaming Conrad in tow.

"It worked out splendidly," he chirped. "I talked to the head of the School of Botany himself, and he was so excited to talk to me. They use my textbook for their introductory botany courses! I'm apparently quite the luminary with the fossils people. Dr. Limeburner even mentioned my autographing a few textbooks before I fly back home, complete with media coverage. You see? This reinforces what I've always said: the farther you get from home, the more —"

Ellie elbowed his ribs. "Tell them what he said about Marion's photo, dear."

"He's going to send a team to Port Campbell tomorrow." He grinned at Nana. "Your trip Down Under could turn out to be momentous, Marion. You might end up with your name on a new species of angiosperm!"

"Are those the ones with the good or bad motility?" Dick Teig inquired.

Conrad went on breathlessly. "And your timing couldn't be better. Dr. Limeburner informed me that in two weeks, the International Society of Botanists meets here, so Melbourne will be crawling with scientists who'll be able to confirm the discovery. I'll warn you right now, Marion, you're going to be famous."

"No kiddin'? Are they gonna need my Polaroid so's they know what they're lookin' for?"

"They should be fine without it. I told Dr. Limeburner they should concentrate on the underbrush along the cliff walk, and to use your pink wildflower as a marker. If the plant is there, they'll find it. Any botanist worth his salt should be able to recognize this variety of angiosperm."

"GIT OUT OF MY FACE, YOU FREAKING DRONGO!"

Toward the rear of the room Lola Silverthorn propelled her husband backward with a two-handed shove to his chest. He hit the wall with a resounding *BOOM!*, then spat out a curse as an oversized art print came crashing down on him in a hailstorm of glass, leaving him in a motionless heap.

Gasps. Cries. Lola nodded with satisfaction and dusted off her hands. "No worries, Hinry. I'll pay the damages." Ruffling her shaggy hair, she thrust out one curvaceous hip and eyed the room at large. "So which one of you handsome mates wants to buy me a real drink?"

Pandemonium erupted. Henry punched a number on his cell. Guy Madelyn corralled Lola and rushed her to a neutral corner. Duncan and Etienne scrambled through the shattered glass to lift the heavy frame off Jake. Several guests attacked the buffet while the waiting line was down. "I'm CPR certified," yelled Conrad as he raced toward Jake's inert body.

Nana hovered close beside me, watching with rapt attention. "You think he's dead?"

"Oh, Lord, he can't be." Two deaths in one day would be pretty extreme even for one of *my* tours.

"That's a crime." Helen Teig waved her punch glass toward Jake. "Reframing that print is going to cost someone a bundle."

"Shhhhhh!" Bernice hissed. "Listen." She glided her hand like a conductor's baton through the air. " *'Que Sera, Sera.'* I haven't heard this in years. No one sings it like Peggy Lee."

"It's not Peggy Lee," Margi piped up. "It's Doris Day."

"Is not," said Bernice.

"Is so," said Margi.

"Are you sure it's not Gisele MacKenzie?" asked Alice.

"Show of hands!" Osmond shouted.

While Osmond tallied the votes, I angled a look at the Polaroid Nana still clutched, my pulse suddenly quickening as I was struck by an improbable thought. *Oh, my God. Could that be why Claire had left the visitor center?*

I fired a glance at Conrad; I fired a look back at the photo. *Uff da.* If my hunch was right, I'd just solved the riddle.

"Sippelspermum australianse," announced Tilly an hour later. We were in my room on the twenty-first floor, decompressing. "Or would you prefer, *Marionspermum austra-lianse?"*

"I'd rather have my name on a candy bar," Nana said as she unlaced her sneakers. "They done that for Babe Ruth. I want mine with caramel and chocolate but no nuts. Old folks can't chew nuts real good,

70

especially if they don't got teeth." She leaned back in her chair, her feet dangling high above the floor. "Awful shame about the 'Meet and Greet' comin' to such a quick end."

I kicked off my shoes and fell back on the bed. "Yeah, policemen and paramedics can have that effect on a friendly gathering."

A team of strapping paramedics had carted Jake off to the hospital, while a couple of seriously buff police officers had dealt with Lola. Made me wonder where Melbourne's emergency services recruiting offices were located. Male strip clubs?

"It was extremely kind of your two young men to ride along with Jake to the hospital," Tilly commented. "Henry assigned the task to the right people. They're quite responsible, aren't they?"

"Responsible. Dependable." I made a sweeping gesture around the room. "Conspicuously absent."

To be fair, Henry would have volunteered for ambulance duty himself if Lola hadn't wrapped herself around his legs, begging him not to abandon her when she was in such desperate need of moral support. So he'd agreed to babysit Lola at the police station and had asked Etienne and Duncan to accompany Jake.

"You s'pose Lola's gonna have to spend the night in the pokey?" Nana asked.

I gave her a palms' up. "That'll probably depend on how kindly Jake is feeling toward her and whether he decides to press charges. Do you think he'll even be able to give the police a statement?"

"His cuts looked relatively superficial," Tilly said. "I doubt they'll keep him overnight. But I'm concerned that Lola may prove to be a disruptive force throughout the whole tour. She's loud; she's obnoxious; and did you notice how she hogged Guy's entire photo session this evening?"

"The only reason he was takin' her picture so much was on account a she was wearin' one a them atomic outfits," said Nana. She lifted her eyebrows and smiled impishly. "He was waitin' for the fallout. Did you see the size a them puppies? When she's my age, she can use 'em for a scarf."

"Well, I think Guy is very generous to take professional pictures of everyone. He probably makes a habit of doing nice things for people" — I stared pointedly at Nana — "like offering them jobs that pay six figures."

"Forgot all about that." Sighing, she pulled some loose photos out of her pocketbook and studied them critically. "I don't know, dear. It's real flatterin' to catch the eye of an expert, but every one a these pictures looks pretty ordinary to me."

"Do you have your angiosperm photo handy?"

She sailed it across the room to me; I scrutinized it under the light. "I have a theory about your photo, Nana, but I need you to double-check something on your laptop to see if it holds water."

"I love listenin' to them theories a yours, dear. They're always so . . ." She whipped the air with her hand as she searched for the right word.

"Wrong?" I offered.

"I was thinkin' more like, 'earnest.' "

"What's our assignment?" asked Tilly.

"Here's the scoop. Claire Bellows told me she had to attend a scientific meeting in Melbourne after our tour ended. Would you access the International Society of Botanists online, and if they have a listing for registrants of the Melbourne conference, see if Claire Bellows's name is on it?"

Nana's mouth rounded into an O. "You think she was a botanist?"

"If she was, it would explain why she went outside, what she was looking for, and why your photo was never returned. You heard Conrad say that any botanist worth his salt would be able to recognize this angiosperm.

73

If she identified the plant when your photos were making the rounds, she could have slipped your Polaroid in her shirt pocket and went out searching for it when Henry announced we were being delayed. She probably had your photo in her hand when she collapsed, and the wind blew it away. If she'd discovered the angiosperm on her own, it would have been her ticket to shattering the glass ceiling where she worked. She told me she'd have to reinvent the wheel to get any recognition. I'd guess that finding a plant that's been extinct for a hundred million years would be the botanical equivalent, wouldn't you?"

"Bellowspermum australianse," Tilly muttered. "Has a nice ring to it."

"We're on the case," said Nana as she re-tied her sneakers.

I regarded her photo once more, another thought occurring to me. "Do you know how many total snapshots you took at the Twelve Apostles?"

"Three film packets, so that'd be twenty-four photos."

"Would you count them when you go back to your room and make sure you have all twenty-four?"

"You bet. Are you thinkin' that Bellows woman mighta run off with more than one?"

"Don't know, but it won't hurt to check." I held up her photo. "Do you want your angiosperms back?"

"How 'bout you put it in your room safe for me, dear. If it's what Conrad says it is, Tilly and me don't want it nowhere around us. Last thing we wanna do is relive Hawaii."

After seeing them out, I slid my closet door open and knelt to examine the small safe located inside. I read the operating instructions, and after ten frustrating minutes of fiddling with the key pad and passwords, finally got the system to work.

Knock, knock, knock.

"Be right there!" I yelled, a little stunned. In the time it had taken me to secret away one measly photo, Nana had completed a major computer search and was back with her results. This was *so* typical. Of course, it probably helped that her room was directly opposite mine.

I opened the door. "What took you so lo—"

Etienne cupped his hands around my head and kissed me with the hot-blooded fervor of his Italian side. Kicking the door shut behind him, he scooped me into his arms and crossed to the bed, lowering all six feet two inches of himself on top me. "Say you'll marry me," he whispered against my mouth.

"Can't," I choked.

"You can't, or you won't?"

"Can't breathe!"

He rolled off. "Sorry, darling. The idea was to coax a commitment out of you, not to crush you." He touched his thumb to the corner of my mouth, his eyes lingering on my lips. "Have I mentioned today that I love you?"

I peered up at him. "Does Duncan know you're here?"

He kissed the tip of my nose. "We seem to have lost track of each other in the hotel lobby, so I'm not sure what he knows."

"How can you both be back from the hospital already? You should still be helping Jake fill out insurance forms."

"It was a slow night in the emergency room. A tetanus shot, a few butterfly bandages, and they sent him on his way. We grabbed a taxi and dropped him off at the police station."

"And you didn't stay with him?"

He shrugged one shoulder with jungle cat ease. "How do you Americans say, 'He's a big boy.' "

I boosted myself to my elbows, eyeing him suspiciously. "A tour guest dies earlier and you don't wrangle your way into the investigation? You take a man to an actual police station, and you don't bother to go inside with him? You *live* in police stations, Etienne. What's wrong with this picture?"

"I'm demonstrating that I can think of something other than work. In fact, I'm thinking of something right now." He trailed a lazy finger up my arm and across my bare shoulder. "Can you guess what?"

"You're having trouble with short-term memory loss again, aren't you? You've forgotten you're a workaholic."

"I don't have to be a workaholic anymore." He nuzzled my throat with his warm, wonderfully soft lips. "As of last week, I have all the time in the world."

"Oh, my God. You got fired."

He lifted his head so that his nose touched mine. "I retired."

"You WHAT?"

"Retired. They even had a little party for me. They gave me a very thoughtful going-away gift." He stretched out his arm and exposed his wrist. "Gold watch. Swiss. Waterproof."

"But . . . you're too young to retire. You're not even thirty-five! What are you going to do for the rest of your life?"

"You mean, besides make love to you?" He tangled his fingers in my hair and kissed me slowly and hungrily, but my mind refused to get with the program. If we got married, would I be able to handle Etienne's retirement? Would I be preparing him three meals a day, watching him take afternoon naps, and listening to him say, "So what are you doing now?" every ten minutes? *Uff da.* This isn't what I had in mind when I suggested he needed to spend more time with me. *Old* people retired. What was he thinking?

I tapped his shoulder. Up went his head. "What?" he said breathlessly.

"We need to discuss this retirement thing."

"It's only temporary, darling. I have something else in mind, but —"

Knock, knock, knock.

He froze. "Don't answer that. It's probably Lazarus."

"I thought you two were buds."

"Closer than brothers. Now, where was I?" He resumed the prodigious task of sucking all the air from my lungs.

Knock, knock, knock.

"Etienne!" I gasped, breaking off his kiss. "I need to answer that. I'm expecting Nana."

"Is she planning to stay long?"

"May I get up, please?"

Groaning, he detached himself from me and assisted me to my feet. "Next time you decide to wear the hot dress, would you schedule more free time into your evening?"

"You was right," Nana said, when I opened the door. "Her name — Whoa." She took one look at me and stumbled back a step. "Why don't Tilly and me come back when you don't got company."

"How do you know I have company?" I lifted my hand self-consciously to my head. "It's my hair, isn't it? Do I have bed-head?"

"Your hair don't look bad, dear, but you know how Helen Teig looks when she accidentally smears her eyebrows across her face?"

"You have the same look going on with your lipstick," Tilly observed. "It bears a startling resemblance to Zulu war paint."

"Ladies." Etienne flattened his palm against my lower back as he came up behind me. "Is this a girls-only event, or can anyone join in?"

"I knew one a you fellas was in there," Nana said, smiling. "Did you buy them international small-cap funds we was talkin' about?"

"The best advice yet, Marion. They went through the roof."

I stared at Etienne; I stared at Nana. I fluttered my finger between them. "The two of you are exchanging financial advice?"

"It's not exactly an exchange, darling." Etienne trailed his fingertips down my naked spine, causing the down on my arms to stand on end. "It's more like a one-way transfer of knowledge from your grandmother to me."

My jaw dropped in shock. "How long has this been going on?"

"Since Italy," said Etienne. "I had little need for financial advice before then."

"Hail, hail, the gang's all here." Duncan tramped down the hallway toward us, breathing heavily and appearing a little ragged around the edges. "I would have joined you sooner, but both elevators are mysteriously stuck on the forty-fifth floor, so I had to take the stairs." He sent a questioning look Etienne's way before gaping at my Bozo the Clown mouth. "So, what have I missed?"

Oh, yeah. Having both "boys" along on the same tour was working out *really* well.

"Not much," said Etienne. "The ladies are getting together for girl talk, and you and I are heading back to our room to allow them their privacy." He nodded to Nana and Tilly and dropped a kiss on my forehead. "See you in the morning, *bella*." He gave Duncan's back a friendly slap and redirected him back down the hallway. "So you had to hike up all twenty-one flights of stairs, did you? That must have been a bear."

Nana nodded toward Etienne. "Isn't that somethin'? For a foreigner, he's learnin' our clichés real good."

"He bought a dictionary." I pulled Nana and Tilly into my room and closed the door behind us. "Did you find Claire's name on the registrant list?"

"You bet," said Nana. "Her name was there, just like you said."

"Her business affiliation was listed as Global Botanicals." Tilly read from a scrap of paper. "According to their website, they're an 'international company involved in research and development of age-reducing cosmetics and organic supplements that help the human body operate at peak performance.' "

"Yes! I knew it! Your photo didn't accidentally blow out the visitor center's door, Nana. Claire Bellows deliberately took it."

She heaved a discouraged sigh. "She mighta took more than that, dear. I counted my pictures like you told me, and I'm missin' two other ones."

"Do you know what they're photos of?"

She shook her head. "I snapped so many shots, I don't got a clue what's missin'."

"If the photos revealed more angiosperms, don't you imagine Claire took those, too?" asked Tilly.

"She mighta snitched all three," said Nana, "but how are we ever gonna know for sure?"

I summoned a mental image of Claire Bellows as she patted down her voluminous travel shirt. "We know that one photo blew away, but I never saw any others. She was wearing a shirt with several pockets, though. Do you suppose the other two photos might have been in one of those pockets when she died?"

Nana's eyes brightened. "If someone finds 'em, you think they'll give 'em back to me?"

A bulb went on over my head. "I'm not sure, but why don't you and Tilly have a seat while I find out."

"Whatcha gonna do, dear?"

I found the card I was looking for in my shoulder bag and sat down on the bed by the phone. "I'm calling the coroner in Warrnambool."

Nana consulted her watch. "It's awful late, Emily. Are you sure he won't think you're bein' rude?"

"He gave me his home phone number and

told me to call anytime a memory kicked in, so I'm about to remember something." I held up a finger for quiet as he came on the line. "Hi, Peter, this is Emily Andrew. We met this afternoon at — Oh, I'm so happy you remember. I apologize for calling so late, but — Uh-huh. Uh-huh. Yup, I did recall something. My grandmother is missing a couple of Polaroid snapshots that she's just now remembering she lent to Claire Bellows, so I'm trying to track them down. I don't know if you're allowed to divulge information like this, but could you possibly tell me if you found any photos in Claire's shirt pockets?

"Uh-huh. I see." I gave Nana and Tilly a thumbs-down. "How about her pocketbook? Anything there? No kidding? Yeah, people used to call them penny postcards, but with the rise in postal rates, it can cost a small fortune to mail them these days." I bobbed my head as he continued. "I appreciate that. Um . . . they're mostly of scenery and stuff but my grandmother takes her photography seriously, so she'd love to get them back. Uh-huh. If I give you my number here, would you give me a buzz if you run into them? Thanks, that's so nice of you." I rattled off the information. "We'll be leaving for Adelaide the day after tomorrow so

— Uh-huh. Sure, I'll be happy to do that. Thanks for your help."

"Well?" asked Nana when I'd hung up.

"He couldn't remember much about her personal belongings other than she was carrying a heap of picture postcards, so he's going to check on the Polaroids and suggested that if I don't hear from him tomorrow, I should call him back in a couple of days. But there were definitely no photos in her pocket."

"You s'pose all three a them blew away after she collapsed?" asked Nana.

"Could be," I reflected. "Maybe the other two are still out there someplace."

"Or maybe Claire didn't take them at all," suggested Tilly. "Maybe someone else did."

I threw Tilly a puzzled look. "They were photos of bushes, and dirt, and rocks. Why would anyone besides Claire *want* them? I mean, a person would *really* have to know their flora to be able to look at those pictures and identify —" I paused midsentence as my brain suddenly caught up to my mouth. "That's it!" I gave myself a V-8 Juice smack on the forehead. "What is wrong with me? Why can't I think outside the box anymore?"

"Might be a good time to apply for government work," said Nana. "I think they're lookin' for folks like that,'specially for them upper-level jobs."

"Where's my guest roster?" I flew off the bed and riffled through the tour documents I'd stacked on the desk. "I was operating under the assumption that Claire was the only botanist on this tour, but for all I know, there could be a whole slew of botanists with us, all planning to attend that same conference." I found the sheet I was looking for and waved it at Nana and Tilly. "Can we go back to your room to check the names on this list against the conference registrant list? I think we're on to something."

"Well, would you lookit that," said Nana ten minutes later. "Diana Squires, Ph.D. in botany from Florida State University, and Roger Piccolo, Ph.D. in the same thing from Pepperdine. You was right, Emily. I guess you can hold off on that government job."

I studied the monitor over her shoulder. "Company affiliations — Infinity Incorporated and GenerX Technologies. Can you check out those websites?"

"Squires and Piccolo," repeated Tilly as she perused the 'mugshot' photos she'd lined up like quilting blocks across the bed. "Here's Diana Squires. Ah, yes. I remember seeing her. The lady wearing the thick theatrical makeup. You have to wonder if that's by choice or necessity."

"I knew them pictures was gonna come in handy," Nana said as she switched to another screen. "And did you notice that I got close enough so's you could read the name tags?"

"Roger Piccolo," Tilly exclaimed, glomming onto a second photo. "I vaguely recall seeing him. He's a rather muscular fellow."

I joined her at the bed for a look-see. "I don't remember seeing him at all." He had a head like a mason jar and no discernible neck, which had to make swallowing really difficult.

"Infinity Inc.," Nana read aloud. "Says here it's some kinda high-tech skin care company, 'specializin' in nonsurgical options to rejuvenate what's been destroyed by the agin' process."

I regarded Diana Squires's photo. Whoa! Most women applied foundation with a sponge; Diana looked as though she used a bricklayer's trowel. Made me wonder if she'd been a guinea pig for an experiment that had gone terribly wrong.

"GenerX Techologies," Nana continued after a few clicks on her keyboard. "Claims to be the largest manufacturer of dietary supplements and nutritional drinks in North America."

"Does it say what kind of supplements?" I asked.

"Natural male enhancement, menopausal relief, and antiagin' remedies. They're claimin' to offer the fountain a youth in 'easy-to-swallow time-released capsules'. Dang. I wouldn't mind tryin' some a them fountain a youth pills, but I'd probably have to OD before they'd do me any good."

"So Global Botanicals, Infinity Inc., and GenerX are all playing to the same audience with their antiaging remedies," I tossed out.

"Which means all three companies are in competition with each other for the largest market share," said Tilly.

Nana turned in her chair. "Which means if them other two botanists recognized my angiosperms, they mighta knowed a discovery like that could be a knockout punch to the competition. You s'pose one of 'em seen Claire take my photos?"

Tilly rapped the floor with her walking stick. "If they did, you can be sure their first order of business would be to wrest the pictures away from her. And we all know what that means."

I sighed. Unfortunately, it meant that

Claire might not have died from natural causes.

She might have been murdered.

CHAPTER 5

A brief look at Nana the next morning at the Ballarat Wildlife Park and I knew I was in for trouble.

She clomped down the stairs of the bus in her teddy bear T-shirt, flowered capris, and kick-ass boots that cocooned her legs like stovepipes. I covered my eyes and gave my head a weary shake. *Oh, God.*

"Mornin', dear. What do you think? Fancy, hunh?" She stuck out a foot that had grown exponentially overnight. "Genuine kangaroo. It's lighter weight than cowhide and guaranteed not to make your feet sweat in the heat. I hardly know I'm wearin' 'em."

Which was saying a lot, considering they were weighed down by fifty pounds of decorative chains and hardware. "I don't imagine you bought those at the neighborhood Farm and Fleet back home."

"Got 'em last night right before the meet 'n' greet. That nice David Jones Department

Store was too far a walk, so I run into the little boutique around the corner from the hotel and found everythin' I needed."

"You needed Gestapo army boots?"

"I needed protection, dear. We all did. You know . . . from the spiders and snakes." She executed a little heel/toe action that caused her chains to jangle melodically. "I was lookin' for gum rubber, but it was the funniest thing, Emily, all's we could find was black leather. Guess they don't cater to the fishin' crowd. We got some real good bargains though. Lotsa styles was on close-out."

"Mostly in large sizes, I take it."

She gazed at her feet. "They didn't have no fives left, so I had to get nines. But I stuffed the toe box with toilet paper, so they're real comfy. I'd a rather bought the ones Bernice got, but I didn't think I could manage them skinny heels." She nodded toward Bernice, who was scuttling toward the entrance gate in the kind of knee-high stiletto boots made popular by lady wrestlers and French streetwalkers. "She wouldn't be struttin' around like that if she didn't have them bunions out last year. Lookit her. She thinks she's Octopussy."

"Missed you at breakfast," said Duncan, massaging my shoulders as he came up behind me.

"My fault. I was awake so much last night that I slept through my alarm. I've bypassed bags under my eyes and gone directly to steamer trunks."

"I have a tried-and-true cure for sleeplessness." He trailed a knuckle down my cheek. "Lazarus family secret. You should have phoned me."

Nana handed him a pencil and notepad. "You mind writin' down your room number? I couldn't sleep last night neither."

"The guided tour begins in fifteen minutes," Henry shouted from the entrance gate, "so that gives you time to use the comfort facilities and buy yourself a cold drink. Most of the wildlife in the park roams free, so be aware that there are surprises on the ground that you'll want to avoid."

Nana elbowed me as Jake and Lola walked past us, hips bumping and arms snaked around each other's backs as if they'd been Velcroed together. "I'll be. Looks like they patched things up."

"Let's see how long it lasts," said Duncan as he ushered us toward the gate. "Henry told us at breakfast that they kissed and made up at the police station last night, but I'm not buying it. Those two have major issues. We'll be lucky if they don't end up killing each other before the tour is over."

My stomach performed an involuntary somersault. Just what we needed. More dead bodies.

The entrance gate funneled us through a gift and coffee shop where patrons could buy cuddly koala backpacks, rubber snakes, Tasmanian devil key chains, and crocodile caps with toothy visors.

"You s'pose the grandkids would enjoy it if I brung 'em back a few snakes?" Nana asked as she approached the bin.

"They'd enjoy them more if they were real," I said, stopping to finger the wombat hand puppets. "But then you'd have that whole quarantine mess at Customs." I slid a puppet onto my hand and brandished it before Duncan's face. "You were between the ages of five and twelve once. What tacky souvenir appealed to you back then?"

"I love you, babe, but how about you do your thing with the puppets, and I'll meet you outside?"

"Ten four," I said, as Diana Squires paused in the aisle opposite me to look over the merchandise. Gee, how handy was that? I meandered in her direction, poking unobtrusively through baskets of change purses and stuffed animals along the way.

"What do you think?" she asked, holding

two coffee mugs. "Should I go kangaroo or crocodile?"

"Is it for you or someone else?" Everything about her reminded me of Veronica in the old *Archie* comic books: the long black hair pulled into a ponytail, the fine features masked beneath a half-inch layer of pancake makeup, the heavily lip-lined mouth and penciled brows, the athletically fit body clad in designer coordinates. Her age was a big question mark, but I went out on a limb and narrowed it down to somewhere in her thirties, forties, or fifties. Go fish.

"It's for a colleague. I never buy junk like this for myself."

"What do you buy for yourself?"

She smiled with the kind of self-satisfied delight a cat would display after polishing off a bowl of cream. "Anything I want. So which mug is it?"

"I'd go with the kangaroo. Nothing says Australia like kangaroos."

"Good point." She set the crocodile mug back on the shelf. "You made that easy enough. Thanks."

"I'm Emily," I said, extending my hand.

"Diana Squires." She gripped my hand with the kind of strength pythons use to crush their prey before devouring them whole. "I guess we would have gotten introductions out of the way last night if it hadn't been for the Silverthorns' theatrical debut. That guy reminds me so much of my old boyfriend. All that swagger and macho bull. If I were his wife, I wouldn't have pushed him into the artwork: I would have pushed him out the window. Did you notice how lovey-dovey they are today? Classic passive-aggressive tendencies. If they don't get help, it's going to get really ugly. And believe me, I know, because I've lived it. How is it that women can be so smart in the business world and so stupid when it comes to men?"

Eh! Was that the reason for all the makeup? Was she disguising physical scars from an abusive boyfriend? I cleared my throat self-consciously. "Is that a rhetorical question or do you really want an answer?"

"Are you married?"

"I used to be."

"Divorced?"

"Annulled."

"See what I'm talking about? Bright girl, bad decision. It's epidemic."

Okay. Maybe. But at least I knew which coffee mug to choose!

"I need help." Nana appeared with an armful of rubber snakes. "I can't decide

94

between the death adder and the king brown for David. All's I know is, it's gotta be creepy enough so's he'll wanna keep it instead a feedin' it to the dog." She dropped her load on the display table and pulled out two remarkably realistic-looking specimens. "Which one looks like it'd be more likely to cause you an agonizin' death?"

Diana regarded the back of Nana's hand. "Do you realize my company has developed a topical cream that can vanish age spots like this? Age spots. Liver spots. Unsightly discolorations."

"No kiddin'?"

"Trust me. It's my life's work." She examined Nana's hand more closely. "Are you allergic to bee stings, peanuts, shellfish, or latex?"

"Latex. You mean like paint?"

"She means like condoms," I whispered.

Nana grinned. "Big negatory on that."

"Then you're a perfect candidate. I can guarantee younger-looking hands in three months or your money back. And there's a bonus. Our cream is a biological rather than chemical product, so you're not required to have blood tests to keep track of liver function, and there are no side effects other than flawless skin. We call it Perfecta."

"Is it a new product?" I asked. "I haven't

seen it advertised."

"It's so new that we haven't even finalized our marketing campaign. But it works. I'm living proof. I used to have a port wine birthmark the size of an Idaho potato on my face." She angled her right cheek toward us as if it were Exhibit A in a criminal trial. "Look closely. Do you see anything? Of course, you don't. It's not there anymore. Do you know why?"

I wondered if observing that it was buried beneath six tons of modeling clay would be too candid.

"It's because Perfecta caused it to fade away. This product performs miracles, and in doing so, it changes lives by inspiring confidence and building self-esteem." She smiled at her own words. "We're going to try to work that angle into our advertising campaign."

Nana scrutinized the backs of her hands as if she hadn't seen them in years. "I s'pose George could take a notion to bein' seen with a woman with younger-lookin' hands, but I hope it don't make him too frisky. He's still got them lower back problems."

"Is George your husband?" asked Diana.

"He's my gentleman companion, and the only reason he's not here is 'cause his grandson's gettin' married next week back home. But he's gonna sign up for our next trip in June. He give me his word."

"By June you could have the hands of a twenty-year-old," Diana enthused. "What would you say to that?"

"I guess I'd wanna know how much it was gonna cost me."

"Miracles don't come cheaply, Marion. We're presently looking at a price point of twenty-five hundred dollars."

Nana's three chins pancaked onto her chest. "For what? A lifetime supply?"

"A quarter-ounce tube. But that should last you a good two weeks, and you'd probably only need six tubes to get the job done."

I gave Nana a resuscitative slap on her back. When her respirations began again, she stared at Diana, speechless. "If I watch the sales real close, I can get me a nice pair a gloves at Wal-Mart for three ninety-nine. Three-sixty if it's a Tuesday, on account a that's when they give us seniors a ten percent discount 'cause we're old."

"EEEEEEEEEEHHHHHHHHHHHH!"

I spun toward the terrified shriek.

"I bet that's a cockatoo," Diana said excitedly. "I've heard they sound almost human. Excuse me, would you?" Dropping her kangaroo mug back on the shelf, she rushed through the doorway into the park proper. Nana looked up at me in bewilderment.

"Did I just hear a scream?"

"Yup."

"Where'd it come from?"

"Outside."

"Oh, good. I was thinkin' it mighta come from me."

Leaving the snakes behind, we hurried outside, joining the curiosity seekers who were running toward the far end of the building. We rounded a corner that said TOILETS and entered a caged area to find three adult kangaroos parked like area rugs in front of the restroom doors.

"I thought they were animal pelts." Helen Teig's voice quavered as she clutched her throat. "And then they moved! How come they're not in cages? Dick, shoo them away so I can use the potty."

Dick aimed his camera and started shooting. "Reach down and pet him, Helen. I think I'm looking at this year's Christmas card photo. That's it. Work it, momma!" His finely tailored Italian trousers were tucked into thigh-high boots with silver toe guards, rhinestone snakes, and chunky acrylic heels that made him only slightly taller than he was wide.

"Hunh. I never would have taken Dick for

a rhinestone kind of guy."

"It was either rhinestones or sequins," Nana explained, "so we decided that rhinestones was less sissified. But it was a real close vote. Six to five."

We left the restroom facilities behind us and walked toward the picnic tables at the opposite end of the gift shop, where a young man in regulation shirt and shorts stood beside a freestanding clock whose hands indicated the next tour would begin at eleven, which was about a minute from now. "All the kangaroos in the park are free-ranging Rid Kangaroos imported from Kangaroo Island," he said conversationally, sweeping a hand toward the giant, jackrabbit-like creatures who lounged on the broad lawn behind him. The area was enclosed by a rail fence and bordered by paved footpaths that were colonized by families of waddling ducks and hungry pigeons. "They're known in Latin as *macropus rufus*. *Macropus*, meaning long-foot, and *rufus*, meaning rid, though they're actually rid-brown in color. Males can reach a height of one and a half meters and can weigh as much as eighty-five kilos. That would be four and a half feet tall and one hundred eighty-seven pounds to you Yanks."

In other words, they were built like Nana only with a really long tail.

"There you are, ladies," said Tilly.

Nana stuck out her right hand. "Tell me the truth, Til, if you was me, would you spend two grand to lose the liver spots and have younger-lookin' skin?"

Tilly tapped the back of Nana's hand. "Bat *guano* and monkey urine. An old Pygmy preparation. Much cheaper."

"G'day, ladies and gintlemen, and wilcome to Ballarat Wildlife Park. My name is Graham, and I'll be your guide today throughout our sixteen hectares of bushland. Australia is home to wildlife found nowhere ilse in the world and it will be my pleasure to introduce you to mini of our native species: koalas, echidnas, wombats, goannas, Tasmanian divils, quokkas . . ."

As he continued his litany, I inched away from the crowd to do a quick head count. All my Iowans were here except for the Teigs, who would probably catch up once Dick filled his memory cartridge with holiday pinups of Helen in her muumuu and leather boots. Duncan and Etienne were posing for Guy Madelyn with a group of young kangaroos; Bernice was making a purchase at the coffee shop window; and Jake Silverthorn was off by himself, studying a corner of the gift shop's overhanging roof.

"We'll ind our tour in the riptile house, where you'll come face-to-face with poisonous dith adders, tiger snakes, and man-eating saltwater crocs," Graham said dramatically.

"Hey!" Bernice shook a small paper sack at Dick Stolee. "Get this on your camcorder. I bet the folks at Channel Six can use it on the 'Senior Doings' segment of their noon show." She dipped her hand into the sack and held out a palmful of feed to a furry little marsupial with a face like Bambi.

Dick sprinted into position. "This is Bernice, feeding a kangaroo."

"Get right profile shots," she instructed him, as a second kangaroo joined the first. "It's my best side."

"If you'll follow me." Graham raised his arm and pointed left. "Our first stop will be around the first bend in the footpath."

As tour guests trailed dutifully behind him, three larger kangaroos loped toward Bernice, crowding around her legs and stretching to their full height to reach her paper sack. "Shoo! Go 'way." She angled the sack over her head to protect it, but the 'roos were smart enough to recognize the mother lode when they saw it. Kangaroos suddenly charged in from everywhere, six more, eight more, clambering over each other to knock the feed bag out of Bernice's hand. "Help!" she screamed.

Dick Stolee moved closer to the foray. "Here's Bernice, rethinking her plan to feed the kangaroos. You have any last words, Bernice?"

"GET THESE DAMN THINGS OFF ME, YOU STUPID SH—" The paper sack flew from her hand. As the creatures pawed and wrestled to reach the seed and grain inside, Bernice's head of wire whisk hair disappeared within a sea of fur. Dick stopped recording.

"I'll make a copy of this for you, Bernice," he hollered at the place where her head had disappeared. "But I'll warn you now, if Channel Six airs it, you're gonna get bleeped." He trotted off after the crowd on the footpath; I rushed toward the coffee shop.

"Bernice?" I called as I circled the perimeter of the animals.

Her hand popped up like the self-timing stick in a Butterball turkey.

"Hang on! I'll . . . I'll get you out." Having no idea what else to do, I let fly a whistle that was shrill enough to shatter aquarium glass. "Move it!" I bellowed, clapping my hands. I whistled again, nearly deafening myself. "Shoo," I yelled. "SHOOOO!"

"I'll hilp you if you promise not to whistle again," Lola Silverthorn called from a distance. She raised a sack of feed into the air and gave it a noisy shake. "Come and git it, you bloody little scamps." She upended the sack, emptying the contents onto the ground like chicken feed.

The pack stampeded toward it, leaving Bernice behind in a minefield of fresh kangaroo droppings. I stared at Bernice; I stared at my new breathable mesh aqua loafers. *Euw.* I tiptoed through the obstacle course and helped her to her feet. "Are you okay?"

She scowled at me as she brushed grit from the seat of her pants. "Don't think this won't appear on your evaluation. You have some nerve, taking old folks to a place where they can be trampled to death. If Erickson doesn't fire you, I'll want to know why." She grimaced at her hands. "I need a moist towelette. Where's Margi?"

"Who's the whinger?" Lola asked, as Bernice strutted off.

"Oh, she's just an overly exasperating member of my group of seniors." I expelled a relieved sigh. "Thanks for helping out. I'm Emily, by the way, and I owe you one."

"No worries." Lola ranged a long look after Bernice. "Nice boots. There's a bunch of old folks that's slapped on lither today. What are they? Some kind of geezer biker dudes?"

"Actually, your husband raised the alarm about poisonous insect and snakebites yesterday, so my guys are addressing the problem by wearing boots. They won't earn any points for style, but you can't fault their common sense."

"Jake's always trying to scare people. The ratbag." Her gaze drifted over to him as he inspected the inner rim of the trash barrel that sat outside the gift shop entrance.

"Do you know what he's doing?" I asked.

She tousled her already shaggy locks. "What he always does; he's lookin' for spidehs, and he knows all their hidin' places — lidges, windowsills, eaves, potted plants, trash containers, the undersides of picnic tables. What's it gonna be, Jake!" she screeched at him. "Are you gonna join the tour or keep your hid stuck in that trash bin all morning?"

He looked our way, his face a scrambled jigsaw of butterfly sutures that made the Frankenstein monster look good by comparison. He tossed Lola an unfriendly "Leave me alone" gesture, adjusted the tilt of his bush hat, then swaggered off toward the restrooms.

"Tin minutes ago he was apples," she complained. "Now look at him. All cheesed off. Acts like he's a picnic short of a sandwich most of the time. He needs drugs, but he won't have nothin' to do with doctors."

"Why is he looking for spiders?" I asked, backtracking.

" 'Cause he collects thim. I bit he has the largest poisonous spideh collection in Murwillumbah. Maybe in all New South Wales. I bigged him to collect something harmless like beer cans or Elvis memorabilia, but nooo. His bugs are his life."

And to think my mother had gotten weirded out about my brother's collection of belly button lint. "Are his spiders dead or alive?"

"He collects thim alive, but a lot of thim ind up did. Then he mounts thim. If he knew what he was doing, they'd all be did, and we'd be rich, but I'm not gonna hold my brith. The last time he was tisting chimicals, he accidintally mixed ammonia with bleach and nearly inded up brain-did. 'Course, with Jake, brain-did would be a step up."

I was sure this would all make perfect sense if I could figure out what she was talking about. "Out of curiosity, what's Jake's line of work?"

"Pist control."

Pissed control? "Is that like anger management?"

"*Pist* control," Lola repeated. "He exterminates household pists. Spidehs. Ants. Roaches. Owns his own company: Bug Be Gone. But what he's workin' toward is producin' a lemon-scinted supeh chimical that'll kill all the creepy crawlies in one fill swoop. If he can mass-produce it, he'll be able to retire, then I can stop frittin' about the ones that go missin'."

I waited a beat. "The pists go missing?"

"All the time."

"But . . . aren't his pists poisonous?"

" 'Course they're poisonous. He don't want thim if they're not. But the little containers he has for thim don't seal like they should because Mr. Pooh For Brains buys the cheap ones." She grabbed her head with both hands. "Why do you think I had that argy bargy with him last night? The fool lit the ridback he found yisterday escape and he niveh bothered to till anyone on the bus. I keep pounding it into his hid, when you lose the didly bugs, you gotta do the courteous thing and *till* people."

I'd never suffered a panic attack before, but my sudden inability to breathe reminded me there was a first time for everything. "Jake was carrying a poisonous spider around with him yesterday?"

"Not *all* day. He says the buggeh wint missing sometime after lunch." Lola knuckled her fist on her hip, the Ann Landers of Aussie advice. "Don't pay no mind to anything Jake ever tills you. Like I say, he likes to give blokes a fright. Ridbacks are more scared of you than you are of thim."

"Wanna bet?"

"They're not gonna bite you unliss you git your fingahs tangled in their wibs."

I swiped a hand down my arms, chasing away phantom sensations that felt suspiciously like spiders. "What if he finds more redbacks today? Is he going to take them on the bus with him?"

Lola's glossy red mouth pinched in irritation. "He can't very will mail thim back to Murwillumbah, can he? The postal authority has real pain-in-the-arse rules about sindin' didly critters through the mail."

"Well, he can't take them on the bus. What if another one escapes?"

"I told you! They're not gonna hurt anyone!"

"Tell that to Claire Bellows!"

She reacted as if she'd just been sucker-punched. Taking a step back from me, she locked her arms beneath her eye-popping bosom and glared at me, a look that would have been truly frightening if her cleavage hadn't migrated to her chin. "Are you accusin' Jake of killin' that woman?"

"He let a deadly spider escape! How do you know she didn't die as a result? He told us himself a redback might have killed her; he just never said *he* was the one who let it loose!"

She paused a half second to study me, shrewdness creeping into her eyes. "If this is the thanks I git for hilpin' you out of a jam, you'll be on your own nixt time."

"You can't let Jake take any more insects onto the bus."

"And who's gonna stop 'im? You?"

"Henry will stop him. I bet he won't appreciate learning that one of his passengers —"

Lola's forefinger catapulted into my face. "You breathe one word of this to Hinry, and it could be the last word you ever breathe. Jake don't like people rattin' on him. No tillin' what he might do if someone spills the beans. He can be so unpredictable. Like I told you, a picnic short of a sandwich."

She looked me up and down as if she'd like to squish me. "See you 'round." She stormed off down the footpath, her wilderness boots clacking like the whole Russian army.

Yup. I guess you could say she was a little passive-aggressive.

CHAPTER 6

By the time I caught up with the group, they were leaving the wooded area that surrounded the Tasmanian devil pen and heading toward a glade teeming with kangaroos and ducks.

"The chain-link cage up ahid isn't a batters' cage," Graham announced. "It's where we house our widge-tailed eagles, which are found everywhere in Australia, can fly for ninety minutes at a time, and often soar to altitudes of two thousand meters, which is more than a mile straight up. Their wingspans can reach two-point-five meters, which is over eight feet. Their most noteworthy characteristic —"

I grabbed Nana's arm and pulled her out of the crowd. "We've got problems."

"You're tellin' me," she said, hauling Tilly along with her.

The odor hit me in the face as the crowd

passed us by. "Oh, my God. What's that smell?"

"Bernice," said Nana. "The koala peed on her."

Tilly clucked disapproval. "The handler warned us that we shouldn't touch the animal anywhere around its face because that makes it agitated. So naturally, when it was Bernice's turn to hold the little feller, she tried to pinch its cheek."

"She didn't know that 'agitated' meant 'go potty'," said Nana.

I tented my hand over my nose. "That is *so* foul."

"I'm told it's even worse when it dries," said Tilly, "so we took up a collection to buy her a new T-shirt at our next stop."

I regarded them proudly. The group might have its differences, but when the chips were down, they could really demonstrate a wonderfully generous spirit with each other. "That's so nice of you guys."

Tilly disregarded the compliment. "Our hearing might be on the skids, but there's nothing wrong with our noses. It comes down to basic survival."

"You gotta convince Bernice to dump the smelly shirt," Nana pleaded with me.

"We can't have people inhaling those fumes all the way back to Melbourne," said

Tilly. "It could make them sick."

"But she's gonna put up a fuss, dear, 'cause she's wearin' her monster truck shirt, and that's her favorite. No way you'll ever get her to trash it."

I looked skyward, searching for the little black cloud that was hanging over my head. "I'll see what I can do about Bernice, but in the meantime, do me a favor and get the word out to the group to avoid Jake Silverthorn at all cost. Tell them not to stand near him, eat at the same table, or sit by him on the bus. *Especially* not to sit by him on the bus."

Nana sidled close to me. "Did he get peed on, too?"

"No, it's just that —" I swallowed the end of my sentence, knowing I'd only frighten them by telling them about the escaped redback and Lola's threat. What if they let it slip to Henry? Would that put them in the crosshairs for Jake's insanity, too? I needed to be smart about how I handled this, and blabbing the situation to the immediate world didn't seem the way to go right now. I needed to think about protecting people, not causing panic. "I got it straight from Lola that Jake likes to peddle fear. Look what happened after his little lecture yesterday." I dipped my gaze toward their feet, putting Tilly's boots on freeze-frame. "Good God. You could puncture someone's lung with those things."

Tilly leaned heavily on her walking stick as she swung her foot out in an uncharacteristically girlish pose. "They spoke to me, Emily. I've never had footwear speak to me before. Do you think they're too over-the-top?"

Black leather? Steel spikes? Silver spurs? *Oh, God.* "They're you," I said kindly. "And who would have thought they'd look so good with madras?" Suppressing a little shudder, I returned to the problem at hand. "Back to Jake. If you hang around him, he'll fill you with so much fear, you'll all be donning body armor, so do yourselves a favor and just stay away."

Nana offered a little salute before craning her neck for a look around her. "Where's your young men, dear? I thought they was supposed to be smotherin' you with attention."

"I'm beginning to think it's a case of bait and switch. Last time I saw them, they were posing for Guy; then all three of them disappeared from the face of the earth. Go figure. You two better catch up to the rest of the group. Looks like there's some kind of demonstration going on at the eagle cage." I nodded toward the Tasmanian devil pen. "Good exhibit?"

Nana shrugged. "We didn't see nothin', dear. We heard some fierce crunchin' from the cave, but he stayed holed up the whole while. David's gonna be mighty disappointed. He wanted me to take a picture of a Tasmanian devil on account a that's his favorite character on the Cartoon Channel. You know what come as a big surprise, Emily?"

"Tasmanian devils are shy?"

"The good programmin' on the Cartoon Channel."

I yanked my Canon Elph out of the side pocket of my shoulder bag. "Well, we can't disappoint my nephew. Now that the crowd's thinned, maybe he's come out of hiding."

Approaching the pen from the tree-lined footpath, I discovered the area was deserted, save for Heath Acres and the thousand-year-old woman who stood arm in arm, studying something behind the chain-link fence. The pen was the size of a one-car garage — an ecologically engineered jungle of trees, shrubs, rocks, hollowed-out logs, and a nifty cave built into a mountainous pile of dirt. I didn't see any furry creatures running around, but I slowed my steps when I heard a loud and unsettling *CRRRRRUNNNCH crunchcrunch.* Euw. It sounded like a garbage disposal grinding up chicken bones.

But it wasn't.

It was a Tasmanian devil devouring its lunch.

"He came out of hiding," I rasped, transfixed by the sight of this broad-headed, small-eyed, piglike marsupial gnawing through the skeleton of a creature who'd been lower in the feed chain. He was black with fur, had pink vampire bat ears, and sported pointy teeth that smacked of the "Big Bad Wolf." I swallowed with difficulty. "What do you suppose he's eating?"

"Another exhibit," said the crone.

I stashed my camera back in my shoulder bag. Stuffed toy was looking like a really good idea for David.

"They look ferocious," said Heath, "but they're inept killers. If not for roadkill, the Tasmanian divil would probably go the way of the Tasmanian tiger. Total extinction." Looking my way, he doffed his Akubra hat and smiled. "I'm Heath. This is Nora."

"Emily." I returned his smile. "You probably see animals like this all the time."

"I live inland, so what I mostly see are desert rats and scorpions."

Inland? "You live in the Outback?"

"I live in South Australia — a little place called Coober Pedy. Have you seen Mel Gibson's *Mad Max* movies? The third flick was filmed near Coober Pedy, so if you remimber the desolate scenery with its scrubby saltbushes and dried-up water-courses, you git a fair picture of the town."

What I remembered about *Mad Max* was how well the terrain conformed to the apocalyptic images of a post-nuclear war landscape. The featureless desert. The unbearable heat. Kinda like Las Vegas without the casinos. "Why do you live there?"

His smile broadened. "Opals."

"Rabbits," said Nora, conversing with the Tasmanian devil through the chain-link fencing. "I've eaten rabbits. But you've gotta skin' 'em first, else the fur gets stuck in yer teeth."

Heath placed a cautionary hand on her shoulder. "Not too close, luvy."

Nora's behavior suddenly seemed as un-nerving as Jake Silverthorn's. I shifted my attention back to Heath. "Coober Pedy is a big mecca for opals?"

"The biggest. It's the richest opal field in Australia. If a man can brave the heat, toler-

116

ate a skyline of brick and corrugated iron, and doesn't mind living like a mole most of the time, he can earn a decent crust."

"Ferrets," said Nora, wagging her finger at the animal. "I've eaten ferrets. But I didn't like 'em much. Too stringy."

"Tell you what, luvy." Heath coaxed her gently away from the pen. "We should catch up to the other gists and let the Tazzy finish his meal in peace. Does that sound like a good idea? You don't want to miss the saltie, do you?"

She twisted around, confusion clouding her brilliant blue eyes. "Where'd everyone go?"

"They've gone on to the nixt exhibit. Come on. Maybe Imily will walk with us."

She tossed me a dismissive look before clutching Heath's forearm. "I don't know that girl. Who is she?" Then in a more animated voice, "Is she from the orphanage?"

"Imily's a gist on our tour. A Yank. You like Yanks."

She nodded docilely. "My da might have been a Yank."

"You coming?" Heath asked me, looking as if he'd appreciate the company.

"So how hot does it get in Coober Pedy?" I asked, as we strolled down the path with

Nora between us.

"Midsummah will average a hundred eighteen degrees Farenheit. Hotter on some days. Not much greenery survives back home. The sun cooks everything."

Including skin. No wonder Nora's face was so wrinkled. I'd probably look the same way under similar circumstances, then be forced to squander so much of my savings on miracle creams that I'd have to declare bankruptcy. Wow. Who'd have guessed that overexposure to the sun had the potential of being as disastrous to a person's finances as investing in survival equipment for Y2K?

"You wanna see my picture?" Nora asked, thrusting her well-handled photo at me.

I angled it into the light, picking out details I'd been unable to see in the visitor center yesterday. A fieldstone wall. An ornamental bench. A young woman with bobbed hair smiling shyly into the camera. She wore a plain housedress and against her bosom hugged two toddlers in frilled pinafores, their heads a riot of pipe curls.

"That's my mum," Nora said proudly. "She lived in England."

"She's beautiful." I held the photo gingerly, fearful that one of the dog-eared corners was going to fall off. "And the children are so adorable. They must be about — what? Two years old? I have five nephews who all went through the terrible twos. Is that you in one of the pinafores?"

"Me and Beverley. See the writing on the back? It says Nora — that's me, and Beverley — that's my sister. Do you see we're dressed alike?"

"Yup. Exactly alike. Are you twins?"

Her breath rattled noisily in her throat and she grew agitated. "I don't want to talk to you anymore. I want my picture back." She grabbed it from my hand. "You're walking too slow," she snapped at Heath. "Slow, slow, slow."

"You go on ahid then." He released her arm. "You won't git lost. I'll find you."

I grimaced apologetically as she barreled down the path with impossible speed. No small feat for a woman with legs like Bilbo Baggins. "Sorry. Wrong question to ask?"

"No worries. As old as she is, talking about that picture still sinds her on an emotional rollah coastah."

"Why did she ask if I was from the orphanage?" I asked as we continued walking slowly down the path.

"Because her mum put her in an orphanage not long after that photo was taken. We think her da died in the war, and her mum didn't have the means to raise her, so the orphanage was the only answer. It was common practice in those days."

"Did her mother eventually go back for her?"

"Don't know. After the war, the child wilfare groups elected to ease overcrowding by transporting hundreds of orphans to Australia. Mind you, they had the bist of intintions. They thought warmth and sunshine would be bitter for English orphans than damp and rain, but the consequinces were horrid. Children were separated from their siblings. Birth certificates were lost. Personal records misplaced. Not Mother England's finest hour."

"Is that what happened to Nora?"

"She inded up in Sydney with only airy fairy memories of her life in England. That photo of her mum is her only link to her childhood. But she was adopted by fine people, who made a home for her in Coober Pedy."

"Did they adopt Beverley, too?"

"She lost Biverley back in England. Her mum put the girls in separate orphanages."

I stared at Heath in disbelief. "Why would a mother separate her own children from each other?"

"To give thim a bitter chance at being adopted. People couldn't afford to adopt two children, and most filt guilty about parting twins, so it was actually an act of kindness on her mum's part. She had to have loved thim a great deal."

"Those poor little girls."

"We've been tracking Biverley down for years, but there's not much of a paper trail to follow. She could still be in England; she could be here in Australia. We've dug up a few documents that's hilped with birth and emigration dates. And there's a couple of new sites on the internet that deal specifically with the English orphan problem. They've given me some good leads. I haven't told Mum yit because I don't want to git her hopes up, but the information is so good, we may be only weeks away from locating Biverley. That would be a happy day indeed."

"Mum?" My voiced cracked in surprise. "Nora's your . . . mother? But she's —" I stirred my hand aimlessly, unable to think of a charitable alternate to "a thousand years old."

Heath laughed. "She's not aged will, but she's fared bitter than most. Life's harsh in the Outback."

As I looked down the path toward the eagle cage, I noticed a small commotion, followed by a scene that I knew was going to end in disaster. I sighed as I turned toward Heath. "Park officials wouldn't allow large, man-eating birds to roam freely around the park, would they?"

"Hard to find man-eating birds in Australia," he assured me. "The bist we can come up with is an emu, and they're harmliss."

I regarded the ostrich-sized bird chasing Bernice across the glade and smiled brightly. "Gee, that's a relief."

"I don't care how much money you collected," Bernice sniped, "you're not gettin' my T-shirt. You'll have to kill me first."

"Told you she was gonna be trouble," Nana said in an undertone.

We'd arrived at Sovereign Hill Park and Living History Museum ten minutes ago and were in the souvenir shop portion of the entrance building, waiting for Henry to hand out tickets. Gold fever had hit Australia a decade after the California Gold Rush, and according to what Henry had told us on the way over, Sovereign Hill had proven to be one of the country's richest deposits. No serious mining took place here anymore, but an authentic gold-mining town had been re-created over the footprint of the original diggings to allow tourists to step back in time and experience a typical day in

1851, from panning for gold to slogging through the mud of the wheel-rutted streets.

"All those in favor of killing Bernice say 'Aye,' " Osmond called out.

Bernice thwacked him with a plastic souvenir pickax. "Stay away from me. All of you! My shirt stays on my back." She swung the pick in a threatening arc. "Don't make me use this."

Dick Teig hitched up the waistband of his trousers and took a brave step forward, which was weird, because Dick never stepped up to the plate to solve problems; he was usually the one who caused them! Wow. This was huge.

"Stow the ax and listen good to what I'm about to say, Bernice." His voice was nasally from the tissue he'd stuffed up his nose. His cheeks ballooned with righteous bluster. "Emily has something to say to you."

Everyone took a giant step backward, leaving me front and center. "Look, Bernice, I'm sorry about your shirt, but wouldn't you agree that your health is more important than an article of clothing?"

"No."

"It's a scientific fact that inhaling noxious fumes can kill you!"

"Emily's right," Alice said helpfully. "You can keel over dead if you inhale carbon monoxide."

"And smoke," said Margi.

"And Helen's perfume when she puts too much on," said Dick Teig.

"You stink, Bernice!" Dick Stolee wailed. "Lose the shirt!"

"All those in favor of Bernice losing her shirt —"

Yup. This was going well.

"Bernice! Just the person I was looking for." Guy Madelyn flagged her down with a black T-shirt with gold lettering. "How hard would I have to twist your arm to be my photographic model for the afternoon? I need someone with great bone structure and presence, and you fit the bill. I'll even buy lunch and provide your wardrobe." He shook out the shirt so we could read the block letters: GO FOR THE GOLD AT SOVEREIGN HILL, BALLARAT, AUSTRALIA.

"Lunch *and* the T-shirt?" She plucked the shirt from his grasp. "Deal. I used to be a magazine model years ago, but you probably figured that out already. Once you have it, you never lose it."

He handed her a zippered storage bag. "For your monster truck shirt."

"My, my." She smiled coquettishly. "You think of everything."

We held our collective breath as she sashayed toward the fitting room and erupted into spontaneous whoops as she disappeared behind the curtain. Dick Teig hammered Guy gratefully on the back. Margi yanked streamers of toilet paper from her nose. Helen grabbed Dick's ear and dragged him off behind her.

"What's this problem you have with my perfume?"

"Sorry about the wait, folks," Henry announced from the turnstiles at the front door. "I have your tickets and visitor maps. The queue starts here. Synchronize your watches. It's twelve-thirty now; we'll meet back in this building at four o'clock."

The group dispersed helter-skelter, leaving me alone with Guy. He winked goodnaturedly. I stared at him in awe. "You do realize that you're about to commit one of the most generous acts in recorded history?"

"I had no choice. I sit directly in front of her on the bus and the drive back to Melbourne will take over an hour. We're talking life or death here."

"I've gotta warn you, she's a handful."

"I cut my teeth on mothers of the bride. Trust me. This should be a cakewalk by comparison."

The fitting room curtain flew open and

Bernice stepped out, a vision in black and gold. "How do you feel about my nose? You think I should get rid of the zinc oxide? I'm not sure pistachio fits our color scheme."

Guy's attentiveness to Bernice boded more than unpolluted air; it meant Etienne and Duncan would be freed up all afternoon! All I had to do was find them. I scanned the souvenir shop and, not finding them in the midst of a buying spree, headed for the next most logical place for them to be.

Conrad Carver occupied a bench in the waiting area outside the men's room, talking heatedly into a cell phone. "Tell them to look harder! I don't accept that. I hope you'll have better news for me later." He punched a button to end the conversation, then muttered a few unintelligible syllables that I suspected might be Polish swear words.

"Problems?" I asked, sitting down beside him.

"Fools." He stared at the phone as if willing it to disappear. "Blind fools."

"Anything I can do to help?"

"You can say a prayer to St. Anthony. Ellie always tells me, 'If you lose something, St. Anthony will help you find it.' Ellie's a believer. Me, I'm not what you'd call a religious man."

"Hey! I pray to St. Anthony when I lose things, and he's never let me down. Honest. It's freaking amazing. And the best part is, he's an equal opportunity saint. He operates under a nondenominational policy."

Conrad looked too depressed to crack a smile. I gave his knee a sympathetic pat. "So, what did you lose?"

"Your grandmother's angiosperms."

CHAPTER 7

"What?"

He squeezed the phone until his hand turned white. "Dr. Limeburner and his team have been at Port Campbell all morning. They can't find anything that resembles the angiosperm I described. They're going to continue searching, but he didn't sound hopeful about finding anything. I could hear the censure in his voice, Emily. He thinks I've lost my edge. He thinks I made a mistake. But I didn't! I know what I saw in your grandmother's photo!" He looked about the room impatiently. "If I wasn't stuck in this damnable place, I'd go look for it myself."

I leaned back in the bench, deflated. "Nana's plant is extinct again?"

"No! If it was there yesterday, it has to be there today. They're not looking hard enough. A plant of that size doesn't disappear overnight, not unless someone dug it up deliberately. And who would have done that? No one even knew it was there until I phoned Limeburner."

Which wasn't precisely true. The person who stole Nana's photo knew the plant was there, so they could have done the digging. But I'd like to think that if someone had dragged a large chunk of landscape onto the bus yesterday, I might have noticed.

"Sorry to make you wait so long, Connie." Ellie bustled over to us. "They ran out of paper towels in the ladies' room, so I had to blow dry my hands. The buzz is that they offer stagecoach rides here. Wouldn't that be fun?"

"I have to use the facilities," he said in a dull voice, "and return Henry's phone."

"I'll do that." I stood up. "I'm headed in that direction anyway. But would you do me a favor? If you see Etienne and Duncan while you're in there, would you tell them I'm heading up Main Street, so they can look for me there?"

Henry was still at the turnstiles, passing out tickets and maps. I took my place at the back of the line and tried not to think about how disappointed Nana was going to be when she heard the news about her angiosperms. Was Dr. Limeburner right? Had Conrad simply identified them incorrectly?

Was it possible that a renowned expert could be so wrong about something?

I scanned the shop while I waited, my gaze lighting on Diana Squires's ponytail as she hefted a huge backpack onto the PACKAGE CHECK counter at the opposite end of the room. Yikes. That thing was big enough to hold a gas tank! I gave myself a mental slap as I gaped. Had she been wearing it earlier today when I talked to her? Had she been wearing it yesterday? Was I blind in one eye and unable to see out the other?

I handed Henry his phone in exchange for my ticket, then idly studied my site map while Diana passed through the turnstile.

"Where are you off to?" she asked, her map already open. "Panning for gold sounds like fun, but that involves water, and I'd prefer not to get wet. Accidents can happen even in shallow water."

Hmm. The Wicked Witch of the West had melted when she got wet. I wondered what would happen to Diana Squires. "Did you bring a change of clothes with you?"

"We're on a nine-hour tour. Why would I do that?"

She'd obviously never watched *Gilligan's Island.* "That backpack you left at the package check counter was a pretty good size.

130

Looked like you could fit your entire wardrobe into it."

"Just the essentials. You know how it is. The older you get, the more essentials you need."

"Were you wearing it yesterday?"

"I wear it every day when I'm on vacation. I guess you were one of the few people I didn't sideswipe with it. How'd you luck out? I get some pretty mean looks when I move the wrong way."

"Were you wearing it at the wildlife park earlier?"

"Sure was."

"How did I not notice something that big strapped to your back?"

"Because it wasn't that big earlier. It's expandable. I buy the expandable model of everything, but I'm downsizing at the moment." She patted the fanny pack at her waist. "I turned the wrong way in the ladies' room and pulled something in my lower back, so I'm giving my muscles a rest." She whacked my arm with her map. "The aging process. See what you have to look forward to?"

"In the oft-spoken words of my grandmother, it beats the alternative."

"Speaking of your grandmother —" She snugged her hand around my forearm and spoke to me from the heart. "I'm afraid I might have scared her off with the price of our product, which is too bad, because it's women like your grandmother — elderly ladies living on fixed incomes — who could benefit most from what Perfecta has to offer."

"Actually, Nana isn't on a fixed —"

"So I'm going to let you in on a little secret that you can share with her. Tell her one of the reasons our product is so pricey is because we have to synthesize a key ingredient in the lab, and we're forced to pass the expense on to the consumer. But I happen to know that one of my colleagues has recently stumbled upon an alternative that grows freely in nature, so there's a possibility we could lower the price to something every woman can afford. Isn't that exciting?" She squeezed my arm as if it were a lemon that needed juicing.

Yow! I looked down at her hand, jerking to attention when I saw something I hadn't noticed before. "Has anyone ever told you you don't know your own strength?"

"All the time. When I'm not in the lab, I'm exercising." She clenched her fist several times. "I'm especially fond of handgrips."

"Is that how you got all those scratches?"

She rotated her hands to examine the angry red nicks that scored her fingers and knuckles. "They're an eyesore, aren't they? Got them yesterday at the Twelve Apostles."

"Really?" I angled my head for a better look. "How'd that happen?"

She hesitated. "You know how most woman go into a clothing store and have to finger all the soft fabrics and fur collars? Botanists are like that, too, except instead of touching merchandise, we're all over the local flora. We can't keep our hands off those unfamiliar leaves and flowers, and unfortunately, nature tends to be thorny." She regarded her hands again. "I had a veritable field day yesterday, but it does look as if I've been clawed by a cat, doesn't it?"

Yeah, a cat with long, manicured nails.

"I'll have to keep applying antibacterial cream. The last thing I need on this trip is a skin infection." She consulted her map. "If I'm going to sign up for the gold mine tour, looks like I walk straight up the street and bang a left. You want to join me?"

I couldn't tell if her smile was sincere, or a dare. "I'm supposed to be hooking up with a couple of people somewhere along the main street, so you'd better go on without me."

"Suit yourself. Catch you later."

My heart pounded in my ears as I watched Diana hike up Main Street. *Uff da!* Had Peter Blunt made the wrong call yesterday? He said they'd found no evidence of foul play, but was there a chance they'd overlooked something as obvious as skin particles under Claire Bellows's fingernails? Was it humanly possible for a technician processing a noncelebrity case outside LA to make a mistake like that?

No. If they'd found traces of skin under Claire's nails, they would have checked everyone in the park for fresh scratch marks.

I blew a puff of air into my face. It struck me then that there was no colleague. *Diana* was the one who'd made the discovery, which meant she'd cut her hands in the puckerbrush, all right . . . *while ripping Nana's plant out of the earth.*

Damn. I had to find out what was in her backpack. But first — I needed something to eat. I was starving.

I glanced up Main Street, wondering if this is what Tombstone or Dodge City had looked like in the 1850s. One- and two-story clapboard buildings with overhanging roofs. Plank sidewalks. Cobblestone gutters. Wooden railings and hitching posts. Teams of horses pulling wagons and coaches.

Ladies in hoop skirts and bonnets sidestepping clumps of manure. Gentlemen in stovepipe hats leaping daringly over it, proving that even though times might have changed, men obviously hadn't.

To my left was Dilges Blacksmith, Forge and Wheelright, Alex Kelly's Bath and Hotel, and the Australian Stage Company. To my right was the Auction and Sale House and a redbrick building that held real potential: HOPE BAKERY.

After a ten minute wait in a line that went on forever, I exited with a boysenberry tart that I purchased from a woman dressed like Betsy Ross. Walking north, I paused in front of the Red Hill Photographic Rooms to admire the souvenir shots of tourists dressed in period costume. Then, spying a bench outside the Post Office, I sat down to devour my tart.

"Do you think if we wait here long enough, a gunfight will break out, and Chester will limp down the street yelling, 'Mr. Dillon! Mr. Dillon!' "

With my mouth full of boysenberry tart, I nearly choked when I realized the man who'd stopped beside my bench was Roger Piccolo. He was short and square, and even though his face ballooned with almost steroidal puffiness, the rest of him looked hard as a sack of grain.

"I remember my granddad watching that show when I was a kid," he went on. "*Gunsmoke,* starring James Arness as Matt Dillon and Amanda something-or-other as Miss Kitty."

"Blake," I mumbled around my tart. "Amanda Blake."

He swung his body around to face me. "I'm impressed you knew that. You don't look old enough to remember the *Gunsmoke* days."

Such a charmer. I swallowed what was in my mouth and smiled. "I used to watch reruns when I visited my grandparents. Grampa ate up Westerns. *The Rifleman. Cheyenne. Bronco Lane.* He loved watching men in ten-gallon hats blow each other's heads off. I think it's a guy thing."

He eyed my half-eaten pastry. "Is that the boysenberry tart? I almost bought one, but the hot cross bun beckoned seductively from behind the glass." He shook the brown paper sack he was carrying. "Mind if I join you?"

I slid to my right to make room. "Has your name on it."

"I know you're on the tour," he said as he opened his bag, "but you haven't worn your name tag long enough for me to see your name."

"Emily Andrew. Sorry. My name tag never seems to match what I'm wearing, so it spends most of its time in my suitcase."

"I'm Roger." He bit into his bun, a heavenly smile appearing on his face. "Unh. *Unnnnh.* God, I'd forgotten how good fresh food can taste."

"Yeah, frozen can be a little hard on the teeth. What do you normally eat? Takeout?"

"Nutritional shakes — breakfast, lunch, and dinner. They're all the body needs. Plus a truckload of dietary supplements. It's one of the perks my company offers. Free product as long as I work for them. I can't remember the last time I visited a grocery store."

I tried to suppress my horror. "You drink all your meals out of a can?"

"Bottle, actually. They redesigned the containers a couple of years ago. But you wouldn't believe how much time and money a liquid diet can save you. My productivity has increased by twenty percent since I made the switch."

"Yeah, but no pizza, no fudge, no soft serve ice cream with colored sprinkles. What kind of drugs are you on for withdrawal?"

"I'm not suffering withdrawal. Believe it

or not, I actually like my diet."

Sure he did. That's why he was scarfing down his hot cross bun as if he'd been given the two-minute warning before the start of the Rapture.

He held up the final scrap. "Just so you won't think I'm a total hypocrite, the only reason I'm eating this is because it's impossible for me to travel with my own food supply, so when I'm on vacation, I'm forced to eat what everyone else does. But once I'm back home, it'll be shakes and supplements again."

"Can you honestly say that drinking nutritional shakes is better for your health than eating steak and potatoes?"

"Spoken like a person who's never heard of GenerX Technologies."

I feigned deep thought by wrinkling my brow. "I've heard of GenerX. Isn't that the company who's developed a new vanishing cream? What's it called? Perfecta?"

"Bite your tongue! GenerX is not, I repeat *not,* the makers of that bogus vanishing cream. You're thinking of Infinity Inc., our scab competitor whose main objective is to peddle snake oil to an unsuspecting public. Bunch of con artists. They're unfit to lick our corporate boots!" He speared me with an accusatory look. "How did you find out about Perfecta? I thought Infinity was keeping it under wraps until they could explode onto the scene with a major ad campaign."

"Word of mouth. There's a guest on the tour who was recommending it to my grandmother. I think she must work for them."

"There's an Infinity employee *on this tour?*" He slapped his thighs in disgust. "Travel halfway around the world, and I still can't escape their propaganda. Whatever she has to tell you, don't listen. It's all smoke and mirrors. And don't point her out to me. I don't want to know." He made a gravelly sound in his throat. "I bet she's planning to attend the conference in Melbourne. I wonder how many people she thinks she can deceive with her phony scientific results. Botany has devolved into a science catering to flimflam artists!"

"But she claimed to have a port wine birthmark on her face that Perfecta erased. If she's telling the truth, this vanishing cream could be the best stuff to come along since —"

"A topical cream *cannot* perform at that level! The implication is that Infinity has found a way to restore a youthful appearance to aging skin. Not true. If you want imperfections removed and elasticity restored, you have only three options: cosmetic surgery, laser surgery, *or*" — he paused for effect — "GenerX Techologies nutritional drinks and herbal supplements. We attack aging from the inside. A strict diet of our product will not only slow the aging process, it will reverse it. We've perfected the nonsurgical face-lift, and I'm a living testimonial. Fifty-three years old and look at me." He leaned toward me and tapped the corner of his eye. "No crow's-feet. No laugh lines. No age spots. My face is flawless."

And the size of a Macy's Thanksgiving Day balloon. "That's really remarkable. Um . . . are there any side effects? Nausea? Insomnia?" I paused. "Unusual swelling in various parts of the body?"

"Nothing. Our shakes are as safe as mother's milk. The important point is, you should introduce our products into your diet while you're still young so you can maintain a youthful glow throughout your life. See that white-haired lady walking out of Clarke Brothers Grocer across the street? I met her last night. Nora Acres. She should have started popping our herbal supplements years ago."

I glanced toward the grocer to find Nora scuttling gnomelike behind Heath while Lola Silverthorn walked hip to hip beside him, her arm entangled in his, her chest pressed to his sleeve as if held there by static cling. Unh-oh. If Jake found Lola cozying up to Heath, I didn't want to be around to witness the fireworks. What was her game? Was she planning to hit on every man on the tour to make her husband jealous?

"Here's the punch line," Roger continued. "If Nora bought into our product, she'd look a hundred years younger in no time."

Considering how wrinkled Nora was, I wasn't sure a hundred years would even make a dent.

"Can you imagine the before and after photos?" His eyes brightened at the prospect. "You know something? This idea has teeth. Nora Acres could be the face of GenerX Technologies, selling our product to the world." He stood up suddenly. "I should speak to them."

He removed a phone from the holster at his waist, punched a couple of buttons, and studied the display screen.

"Is that a satellite phone?" I asked. "I thought they were a lot bigger."

"Global Positioning System. I'm marking

waypoints where interesting things happen to me on this trip. I press this click stick on the front and it assigns a three-digit number to the place where I'm standing. Then when I highlight the number, it gives me exact latitude, longitude, and elevation. I find an obscure specimen I'd like to investigate in an out-of-the-way place? I mark the waypoint and I can walk right back to it. Nothing ever gets lost. It's an invaluable tool in my line of work."

He fidgeted with the unit before showing me the display screen. The number zero-one-four appeared inside a rectangular flag. Below it was an array of digits signifying location, elevation, distance, and bearing.

"So where's zero-one-four?" I asked.

"That's —" He hesitated, his eyes flickering with sudden unease. "That's one of the places we stopped yesterday."

"Port Campbell?"

He clicked off the power button and returned the unit to its holster. "Yeah, probably. Look, I want to catch Nora before she heads farther up Main Street. Great talking to you."

"Have you ever heard of a company called Global Botanicals?"

"Another competitor," he said as he backpedaled into the street. "What of it?"

"Did you know that the woman who died yesterday was a research botanist who worked for Global Botanicals?"

He puffed out his bottom lip in a miserable attempt at surprise. "Guess she'll miss the conference. That's too bad. It's supposed to be a good one."

I wagged a cautionary finger at him. "Before you go any farther, you better turn around and watch where you're —"

Squish.

"— stepping."

After helping Roger locate a restroom where he could clean his shoes off, I window-shopped my way up Main Street, tempted by boiled lollipops, soaps, spices, and fudge, but my mind kept drifting to the zero-one-four on Roger's GPS. What did it signify? Was it a general marker for the national park, or was it more sinister? Could it mark the exact spot where Claire Bellows had died? If it did, what did that imply? Had Roger recorded the death of a competitor simply because it was a momentous event, or because he'd had a hand in her death?

Now *there* was a sobering thought. But let's face it, there was so much rivalry between Global, Infinity, and GenerX, it wouldn't surprise me if knocking off the competition was part of a new corporate strategy to increase market share.

I sighed as I trudged up the plank stairs to the next level of sidewalk. No way was I ready to throw accusations around yet. Before I started pointing fingers, I needed to find out if Roger had actually followed Claire out onto the cliff yesterday. If he'd stayed inside the visitor center to wait for the bus to be repaired, there was no way he could possibly be involved in anything suspicious. Unless —

I paused before a shop window.

Unless the waypoint he'd marked was the location of Nana's plant. Could he have seen Nana's photo, gone out searching, and found it himself? Was it possible that the plant wasn't in Diana Squires's backpack after all, but was simply camouflaged by all the undergrowth at Port Campbell? Could he be planning to return to the park after his conference to cash in on his find and deliver a knockout punch to the competition? Was it possible he could be involved with the angiosperms and *not* with Claire's death?

With my brain twisted into more knots than a macrame rug, I stared at the merchandise in the window, perking up a little when I realized what I was looking at. *Ooooooh! Jewelry.*

The name of the establishment was Rees and Benjamin Watch and Clockmakers, but the display in the window showcased more than antique timepieces. There were trinket boxes shaped like hearts, octagons, and coaches. An egg-shaped case lined in scarlet satin that held a dainty manicure set. Earrings and brooches in intricately carved jet. Lockets encrusted with tiny pearls. Gaudy Victorian necklaces set with amethysts that were big as quarters. And an elegant gold band in a lacy filigree pattern that was quite the most beautiful ring I'd ever seen.

I looked down at my fingers. I looked at the band again. I walked into the shop.

"Could I trouble you for a closer look at the gold ring in the window?" I asked the young woman behind the counter. She was dressed in a poufy pink gown trimmed with black piping and wore her hair pulled back into a tidy chignon that might have been the "in" thing at Tara.

"You're from away," the girl greeted me. "We've had news that the *Charlotte* made safe passage from England a fortnight ago. Were you aboard her?"

I stared at her dumbly. Oh! I got it. Since Sovereign Hill was a living history museum, all its employees were "living" in 1850, which meant, so was I. Okay, given my degree in theater arts from the University of Wisconsin and my brief stint on Broadway, I could play along; I could even embellish. "I'm recently arrived," I said seriously, "but not aboard the *Charlotte*. I was traveling on a ship that wrecked near Port Campbell and if not for a perfect stranger who could dog paddle like a Labrador retriever, I would have drowned." I winced as I thought about my previous trips abroad. "I don't seem to have good karma with water."

"We've suffered terrible wrecks along that stretch of coast, and few people have survived. I'm so happy you were one of the lucky ones." She patted my hand before removing the ring from the window and placing it on a velvet cloth before me. "What ship were you on? News travels so slowly here. We're often ignorant of naval disasters until months later."

"It was the —" What had Guy Madelyn said? *Mermaid? Meredith?* I remembered it sounded like something you'd take for insomnia or erectile dysfunction. *"Meridia!"*

The clerk clutched her throat and gasped,

her eyes bulging with horror. I couldn't tell if she was choking on a Tic Tac or being suffocated by her corset.

"How is it possible you were aboard the *Meridia?* You claim to be recently arrived on our soil, yet the *Meridia* wrecked over forty years ago."

I was relieved she wasn't choking. I wouldn't be able to use the Heimlich maneuver for another hundred years. "Umm, it must have been the *Meridia II.* The Roman numeral probably washed off in high seas when we were rounding the horn, or the Cape, or something. I'm not exactly sure which route we took." I touched the lacy scrolls and arabesques of the gold band. "Would it be all right if I tried this on?"

"Allow me." She slid it onto my ring finger, cooing at the fit. "We wouldn't have to make any adjustments. It's as if it were made for you."

It certainly was unusual, combining the serpentine grace of Florentine and Celtic designs. I loved all the twisty-turny spirals and loops.

"It washed up on the beach at Loch Ard Gorge, probably from one of the many wrecks. It looks to be the kind of bauble a gentleman might present to a lady when he proposes marriage, doesn't it? One only hopes the gentleman lived long enough to take a bride. Shall I wrap it up for you?"

I checked the price on the attached tag. *Eh!* Even with the favorable exchange rate, in order to pay for it, I'd have to omit either food or rent from my budget. I rechecked the tag and winced. Maybe both. "It's a teensy expensive," I said as I slid it reluctantly off my finger.

"You're paying for the fine craftsmanship."

I stared at it forlornly. It was speaking to me. Nuts. I wondered if the clerk would think me too weird if I clapped my hands over my ears.

"By any chance, would your last name be Madelyn?" the clerk asked in a curious tone. "There were several members of the Madelyn clan who survived the wreck of the first *Meridia.* Might you be a relative?"

"You know about the Madelyns?"

She smiled indulgently. "Everyone in this part of Victoria knows about the Madelyns. They were heroes, risking life and limb to save drowning passengers. Carrying them to safety up those treacherous cliff paths. They became such a vital force in the communities they married into that we often refer to them as Victoria's First Family. Next to the Queen, they're our closest link to royalty."

"I *know* one of the Madelyns!" I enthused. "You should talk to him. He'd be so excited to hear what you —"

"Forgive me for stealing your customer," Etienne apologized to the clerk as he circled his arm around my waist and herded me out the door, "but this can't wait." He hurried me across the street toward the New York Bakery, sent surreptitious glances north and south, then feinted left, ducking onto the street that ran behind the eatery. In the absence of foot traffic, he pinned me to the restaurant's rear wall and kissed me with the urgency of a man whose Viagra fix was about to expire. His breathing was rapid; his mouth was hot. This was the perfect moment.

"Back to the retirement thing," I mumbled against his lips.

"Shhh. I'm trying to make love to you."

"In an alleyway?"

"I'm desperate. Kiss me, Emily."

"There you are, Miceli," Duncan called from a distance.

Etienne stiffened like a sprung trap. *"Merda."*

Uh-oh. I knew what that meant, and it

wasn't good.

"I turned around and you were gone." Duncan entered the alleyway at a quick clip, sounding a little breathless. "I thought you'd had a Madelyn sighting and were taking evasive action, but I obviously drew the wrong conclusion. You were hungry for sweets." He gave me a sizzling once-over and smiled.

"What *is* it with you two and Guy?" I looked from one to the other. "He's a very nice man, but don't you think the photography thing is turning into a bit of an obsession?"

Duncan raised an eyebrow at Etienne. "You haven't told her yet?"

"Told me what?"

Etienne's face flooded with color. "Madelyn wants to branch out into fashion photography, so he's putting a portfolio together. His photos of Lazarus and me have apparently turned out so well that he's planning to submit them to several high-fashion magazines."

"No kidding?" Where was the justice? Guy's photos of me end up in cyber trash; his photos of Etienne and Duncan end up in *GQ*. "So that's why he's been monopolizing the daylights out of you. Congratulations on being so photogenic! Wow. Does this mean the two of you could be responsible for making him even more famous than he is now?"

"This is where it gets a little tricky," Duncan hedged. "He thinks that once he submits the photos, Miceli and I are going to become the famous ones. He's expecting us to create the same kind of sensation that Burt Reynolds caused when he posed in the altogether for that centerfold in *Cosmo* years ago, only we'll have clothes on."

"Oh, my God! The two of you are going to become glitterati?"

"NO!" they replied in unison.

"We're not models," Etienne scoffed.

"Or girly boys," Duncan added.

"Do we look as if we could exercise judgment that poor?" Etienne asked. *"Papparazzi?* Crazed fans? *Entertainment Tonight?"*

"You don't want to be famous?"

"NO!" they replied again.

"Have you told Guy?"

"YES!"

Boy, they had the unison thing down to a science.

"We've told him to submit the photos if they can further his career, but not to meddle in ours," Duncan said, glancing back toward Main Street. "We want to remain anonymous."

"We've also told him no more photos," Etienne added, "but he's having a difficult time keeping his finger off the shutter button. He's a half step shy of stalking us."

"Hey, guys, I have good news. You don't have to worry about him pestering you the rest of the afternoon because he volunteered to keep Bernice occu—"

"He's headed our way," Duncan warned. "Come on, Miceli. We're outta here."

"Sorry, *bella*." Etienne blew me a kiss.

"But —" They were gone before I could finish. "Can't you just tell him to bugger off?"

I sighed. *Men.* They simply had no idea how to say it tactfully. Guess I'd have to show them how it was done. Dealing with Bernice had turned me into a master of tact.

I stepped out of the alleyway, prepared to confront Guy, but the street was deserted. I jaunted up to Main Street and looked both ways, but I still couldn't see him.

Huh. That was funny. Or was it?

Either Duncan's eyes were playing tricks on him or he and Etienne were playing a game much different than *Survivor.*

They were playing keep away.

CHAPTER 8

Alone once more, I decided to "power tour" Sovereign Hill before breaking for lunch. In the space of an hour I hiked to the far end of Main Street to sign up for a gold mine tour, watched a bald guy melt a bar of gold into liquid that could be poured like orange juice, listened to the far-off report of musket fire, bought a lace doily for my mom at David Jones Criterion Store, took a few pictures of a supply wagon whose cargo of canvas bales rose higher than the roofs of most buildings, then bypassed the Victorian dining experience offered at the United States Hotel and New York Bakery in favor of something more my style: The Refreshment Kiosk.

The kiosk offered cafeteria-style dining, so I paid the cashier at the end of the food line for my hot dog, chips, and soft drink, then scoped out the picnic tables in the overcrowded dining area for an available seat.

Henry walked toward me, carrying an empty tray. "You can have my seat if you hurry. Table in the lift corner, nixt to the wall. Some other tour blokes are there to keep you company."

"Thanks!" Gee, that was lucky. It was only after I arrived at the table that I wished I'd taken the elegant dining option. There were nine people at the table and only one seat available, right between Diana Squires and everyone's favorite fear monger, Jake Silverthorn. Damn.

"Hi, there, Miss Emily." Guy Madelyn stabbed his fork at the empty space. "Feel free to join us if you can handle the tight squeeze."

"My money says she'll pass," Jake said, rolling his toothpick from one corner of his mouth to the other. "Looks too skittish to abide small spaces."

Lola sat at the end of the bench, directly opposite Heath and Nora. She stared at me, her eyes issuing a challenge. "Bite ya bum, Jake. Make room for the lady. I'm sure there's nothin' she'd like bitter than to cuddle up nixt to you while she's eating her weinah. Isn't that right, Imily?"

I wasn't sure what kind of game these two

were playing, but if they thought they could scare me —

Well, they *were* scaring me, but Jake's plate was empty. Chances were, he'd be leaving soon.

"Come right over here and set your keister down beside me," Diana said. She nudged Bernice, who anchored the bench on her right, "Would you mind sliding over?"

"WHAT?" Bernice shouted.

Guy held up his hand in apology. "You'll have to forgive her. The musket-firing demonstration seems to have short-circuited the hearing aid in her one ear and deafened her in the other. But it's nothing to worry about. They tell me this happens to people all the time and the effects are only temporary."

"WHAT?"

Oh, God.

"SLIDE DOWN, BERNICE!" Lucille Rassmuson gesticulated wildly from across the table. "MAKE ROOM FOR EMILY."

In an effort to prevent us all from going deaf, I set my tray on the table and squeezed nimbly between Jake and Diana. "Well, would you look at that? I have room and then some, so you can tell Bernice to stay right where she is."

"You tell her," Lucille fussed. "Your vocal cords are younger."

Nora Acres stared at me with her too-blue eyes. "If you don't live in the orphanage," she asked in her sandpaper voice, "where do you live?"

"I live in the United States, in the middle of the country, not too far from the city of Chicago. Have you heard of Chicago?"

"Is that near the Big Apple?"

"West of the Big Apple."

"I live near the Big Winch."

Heath draped his arm around his mother's shoulder. "Coober Pedy's most famous tourist attraction is the Big Winch."

"Winch or wench?" asked Roger. "If it's wench, you've got my attention."

"It's a gigantic bucket hanging from a crosspiece that has a crank on each ind," said Heath. "A winch. All that's missing is a will."

"I've seen the Big Banana," Nora muttered.

"The concrete thing at Coffs Harbour?" asked Lola. She dismissed it with a flick of her wrist. "Too cheesy for words. But Jake *loooved* the theme park, didn't you, Jakey?"

Jake fell into the kind of silence that usually precedes volcanic eruptions. I shoved

156

half my hot dog bun into my mouth and chewed furiously, hoping to get out of here before the ash began to fly.

Roger Piccolo caught Heath's eye. "This is pure speculation, but would I be right to assume that Coober Pedy is intensely hot throughout the year?"

"Coober Pedy's so hot, the divil moved out a few years back," Heath teased.

"Wreaks havoc on the skin, doesn't it?"

Heath arched an eyebrow. "We're not a town of beauty queens, mate."

"I've visited the Big Oyster," said Nora. "It has searchlights for eyes."

Roger pinched the bridge of his nose in frustration. "What I'm trying to ask without sounding too insensitive is, do most of the people end up looking like your mother?"

Heath's expression grew hard. "You'd bitter mind what you're saying."

"I'm trying to help! I'm a researcher for a company called GenerX Technologies, and I'd like to work with your mother to freshen her complexion. I can reverse sun damage and any visible signs of aging without scalpels or harsh chemicals and have her looking decades younger in a matter of months. Wouldn't you like to see her lose the wrinkles? She could become the poster child for the nonsurgical face-lift. We could feature her on infomercials and follow up with a documentary that would go directly to DVD."

"All the tables in the room, and I have to pick the one with the resident con artist," Diana Squires groaned. She jabbed a cautionary finger at Heath. "Don't believe a word he's telling you. He'll take you to the cleaners and leave your mom with the same number of wrinkles she has now. That garbage he sells might even give her a few more."

Roger's flabby cheeks puffed with indignation. "Well, well, well. I heard the competition walked among us. So, you're the Infinity maggot. Kee-reist, I knew the stench in here was coming from more than just the boiled hot dogs."

My hot dog was boiled? I stared cross-eyed at the uneaten portion sticking out of my mouth. *Euw.* I hated boiled hot dogs.

"What you're smelling is success," Diana shot back. "Considering the pathetic results GenerX has had with its product, I can understand why the scent is foreign to you."

"I don't know how industry maggots acquire their information," Roger challenged, "but yours is all wrong. Your company would kill for GenerX's market share, but it ain't ever gonna happen because your product is crap."

"I've visited the Big Bull," said Nora. "It's got bollocks wot swing in the breeze."

Jake sailed a scrap of paper across the table at Roger. "What's that?" Roger snapped, salvaging it from the clutter on his tray.

"Business card. For a small fee, I can take care of maggots for you. Jake Silverthorn. Bug Be Gone. No pist is too tough for me to tackle. Ants, roaches, spidehs, snakes, and" — he looked from Roger to Diana — "the occasional maggot."

Diana sucked in her breath and stared at him, aghast. "Are you threatening me?"

"What *is* it with you people?" Lucille hollered. "Can't you see some of us are trying to eat? Maggots. Ants. Enough with the bug talk already!" She shot menacing looks at Jake and Roger before shoving a forkful of macaroni and cheese into her mouth.

"What's your problem?" Jake taunted in an oily voice. "Bugs make you squeamish?"

She slammed her fist down so hard, our trays jumped. "Listen, spider man, before my Dick passed away, he operated the largest pest control company in Windsor City, Iowa. Our retirement fund was built on the backs of dead bugs, so don't accuse me of being squeamish."

"I bit your Iowa bugs can't kill you."

"Maybe not," Lucille conceded, looking Cheshire Cat smug, "but our bugs are a damned sight uglier than the ones you've got here! So there."

Way to one-up the guy. Tell him we have uglier bugs.

"I've seen the Big Prawn," said Nora.

"Mrs. Acres," Diana implored, "the man sitting beside you is a fraud. You mustn't listen to him. I'm the only person at this table who can make promises and follow through with results. I can make you younger, more beautiful. And when the world sees what we've done, your face will become the most celebrated image in the world."

Nora nodded vacantly. "The Big Lawn Mower. The Big Koala. The koala didn't have bollocks 'cause it was a girl. The Big Merino —"

"If you're a prime example of what she can expect, let's hope she does the smart thing and runs like hell," Roger interrupted. "What's buried under all that facial cement you're wearing? Jimmy Hoffa?"

"You've niveh seen ugly 'til you've seen a three-horned dung beetle," Jake drawled. "A prehistoric body encased in indestruc-

tible black armor with horns that can pierce
—"

"European corn borer!" Lucille yelled.
"The grossest, ugliest — TV stations had to
stop showing it in commercials over the dinner hour because it was making folks sick."

"Pimple-faced bush cricket."

"Rootworm. Cutworm." She added a
pinch of horror movie vibrato to her voice.
"Alf*aaaaal*fa weevil."

"Topless cannibal ant!"

Back home we put our ants in farms; here,
they put them in strip joints. Cool.

"Would you all stay where you are so I
can get a group photo?" Guy asked as he
muscled himself off the bench.

"Emily warned us to stay away from you,"
Lucille raved at Jake. "I never listen to her
'cause she's usually wrong about everything,
but she was right about you!"

"Is that so?" Jake spat out his toothpick
like a dart from a blowgun. It whistled onto
his plate, spearing a half-eaten fuscilli
noodle.

Whoa! Anyone who could spit with that
degree of accuracy shouldn't be killing bugs.
He should be playing major league baseball.

He angled around to face me. "What
exactly has Imily been saying about me?"

"Go ahead, Emily," Lucille prodded. "Tell him."

Tell him to his face that he was a threat to humanity? Right. Why didn't I just paint a target on my chest and hand him an Uzi? "Umm . . . just out of curiosity, do you have professional baseball in Australia?"

"Would everyone on Emily's side of the table squeeze in a little tighter?" asked Guy. He looked through his viewfinder. "Bernice and Lola are still out of frame."

"WHAT?" yelled Bernice.

"Ouch!" I shifted position as Jake pressed against me, driving something hard and intractable into my thigh. I stared down at the lump in the hip pocket of his shorts. "What are you packing? A lunch pail?"

He wriggled his hand into his pocket and removed a clear plastic cube that he slammed onto his tray.

"Hold that pose," Guy instructed as he pressed the shutter.

"What have you got inside there?" Roger asked, scrutinizing the container. "Some kind of carpenter ant?"

"Spideh," said Jake as he yanked off the lid.

Holy shit. I shot off the bench like a Jack-in-the-Box, elbows and legs flying. Roger burst out in raucous laughter. "Calm down,

Emily. It's not a tarantula." He leaned across the table for a better look. "It's pretty good-looking as far as spiders go. No hair. Compact. Nice glossy exterior. Looks like a garden-variety arthropod. What's so special about it?"

Diana shrieked as the creature landed on her nose.

"It's a jumpeh," said Jake.

"EHHHHH!" Diana swatted it off.

"Oh, my God!" I cried, as it leaped onto the table. "Is it poisonous?"

Jake's mouth slid into a lazy sneer. "What do you think?"

"Run!" Diana screamed.

"WHAT?" yelled Bernice.

Lucille hoisted herself to her feet. "RUN FOR YOUR LIVES!"

The terror in Lucille's voice started a buzz that prompted rubbernecking, uncertainty, foot shuffling, and a chaotic stampede out the doors. Jake grinned at the disorder, while Heath stood over his mother, tugging on her elbow.

"C'mon, luvy. We need to go."

"Leave me be." She shooed him away. "I'm not through eating."

"Could you use some help?" I asked, running around the table to them.

Heath nodded his thanks. "Up you go, Mum. Imily will carry your tray outside for you."

Jake snatched up his plastic container and stalked the table. "All right ladies and gints, where's the little buggeh hiding?"

I screeched as it leaped onto Nora's tray.

"Mum! It's not safe to sit here!"

Nora smashed her fist on top of it, smiling serenely. "It is now."

"It wasn't poisonous after all?" said Guy, as we descended the long flight of stairs leading to the gold mine. Bernice had taken one look at the stairs and said she'd rather shop, so it was just the two of us.

"Nope. Henry made Jake fess up. It was just a harmless jumping spider, which was a good thing for Nora. Henry said there are some insects so deadly, you can get poisoned simply by touching them."

"Do you think she knew what she was doing?"

I shrugged. "I'm not sure she's operating on all cylinders. She's apparently been on a decades-long quest to find her twin sister Beverly, and I think the stress has taken its toll. But Heath has found some new leads on the internet, and he's hoping to locate Beverly within a few weeks. Maybe that'll give Nora's mental health a boost."

"Any repercussions for Jake?"

"Big-time. Henry confiscated his plastic container and warned him that if he instigated any more bug incidents, he and Lola would be sent packing. Lola complained that she had nothing to do with the incident and resented both the threat of punishment and Jake's moronic smirk. So she cussed them both out, vowed to get even with Jake for causing her so much embarrassment, and stormed off for destinations unknown."

"What was Henry's reaction to her theatrics?"

"He gave Jake his email address. In his off-hours, Henry apparently does a little moonlighting as an online marriage counselor."

Arriving at the bottom of the stairs, we headed uphill toward a weathered clapboard shelter that appeared to be the waiting area for the gold mine tour. Sheer cliffs flanked us on the right. Scrubby trees flanked our left. Mining cart tracks led to nowhere. Wooden planks shored up the cliff wall and framed an entryway that tunneled deep into the mountainside. I skidded on some loose pebbles and yelped as my legs gave way beneath me.

"Easy there." Guy grabbed my arm, right-ing me. "No twisted ankles allowed."

"Thanks." I regarded the gritty terrain with a bit more respect. "I guess I need training wheels, or a keeper."

"I thought you already had one. Or is it two?"

"Funny you should mention that."

"I don't know many women who can brag about having two such good-looking bucks chasing after them. Neither one of them can stop talking about you. Why don't you do one of them a favor and marry him?" He paused for a moment's contemplation. "Unless you think marriage is for old fogies and you're into something more kinky."

"No! I want to get married, and this trip is supposed to help me get to know both Etienne and Duncan a little better. The problem is, they're spending so much time in front of your camera, you're getting to know them better than I am."

Guy winced. "Ouch."

"Exactly."

He held up his hands in surrender. "*Mea culpa.* I didn't understand the situation. No more photos. But I couldn't help myself. Bone structure like theirs comes along once in a lifetime. I thought I could make them famous."

"They don't want to be famous."

"If that's what they told you, they're lying. Everyone wants to be famous. It's part of our culture. Ask my kids. Fame is the in thing, and I'm talking about more than just fifteen minutes of it. You can slink through life unnoticed, or you can choose to make a splash."

"And you think splash is better?"

"I know splash is better. I've had it both ways, and I'll take splash any day."

"In other words, you think Etienne and Duncan are being shortsighted."

"I'm not walking in their shoes, Emily, but I'll tell you this. My father would have killed to be someone, with a capital S. He envied everyone. He wanted what everyone else had. When I earned some notoriety, he wanted to be me. On his death bed, he said if he had to do it all over again, he'd do everything differently so that he'd be the person everyone wanted to be. I don't think he was happy for more than a minute throughout his entire life." He shook his head and raked his hand through his hair. "He died just about a year ago."

"I'm so sorry, Guy."

"Thanks. It's a real shock to lose someone when he's in perfect health."

"Excuse me?"

"Prior to being broadsided by a semi, there'd been nothing wrong with him. Afterward, he had so many internal injuries, they couldn't piece him back together again. His kidneys stopped functioning, so I volunteered to donate one of mine, but preliminary tests showed that I'm diabetic, so that eliminated me from the donor pool. By then it was only a matter of time. He never lived long enough to undergo surgery. That was a hell of a month."

"It's too bad he never got to talk to the clerk in the jewelry store here. She would have made him feel *really* important. She knew all about your family history. Were you aware that in Victoria, the name Madelyn is right up there with the Queen? You should talk to the clerk. She'll make your head swell."

"Is that right? Yeah, my dad would have eaten up the attention and been on top of the world. He might have even been happy for a day. Guess my kids will have to experience the excitement for him. They're going to be so full of themselves. But they're good kids. They deserve the attention."

I saw a few familiar faces when we arrived at the shelter. Lola Silverthorn sat on a bench in the bright sunlight, slopping lotion on her legs. Diana Squires waited in the shade beneath the building's overhanging roof, hardly recognizable in her floppy hat and sunglasses. Roger Piccolo paced the grounds in what looked to be a futile search for rare vegetation. And the two Dicks exchanged belly laughs as they huddled near Lola's bench.

"Will you excuse me?" Guy asked as he powered up his camera. "Since your beaus are off-limits and Bernice is *in absentia,* I find myself in the market for willing substitutes. Wish me luck."

"Have you ever tried looking at people face-to-face instead of through the viewfinder of your camera?"

He laughed. "Too late for that. I don't know any other way."

"The tour begins in two minutes!" a man called from the mine entrance.

I caught up to the Dicks, whose belly laughs diminished to giggles when they saw me. "Hi, guys. I see the ladies cut you loose. So what are they up to?"

"Fanning their muumuus in front of the electric hand dryers in the ladies' room," Dick Teig howled. "One minute we're panning for gold at the edge of a mighty river, and the next minute —"

"Splat!" said Dick Stolee, slapping his

hands together with belly flop loudness. "Helen stumbled into Grace and they both went down like Sumo wrestlers. It was hideous. The screams. The flailing limbs. The wails for help."

"I thought they were goners," said Dick Teig.

"Oh, my God! What did you do?"

"Jumped in after 'em."

"But you can't swim!"

"A man's gotta do what he's gotta do," he said humbly.

"That was so heroic!" I gave him a congratulatory pat on his shoulder, suddenly struck by something very peculiar. I stood back, eyeing him up and down. "So you jumped bravely into the river and hauled the girls to shore."

"Yup."

"How come your clothes aren't wet?"

Dick Stolee wheezed with laughter. "Because the water's only two inches deep!"

"Two inches deep?" I scoffed. "That's a creek!"

Dick Teig stuck his jaw out defensively. "In Iowa it'd be a river."

"This way, folks," our tour guide called out. "Have your tickets riddy. A hundred and fifty years ago, if you worked a mine like this, you could be as young as thirteen years old, and you'd most likely be Chinese. It was dark, dirty work, but the money was good. If you could stay alive, you prospered."

I let people file in front of me as I paused to dig my camera out of my shoulder bag.

"I hope this tour's a beaut," Heath remarked, stopping beside me. "I admire the commercial genius who came up with the idea of having blokes pay to explore a fake gold mine. We should do that in Coober Pedy. We've got plinty of real mines to go tramping around in."

I glanced curiously left and right. "Where's Nora?"

"She's afraid of dark places, so Hinry's looking after her for a spill. He mintioned taking her down to the creek to pan for gold. She's fond of being in the sunshine. Be nice if she could strike it rich."

Better still, it would be nice if she could avoid Jake for the rest of the afternoon. He'd been seriously ticked off when she hammered his spider. Considering what a nutcase he was, there was no telling how he'd get even, but I suspected he'd find a way. Poor Nora was probably in Jake's crosshairs and didn't even know it. I applauded Heath's ability to entrust her to

Henry's care. If she were my mom, I'd be hard-pressed to let her out of my sight.

I sighed at my own frailties. I was so freaking neurotic.

"Would you like me to git a picture of you in front of the mine?" Heath asked, as we walked toward the entrance.

"How 'bout I get a picture of you? I bet you're a lot more photogenic than I am. I can use it in the newsletter I write for our travel club. You'll add a dash of local color." Not to mention a ton of sex appeal. I'd entitle it, *The Wonder Down Under.*

We handed in our tickets, then lagged behind so I could set up my shot. "Right about there is good," I said, as Heath leaned his shoulder against a vertical support beam.

"Don't even think of taking a picture without me in it," Lola cooed as she appeared out of nowhere and muckled onto his arm. She tousled her hair and pressed her cheek against his. "We're riddy. Shoot."

Oh, this was nice. I had a perfect shot highlighting half of Heath's face and all of Lola's silicone-enhanced chest, but I'd be damned if I'd allow her to ruin my idea. I clicked the shutter. "Great shot!" I'd entitle it, *Australian Flotation Devices.*

Lola ended the session by cradling Heath's face and kissing him like a Power Vac intent on sucking the lips off his face. "C'mon, you luscious hunk of man," she drawled, as she pulled him into the tunnel. "I'd feel terrible if you missed anything because of me."

He stumbled after her, managing a wild gesture in my direction before being consumed by darkness. I glanced around the deserted grounds, looking from cliff top to forest, creeped out by the sudden quiet and feeling terribly exposed. Hearing a twig snap, I spun around, wondering if Jake could be out there someplace, spying on us.

For Lola's sake, I hoped not.

Shifting the power switch on my camera to off, I hurried into the mine.

CHAPTER 9

"Don't surprise me they can't find them plants," Nana reasoned late that night. "Your grampa could never find nothin' neither. Menfolk are like that, dear. I think their ho-hos cause some kinda chronic visual impairment."

Nana, Tilly, and I were gathered around a table in the hotel lounge, winding down after our big evening of Broadway entertainment at the Princess Theater. While Etienne and Duncan ordered drinks at the bar, I relayed the information I'd scavenged throughout the day.

"Is the university group going to continue searching?" Tilly asked.

I shrugged. "Conrad insisted they not give up, but I'm not sure the plant is even there anymore. I have a sneaking suspicion Diana Squires might be carrying it in her backpack."

"No kiddin'?"

I regarded the other tour guests who'd stopped off for a nightcap. "Either that, or Roger Piccolo may have done something to camouflage it temporarily, with the intention of going back for it during his conference. He has a number plotted on his GPS unit that could very well be Nana's angiosperms."

Nana sucked thoughtfully on her dentures. "So you think one a them followed the Bellows woman outside, knocked her off without no one seein', made it look like natural causes, grabbed my Polaroids, found the plant, and either stuffed it into a backpack or sent a beam into outer space that'd mark it for future reference?"

Why did my theories always sound more credible before someone repeated them out loud?

Nana gave a little nod. "I like it."

"You do?"

"It's completely implausible," said Tilly. "Your time line is a farce. You flout the laws of nature and physics. Your explanation smacks of wizardry and lone gunman theories." She nodded her approval. "I like it, too. Sounds like something straight out of the Warren Commission."

"So how we gonna nab 'em?" asked Nana.

I motioned them to huddle closer. "First

thing we need to do is find out what's in Diana's backpack."

"Airport security should be able to help with that tomorrow," said Tilly. "If the X-ray machine indicates she's carrying a plant, they'll definitely want to take a look. The Australian government is very strict about what they allow passengers to transport across state lines."

"Tilly and me'll get in line with her so's we can keep an eye on what's goin' down."

"Good. One of you in front of her and one of you behind. And I'll go through security ahead of you so I can corner her if she gets pulled aside. I'll be dying to hear her explanation of how a hundred-million-year-old plant got into her backpack."

Nana raised her chubby little forefinger. "Emily, dear, which part a them angiosperms is s'posed to be the good part? The leaves, the root, or the stem?"

"Uhhh — Beats me." I looked to Tilly for assistance. "Do you know?"

"It might be all three. There's no way of telling until they get it into the laboratory for testing."

"If the plant dies, can them folks in the laboratory still run tests on it?"

"Uhhh —" I looked to Tilly again.

"Not being a botanist, I'm not sure how

176

to answer that, Marion, but I would assume that the scientists at Infinity would prefer the plant be alive."

"That's what I figured. What I can't figure is, how she plans on keepin' the thing alive for the next two weeks if it's all squushed up in her backpack. The leaves are gonna crumble like dried oregano." Nana shrugged. "Maybe she can use 'em to make hundred-million-year-old spaghetti sauce."

"If I could get my hands on Roger Piccolo's GPS, would either of you know how to use it?" I asked.

"Your father would know how to use it, dear. He's got one on his harvester, between the mini-refrigerator and the portable cappuccino maker."

Personal GPS units hadn't caught on in Iowa, mostly because Iowans never get lost. We're all born with internal compasses in our brains that make street signs, road maps, and AAA Trip Tiks completely unnecessary. It's the neatest perk of hailing from a landlocked, tornado-ridden state in the middle of nowhere.

Well, that, and the Iowa chops.

"My apologies for the delay with your drinks, ladies. One Shirley Temple with extra cherries" — Etienne set a glass down in front of Nana — "and one Professor and

Mary Ann." He placed the other highball in front of Tilly, who clasped her hands with girlish pleasure.

"What a delightful surprise, Inspector Miceli. I had no idea there was a cocktail named for us stodgy old academics. I'm honored."

"It's just Etienne, Ms. Hovick. My police inspector days are behind me." He kissed the crown of my head and trailed his thumb across my cheek. "Be right back with the rest of the order."

"What'd he mean about his police inspector days bein' behind him?" Nana asked, plucking a cherry off its skewer and popping it into her mouth.

"Did I forget to mention the latest? Etienne took it upon himself to retire from the police force. They gave him a gold watch and everything."

Tilly swished her cocktail around in her mouth like a professional wine taster. "This is quite tasty. I believe I detect apricot brandy, vodka, and a hint of lime. Has he told you what he plans to do with himself for the rest of his life? He's rather young to be sitting around, gathering moss on his north side."

"He can do anything he wants," Nana piped up. "He's loaded."

I lasered a look at her. "About that — You were giving him financial advice on the sly and never bothered to tell me?"

"Do I look like a snitch?"

"No, but — Joblessness? Lavish wealth? This is a lot to have dropped on me all at once."

Nana sighed. "That was probably your grampa's last thought, too, when the roof a that ice shanty come crashin' down on him like it done." She patted my hand. "It's not so bad, dear. Trust your young man. He knows what he's doin'."

"Here you go, pretty." Duncan slid a shot glass onto the table then, with a pint of Guinness in hand, sat down beside me. "Try that out for size." It was white and frothy, with a consistency like melted Marshmallow Fluff.

"What is it?" I gave it a sniff.

"Looks like Kaopectate," said Nana.

I tongued some froth into my mouth.

"No, no, no," Duncan said, laughing. "Don't sip it. It's a shooter. You're supposed to knock it back in a single slug."

"Like chugalugging? I've never been good at that. Everything always comes back out through my nose."

"I'll try it," Nana volunteered. With Duncan's blessing, she knocked it back in one swallow.

"Well?" I asked.

She broke out in a giddy smile. "Not bad. It's got a better kick than Kaopectate."

"Try this, *bella*." Etienne placed a champagne flute before me. "It's much more your style. Meant to be sipped rather than chugalugged." He exchanged a defiant look with Duncan before circling the table to an empty chair.

I held the glass up to the light. Bubbles effervesced to the surface like a galaxy of shooting stars. "Champagne. Yum. What else is in it?"

"Peach brandy and orange juice."

"It's an AARP cocktail," Duncan teased. "Did Miceli tell you he's on their mailing list now that he's turned in his badge?"

"Buttati in un mare pieno di merda come te," Etienne said with quiet restraint.

"Vaffanculo," Duncan returned calmly.

I looked from one to the other. "I *hate* it when you guys do that! Come on, what did you just say?"

"Drink up what's in front of you, darling. There's more coming."

"I propose a toast," said Duncan, lifting his Guinness. "A little Irish blessing: 'There are good ships, and there are wood ships, the ships that sail the sea, but the best ships are friendships, and may they always be.' "

Aw, that was so sweet. We clinked glasses all around, and I took a sip of my champagne. I licked my lips, savoring the taste. "Wow, this is the best stuff I've ever drunk out of a champagne flute. The peach and orange really pop." I took another sip. "What's it called?"

Etienne's lips slid into a slow, sensuous smile. "Sweet Surrender."

Duncan rolled his eyes. Mumbling something under his breath, he took a swig of his stout.

I toasted Etienne. "An exquisite choice."

"Exquisite choices are my specialty," he said, drilling me with a look that made my tummy tingle.

Duncan drained his mug and thumped it onto the table. "I'm ready for another round. Anyone care to join me?"

Etienne motioned toward the bar. "It's on its way."

"By the by," I said with a dramatic flourish, "you'll be happy to know that I talked to Guy today and convinced him to stop monopolizing the two of you, so you're officially off the hook and free to spend your time as you please." I smiled impishly.

"Thank you very much; it was nothing."

Both men whipped Palm Pilots out of their jacket pockets. "I have dibs sitting beside her on the plane tomorrow," Duncan said, moving his stylus over the display screen.

"No can do." Etienne consulted his own screen. "I have that marked in stone. See?" He flashed it at Duncan. "You can sit beside her on the bus ride from the airport to Adelaide."

"A ten-minute ride? I don't think so. I want her for the plane ride and miscellaneous free time tomorrow afternoon. You can borrow her for dinner, then the three of us can do something afterward."

"I have plans for her tomorrow evening after dinner, and no offense, old bean, but they don't include you."

Duncan smiled stiffly. "If you get her for after-dinner activities tomorrow, I get her for the entire day in the Barossa Valley, *plus* dinner alone with her and any postdinner intrigue we care to engage in."

"Interesting take on equal time," Etienne said in amusement.

"Works for me, *old bean.*"

"Do I look entirely obtuse to you?"

"How honest do you want me to be?"

"Bischero," rasped Etienne.

"Farabutto," Duncan snapped back.

Oh, yeah. Guy's not monopolizing them anymore was working out *really* well. I glanced around the bar. Where was he? Maybe I could convince him I'd only been kidding.

"Evenin'." A barmaid carrying a tray of colorful mixed drinks arrived at our table. "Who gets the Shirley Temple with extra cherries?"

Nana raised her hand.

"The Professor and Mary Ann?"

"I'll take it," said Tilly.

"Dry martini with a twist?"

"That would be me," said Etienne.

She held up a highball glass whose contents resembled a Pepto-Bismol shake. "Strawberry Kiss?"

Etienne nodded toward me. "The young lady."

She plucked the final glass off the tray. "Old Bastard?"

"Here," said Etienne, slapping the table in front of Duncan.

Duncan's mouth inched into a crooked grin. *"Maleducato,"* he said, bowing his head politely.

"Zoccolo." Etienne nodded back.

"Anything else I can bring you right away?" the barmaid asked.

"I wouldn't mind havin' a refill on my Kaopectate shooter." Nana waved her empty shot glass at Duncan. "What'd you say it's called?"

"A Screaming Orgasm."

I hung my head. *Oh, God.*

Nana handed the shot glass to the barmaid. "Could you make it a double?"

"I need to call it a night, guys. My head is fuzzy."

"It's only a little past midnight," said Etienne, as we stood outside my door. "We have the whole night ahead of us."

"I think you should invite us in for a nightcap," Duncan urged.

"The only thing in my room that's even marginally alcoholic is mouthwash. I'm going to bed. Six o'clock comes early, and I still have to pack." I unlocked my door and blew each of them a kiss. "Night, night. Thanks for a fun evening."

"But, Emily," they pleaded, doing the unison thing again.

I closed the door and slumped against it, my attention drawn immediately to a red light that was blinking rapidly in the darkness. I flipped on the light switch and walked to the phone, feeling a moment's dread as I regarded the indicator light signaling a message on voice mail. I hated unexpected phone calls when I was traveling. They always made me fear the worst. I picked up the phone and punched a button.

"Imily, hi, this is Peter Blunt from the coroner's office. Wanted to git back to you about your grandmother's photographs. We didn't find any Polaroid snapshots among Ms. Bellows's belongings, just the postcards, so I hope they turn up for you someplace ilse. Sorry I don't have bitter news for you. My apologies to your grandmother."

I replaced the phone on its cradle, this new information causing my brain to grow even more fuzzy than it was before. So if Claire Bellows didn't have Nana's photos, who did?

"I thought for sure they was gonna pull her over to search her backpack," Nana said in a conspiratorial tone the next morning, "but she cleared security slick as a whistle. Didn't matter, you gettin' stuck at the back a the line, dear. There wasn't nothin' to see."

I'd been waylaid helping Bernice drag her luggage to the check-in counter after one of the wheels fell off her pullman, so I went through the security line last rather than first. "The plant can't be in her knapsack, then."

"And she wouldn't a packed it in her grip 'cause it'd get her clothes all full a dirt and prickles," said Nana.

Tilly leaned heavily on her cane. "If she didn't pack it in either her knapsack or her suitcase, should we assume she didn't take it at all?"

We were huddled behind a self-serve display case in an airport candy shop, surrounded by chocolate penguins, koalas, kangaroos, and wombats that produced an aroma like Hershey-bar-scented room deodorizer. Inhaling too deeply would probably cause serious weight gain.

"The only thing I'm gonna assume is that them chocolates taste so good, I need to get me a box," Nana said, grabbing a serving tray and tongs. "I'd buy some for the boys, but I'm afraid they'd melt before we got home."

"Our hotel rooms should be equipped with mini-refrigerators," I reminded her, "so you'd probably be safe."

"The place they'd melt would be in my mouth, dear. When it comes to chocolate, I got no self-control."

"Ladies," Tilly interrupted, "we're getting off topic. If Diana Squires doesn't have the plant, should we delete her from our list of suspects who might be responsible for Claire's death?"

"I wish we could go back to Port Campbell," I said in frustration. "If the plant is still there, we wouldn't have to —"

"S'cuse me, dear." Nana nodded toward the main concourse. "What do you s'pose that's all about?"

Just outside the candy shop, Duncan stood mutely while Diana circled her arms around him in an affectionate bear hug. She cooed and laughed while he nodded; squeezed his arm while he smiled.

"Looks like she's hittin' on 'im," said Nana.

"I find that rather surprising considering the age gap between them," said Tilly.

"How old do you s'pose she is? I can't tell for all the makeup."

I watched the encounter with curiosity. Duncan was always open and friendly with people, but I wondered what he'd done to merit all the extra attention. Diana stood on her tiptoes to give him a peck on his cheek, then trundled off with her knapsack strapped to her back like an iron lung.

"I have no idea what prompted that," I said, "but I know we're all itching to find out."

I caught up to him halfway to our gate. "You walk too fast," I teased as I took up stride beside him.

He took my hand and smiled. "Hey, Em, what's the good word?"

"Mmmm" — I cocked my head as I regarded his cheek — "lipstick."

He paused for a nanosecond before swiping his hand down his face. "Is it gone?"

"Almost." I rubbed his cheekbone with my fingertips. "For future reference? Deep burgundy isn't your best shade."

He grinned. "A souvenir from Diana Squires, who stopped to express her gratitude. That woman gives me the willies, Em. She looks as if she learned to apply makeup from an undertaker."

"What was she expressing her gratitude about?"

"A random act of kindness. She was trying to manage a huge box plus her luggage this morning, so I offered to carry the box for her. It was no big deal, but she was acting like —"

"She left the hotel with a box?" My voice became a squeak. "Where is it now?"

"Back at the hotel. The front desk clerk was going to mail it for her."

"Are you serious?" I clenched my fists. No wonder her knapsack hadn't sent up any red flags. Damn! "Did you see the label? Do you know where she was sending it?"

"I caught a glimpse. A company called Infinity Inc. in Wilmington, Delaware."

"Was it heavy?"

"Not for me."

"Did she want it overnighted?"

"Emily —"

"Do they *have* overnight mail in Australia? With the international dateline thing, it could arrive in Delaware even before she sends it."

He clapped his hands on my shoulders and gave me a narrow look. "Would you mind telling me why you're so freaked out about Diana Squires's box?"

My mouth fell open. "This isn't freaked out. Yesterday at lunch? When Jake let his spider loose? *That* was freaked out."

"Is this a private party or can anyone join in?" asked Etienne, pausing beside us with Nana on one arm and Tilly on the other. "I couldn't resist picking up a couple of good-looking young ladies along the way."

"Anyone want a chocolate?" Nana flipped open the lid of a small white box and offered up the contents. "I bought a whole Noah's Ark a local wildlife. If you're one a them vegetarians, it's a good way to try kangaroo."

The guys happily depleted much of Nana's menagerie as we moseyed toward our departure gate. However, unlike M&Ms, this chocolate melted in their hands as well as their mouths, so they had to make a pit stop at the men's room. When they'd gone, I herded Nana and Tilly to a quiet corner in the gate area.

"Do you know why no one could find Nana's plant yesterday? Because it wasn't there anymore. Diana mailed it to Delaware!"

"No kiddin'?" Nana said, wide-eyed.

"No kidding. She packed it in a big box, and Duncan carried it to the front desk for her this morning."

"That was nice a him," said Nana. "His parents raised him real good."

"Did she actually tell Duncan what was in the box?" asked Tilly.

"Well, no, but it was addressed to Infinity Inc. What else could it be?"

Nana shrugged. "Could be she's mailin' all her dirty laundry back home so she'll have room in her grip for lots a new stuff. Some folks haven't figured out it's cheaper just to spring for another suitcase."

Tilly rapped her cane on the floor. "If you

turn around, you'll notice she's right over there. Perhaps we should simply ask her."

She was standing in a tight circle with Roger Piccolo and Heath Acres, her hands flying into the air as she railed at Heath.

"What do you s'pose them three's got to talk about?" asked Nana.

Heath was shaking his head, looking as if he wanted to escape, only to appear more desperate when Roger started ranting, too.

I made a shushing sound that echoed my disgust. "I bet you anything they're arguing about Nora. They're probably trying to cram incentives down Heath's throat so he'll convince his mother to endorse their company products. I hope he doesn't sell out. I think they should just leave the poor woman alone. Who cares how many wrinkles she has?"

"Obviously, Infinity and GenerX care," said Tilly. "Why else the hard sell? Do you suppose they think they've found the goose that laid the golden egg?"

"I gotta sit," Nana declared as she limped toward a row of unoccupied chairs. "My kick-ass boots are killin' my feet."

"I'm so relieved to hear you say that," Tilly admitted as she limped to the chair beside her. "If I had to do it again, I'd buy the ones with the orthopedic inserts."

I sat down next to Nana. "You know, ladies, if you switched to closed-toe walking shoes, you could probably lose the boots and still be protected."

They leaned over to regard each other's footwear with the kind of adulation people normally reserve for newborns and Lamborginis. "We don't wanna lose 'em, dear. Once you look this hot, it's hard settlin' for ordinary." She leaned back in her seat and smiled. "You wanna see some pictures? I got a new batch."

I gestured to Conrad and Ellie while Nana plowed through her pocketbook. "Are you all set to leave Melbourne behind?" I asked as they joined us.

Conrad looked so miserable, even his mustache was drooping. "I've failed you, Marion. The university has failed you. My sincere apologies. It pains me to think what might have been."

Ellie nodded in sympathy. "Connie knows a scientist in Sweden who has a long-standing offer to award one million American dollars to anyone who can provide him with samples of plants previously thought extinct. Just think. The two of you might have ended up splitting all that money."

"I'm a scientist," Conrad said dismissively. "The last thing a scientist ever concerns himself with is money."

Ellie stared at him as if his nose had suddenly been injected with growth hormone. "That's not what you said last night when you were fretting about how you were going to scrape together the down payment on the new condomin—"

"These ladies *are not* interested in our financial affairs," he snapped, cutting her off.

"Well, you're an old fool if you can stand there and claim that five hundred thousand dollars wouldn't solve a lot of our retirement problems."

She glared at him. He glared at her. Nana handed them a photograph.

"That there's Bernice when she was gettin' chased by the emu. I got a real good angle showin' off her new boots.

"This is the stain on Bernice's shirt after the koala peed on it. I'm real happy we're not doin' scratch and sniff.

"Here's the stagecoach at Ballarat. Them two fellas makin' horns behind their wives' heads are the Dicks.

"This one is a little four-legged critter what I found runnin' around. Couldn't figure out what it was."

Conrad studied the last photo in lengthy

silence. "Where did you shoot this, Marion?"

"I think it was down by them trees 'fore you get to the gold mine."

"Have you any idea what this creature is?"

"I was leanin' toward chipmunk."

"This is a desert rat kangaroo!" he said excitedly.

Nana froze. "THERE WAS A RAT RUNNING AROUND THAT PLACE WE WAS AT YESTERDAY?"

"That's not the point, Marion. It hasn't been seen since nineteen-thirty-five!"

CHAPTER 10

I was missing something. I *knew* I was missing something. But what?

Upon arrival in Adelaide, we'd boarded an air-conditioned bus for a tour of the city and its environs. Adelaide seemed a sleepy, genteel place, big on city parks and Parliamentary-style buildings, and short on skyscrapers and kamikaze traffic. Mothers pushed fancy prams down city sidewalks. Children were meticulously dressed in school uniforms. Everyone looked healthy, happy, and incredibly handsome. It had such a 1950s *It's a Wonderful Life* feel to it, that if I lived here, I expected my neighbors might be Ozzie and Harriet, or Wally and the Beav.

Our hotel sat cheek to jowl with the shopping district and was pretty upscale with its sliding glass doors, balconies, posh bathrooms, and computer hookups. I was sharing a two-bedroom suite with Nana and Tilly, who were exploring Rundle Mall while I sat at the desk in our living room, staring at Nana's computer screen.

From the web, I'd discovered that Conrad Carver was exactly who he said he was. He'd had a distinguished career as a paleobotanist at the Smithsonian Institution, authored several university textbooks, and enjoyed bird-watching, World War II documentaries, and championing environmental issues that promoted the survival of native wildlife on a global scale. There was nothing in his background that hinted of unscrupulous behavior.

So why was I haunted by the feeling that something wasn't quite right? That some critical clue was staring me in the face, but I couldn't see it?

I recalled the scene in the airport this morning, pinpointing the moment when I'd begun to toy with another theory.

It was when Ellie mentioned the money.

Conrad had been so irritated with her. Why? Was he embarrassed about having his financial difficulties revealed, or simply angry that she'd spilled the beans about the million-dollar award? Had he been planning to sell the plant on the sly so he could pocket all the loot himself? Not that Nana would care. Since her big lottery win, five hundred thousand was chump change to her, but if that had been his intent, it was so dishonest!

Dishonesty aside, however, the question that baffled me the most was how could he sell a plant that no one could find?

I drummed my fingers on the desk as I studied Nana's infamous Polaroid. How could a team of university botanists miss this thing? Granted, it looked common as dirt, but these guys were experts. Shouldn't at least one of them have stumbled on it?

I stopped drumming as another thought hit me. *They should have, unless Conrad had been lying to us right from the start.*

Uff da. I typed an entry into the laptop, clicked on a couple of links, wrote down the number that appeared on the screen, and turned off the computer so I could use the phone.

"University of Milbourne, Botany Department," announced the woman who answered. "This is Liz."

"Hi, Liz, I need your help. Is the big international botany conference taking place this week?"

"That would be the week after nixt, luv, on the twenty-fourth."

"Oo-kay. That's what I thought, but when I stopped by the department yesterday, lots of people were gone, so I was afraid I'd mixed my dates up."

"No, no. A group of thim were on a field trip to Port Campbell yesterday. But it turned out to be more of a wild-goose chase. If you need to talk to anyone, do yourself a favor and don't stop by today. Come tomorrow." She lowered her voice to a discreet whisper. "They might be over their grouchies by then."

I rang off and powered up the laptop again, frustrated that my hunch had been off the mark, but glad for the verification. Conrad *said* he'd contacted the university, but how did we know he'd been telling the truth? He could have made up the whole story, and we never would have known the difference. But he *had* contacted them, and they *had* sent a search team, and they'd come up dry. So where did that leave me?

I turned in my chair as the door rattled open. "Hi, ladies." As Nana and Tilly trooped down the long hallway to the living room, I typed the word, angiosperms, into the computer.

"The shoppin' in that mall area is real good, Emily. They got a David Jones store

what sells lots a Queen Elizabeth h
four and five hundred bucks, and
fancy boutiques with scarves and n
and pretty opal earrings."

"Uh-huh." I clicked on the first site listed
and scanned the text.

"We bumped into Conrad and Ellie while
we was out. Conrad said he called Sovereign
Hill to tell 'em they got a desert rat kangaroo runnin' around the grounds. The official he talked to didn't know what that
was, so Conrad called the University a Melbourne's Zoology Department and told 'em
they needed to send a team a experts to Ballarat to look for the critter."

"I bet they could hardly contain their
delight." I scrolled down the page.

"He's sure got a good eye for findin'
stuff."

"*You* have the eye for finding it," Tilly corrected. "*He* has the eye for identifying it."

"Ellie asked if she could hang out with
me and Til' while Conrad run off to the
potty, and she really let loose when he was
gone. She didn't take kindly to him gettin'
cross at her this mornin', so she had lots to
vent about."

"Like what?"

Tilly hovered by my elbow. "Like the decision he made to buy chicken feed futures in

China. When the avian flu hit, the commodity price tanked, and so did his investment. Ellie said it ruined them financially."

"It really depressed her that she didn't have no money to buy one a them gaudy bonnets at David Jones," said Nana. "If you was to ask me, there's times when financial ruin can be a real blessin'."

Words leaped off the web page at me: epiphytes, synapomorphies, *Amborella trichopoda*. Oh, yeah, this was helpful. "How could they afford a trip to Australia if they're in such dire straits?"

"It was a gift from their children for their fiftieth wedding anniversary," said Tilly. "But I take it they don't have much spending money."

"All flowering plants are classified as angiosperms," I said, referencing the screen. "But what if the team from the university wasn't looking for the right one?" I scrutinized Nana's photo. "What if Conrad had them deliberately looking for a plant that wasn't there?"

"That don't make no sense, dear. Why would he do that?"

Puffed up with excitement, I grabbed the Polaroid. "Because —"

I gawked at Nana . . . and blinked. "Out

of curiosity, why do you have a latex gl~
hanging from your ear?"

"It's on account a the girl what pierced
my ears was doin' it for the first time. She
was usin' one a them guns, and she had an
oops. Missed her finger, but she got the tip
a the glove real good. At least there wasn't
no blood. I expect she'll get a mite better
with practice." Nana waggled her earlobe.
"What do you think? Genuine opal."

"The poor girl grew so hysterical, we had
to sit her down and put her head between
her knees," said Tilly. "The store manager
finally had to escort her off the floor, which
is when your grandmother and I decided to
leave."

"With the glove still hanging from your
ear?" She looked as if she had a small udder
attached to her head.

"The manager said someone was gonna
have to cut the thing off with surgical scis-
sors, and he didn't have none, so we're
s'posed to go back tomorrow night. His
wife's a nurse, so she'll be able to do it. But
never mind about me. Finish what you was
sayin', dear."

What *had* I been saying? Oh, yeah. "Remember the night when Conrad discovered
Nana's photo? He threw lots of botany
speak at us, but *I* was the person who sug-

201

gested we report the find to a higher authority."

"I remember that, dear. That's when he said he'd call the University a Melbourne."

"He'd call them before *I* called them. Think about it. Do you see what I'm getting at?"

"I do," said Tilly. "If you called them, they'd need to see Marion's photo to identify the plant, but if Conrad called them, he could tell them anything. He could even tell them to search for another family of plant altogether, and no one would be any the wiser."

Nana sucked in her breath. "Tell 'em to search for the wrong plant. Dang. That'd be real smart a him. Then he could go back to find the real plant and keep that million-dollar award all to hisself. You s'pose he's the one what took my other two snapshots?"

"Now there's a thought," I said, warming to the idea. "Maybe he's playing a shell game with us. While our eyes are locked on one photo, he's playing fast and loose with the other two."

"What if Marion's missing photos show something even more incredible than an extinct plant?" ventured Tilly. "What if she photographed a rare butterfly, or . . . or . . ."

Jake and Lola sat at a corner table w.
Conrad and Ellie, whose body language
indicated they were still miffed at each
other. The rest of my Iowa contingent were
scattered in foursomes throughout the
room, passing envelopes back and forth
between tables.

"What's up with the envelopes?" I asked
Nana.

She craned her neck for a look-see. "Must
be the photos they got back from the one-
hour developin' place this afternoon."

"They're having film developed already?
But we're only four days into the trip."

Tilly smiled archly. "Your grandmother's
success with her photography has sparked
the competitive spirit in everyone else."

"They're all lookin' for a piece a my action," Nana quipped.

"If any of you would like a dish that won't
burn the skin off your tonsils, you might
want to try the yogurt chicken," Duncan
suggested.

"Or the Tandoori chicken with a side dish
of cucumber raita," said Etienne.

"What if you don't got no tonsils?" asked
Nana.

While the boys filled Nana and Tilly in on
the particulars of Indian spices, I watched
Dick Teig swagger over to Conrad and hand

him a stack of photographs. He was soon joined by Alice Tjarks and Osmond, who fell into an orderly queue behind him, and Margi Swanson, who studied her menu while she waited, probably looking for the Indian equivalent of a burger and fries.

Not to be outdone, Dick Stolee presented a handful of photos to Guy, who studied them politely while Helen Teig, Lucille Rassmuson, and Grace jumped in line and began to fuss about who had cut in front of whom.

Oh, God. Just what a posh Indian restaurant needed. Conga lines. What would be next? *The Hokey-Pokey?*

"What looks good to you, *bella?*"

"Huh? Oh —" I turned back to my menu. *Eenie, meenie, meinie* . . . "How about this?"

"A gutsy choice," Etienne whispered, caressing my knee beneath the table. "You never cease to surprise me."

Nana tapped my other knee. "Incoming."

"I'm sorry to bother you." Diana Squires was all smiles as she greeted us. "We're in the middle of a discussion at our table, and I need some backup. Marion, dear, have you thought any more about the Perfecta treatment for your hands?"

"Yup. I'm thinkin' I'll keep the age spots."

Horror filled Diana's eyes. "A whole new you is there for the asking, and you're choosing the old you?"

"I'm pretty fond a the old me. A new me would only confuse George."

"Really? That's disappointing." She glanced back to her table. "Look, I really need you to say something terrific about Perfecta to Heath and Nora. She's in desperate need of this product, Marion, and he's being a twit about the whole thing. The treatment will be free, for God's sakes. What more could he ask for?"

"Maybe he don't want you folks exploitin' her."

"Who's talking about exploiting her? I'm merely trying to improve her quality of life."

"Perhaps the quality of her life doesn't need improvement," Etienne said in a tight voice.

Her eyes lengthened to mean little slits. "Did Roger tell you to say that? He's gotten to you, hasn't he? The pinheaded little twerp. Let me give you some advice: never listen to a man whose face resembles an auto-inflating mattress."

"Do you think he's suffering from a glandular problem?" asked Tilly, glancing toward him.

"What he's suffering from is the effects of

one too many GenerX nutritional shakes. His company has a dirty little secret that they refuse to make public: a steady diet of their crappy product will kill you."

"Maybe they oughta think about warnin' labels," said Nana.

"Speaking of labels," I leaped in a little awkwardly, "would I be terribly rude if I asked how much you paid to mail your package this morning?"

Diana's face twitched with movement that might have been a scowl, a frown, a smile, or all three. It was hard to tell beneath the makeup. "Why do you want to know?" she asked coolly.

"I have to mail a truckload of purchases that won't fit in my suitcase. It's a chronic problem. I always pack too much and don't leave any room for souvenirs and gifts."

"That's too bad, because you'll be forking out big bucks for postage."

I winced. "I was afraid of that. My stuff is really light — balsa wood and paper — but I suppose it'll still cost me an arm and a leg to mail."

Diana eyed me curiously. "What did you buy? Chinese lanterns?"

"Kites," I lied. "For my nephews. What did you buy?"

"Sovereign Hill T-shirts," she said after a

slight hesitation. "For the guys in the lab. I really stocked up. I always send them back something to let them know I'm thinking about them. I've learned that a little kindness directed at the grunts can result in huge dividends when I need samples tested ASAP." She rapped her knuckles on the armrest of Nana's chair. "Marion, dear, we'll talk later."

Etienne bowed his head toward me. "She's lying."

"You don't think she'll talk to Nana later?"

"She's lying about what she bought."

"You're sure?"

"I've spent a dozen years interrogating people, Emily. I know when they're lying. Although I'm not sure why anyone would feel compelled to lie about something as trivial as shopping purchases."

I watched as she returned to her chair. Why indeed?

Our waiter arrived — a tall, angular gentleman dressed in pajama-like pants and a white chef's coat with a mandarin collar. "Good evening." He bowed with practiced elegance. "Welcome to Jasmin. Would you care to order anything from the bar?"

"You bet," said Nana, unable to contain her enthusiasm. "I'd like to have one a them Screamin' Orgasms."

The waiter affected a droll smile as he looked down his aristocratic nose. "Honey, wouldn't we all."

CHAPTER 11

"The Barossa Valley was sittled around eighteen-thirty-six by Lutheran farmers from Germany and Poland who were fleeing religious persecution," Henry informed us over the bus's loudspeaker the next morning.

We were traveling northeast from Adelaide, through gorges of raging river water, hills forested with leafy gum trees, and grassy meadows in shades of green that Sherwin Williams could never duplicate. Vineyards dotted the landscape. Towns gave off an Oktoberfest air. In culinary terms, if Australia's interior was desiccated flat bread, the Barossa Valley was Bavarian cream pie.

"The sittlers built their towns, then planted vineyards that have produced the finest wine ever to tease the human palate. And you needn't take my word for it. You'll be able to judge for yoursilves whin we visit two of the valley's most renowned wineries later today."

"If we have to pay for it, you can count me out," Bernice shouted from the back.

"You don't have to pay to taste wine," Dick Teig mocked. "Everyone knows that."

"Max Schubert's Grange Hermitage is called the bist rid wine in the world," Henry continued. "Australia has mini distinctions like that. For instance, did you know we're home to the world's largest monolith? Anyone know what it is?"

"Ayers Rock," called Tilly. "Although I believe it's now referred to as Uluru, which is the aboriginal name."

"Brilliant. We also boast the largest living thing on earth. Care to giss what that might be?"

"Dick Teig's head!" yelled Bernice.

"The Great Barrier Reef," Nana called out. "I seen it on a Travel Channel special."

We pulled into a parking lot surrounded by a forest of pine, tall red gums, and dense scrub. Beyond the trees was a lake that looked deep enough to moor a luxury liner, but I saw no yachts, no speed boats, not even a dinghy. Australia probably hadn't been populated long enough for folks to figure out how to spoil a quiet mountain lake.

Henry killed the engine and powered the doors open. "Wilcome to the Barossa Dam and Riservoir, which feeds water to regions in the south. The dam was completed in nineteen-oh-three and was such an engineering marvel, it was highlighted in *Scientific American* magazine. The retaining wall curves backward aginst the prissure of the stored water, and the resulting structure provides a doozie of a surprise. I'm not going to till you what it is, but the first person who figures it out gits a free drink."

That's all he had to say to start the stampede. Out the exits they flew, practically trampling each other in their quest for a freebie. When the dust cleared, the only guests remaining on the bus were Etienne, Duncan, and a bewildered Nora.

"Where's Heath?" she asked, as she struggled to her feet. "I've gotta use the toilet."

"I can help you, Nora." I scurried over to her, Etienne and Duncan close on my heels.

"I can take care of her if you'd like to be in the running for a free drink," offered Etienne.

"You grab one arm, Miceli," Duncan instructed. "I'll take the other."

"It's okay, guys." I gave them each a grateful pat on the back. "This is girls' work, right, Nora?"

She crimped her eyes at me. "You're the girl wot's from the orphanage, aren't you?"

What the heck? Maybe it was time for me to live in her reality rather than expect her to live in mine. "You have a good memory, Nora. That was a long time ago."

"Not so long," she said, looping her arm in mine.

"Go on ahead," I said to the guys. "I'll catch up."

"Are you going to help me find Heath?" she asked, as I walked her to the comfort station directly opposite the bus.

"We can both look for him after you're done," I promised, guiding her through the door. I suspected Diana and Roger had him cornered someplace, so he'd probably be pretty easy to find.

While I waited, Henry jaunted down the front exit of the bus and sat down in the step well, clipboard in hand. "A tour guide's work is niveh done," he said, groaning when a chirpy digital tone rang out. "Cill phones. As to their benefit to society, I rank thim up there with the Spanish Inquisition and boils." He unholstered his phone. "This is Hinry."

I watched his expression mutate from an-

214

noyance to concern as he listened for a full minute before uttering a word. "An arrist warrant? I'll be damned. Nothing like this has ever happened before, has it?" He paused. "I didn't think so. Buggeh me. No, I won't lit on."

Nora shuffled out of the ladies' room. "I wanna go back to the bus. Heath'll know to look for me there. He'll fret if he can't find me."

"Gee, Nora, are you sure you don't want to stretch your legs a little before —"

"I'm tired. I couldn't sleep last night. I wanna sit down."

"Okay, I'll take you back."

"Did you see my mum when she brought me to the orphanage? I got a picture of her if you can't remember wot she looked like. You wanna see?"

"Sure," I said softly, "I'd love to see your mum."

After getting Nora settled back on the bus, I stopped to speak to Henry, who hadn't budged from the exit stairs. "I can't pretend I didn't hear what you just said over the phone."

"That's the other problem with cill phones," he complained. "Not only can the conniction be dodgy, the whole world hears what you're saying."

"Arrest warrant?"

"Do me a favor, Imily. Pretind you heard nothing."

"If arrest warrants are being issued, I think you'd better tell me what's happening."

"I'm a tour guide, luv. When my supervisor warns me to keep something under my hat, I do exactly what I'm told because I like my job, and I want to keep it."

"Has there been a break in the Claire Bellows case?" I asked quietly. "Oh, my God! Have the police figured out there was foul play? That's it, isn't it? I *knew* it wasn't as cut and dry as it appeared. I just knew it."

He leaned forward, checked left and right, and motioned me closer. "No one is to know about the warrant. Mum's the word until the police arrive to haul their suspect away. It would go badly for both of us if the suspect should overhear something and decide to part our company prematurely. You know nothing, and I know nothing. Understood?"

"Absolutely." I lowered my voice to an undertone. "When are the police going to arrive?"

"My thinking is, they'll git here whin they git here."

I recognized the look he gave me as the

same one I gave my mom the day she decided to alphabetize the contents of my freezer. I hadn't minded that she'd dived into my freezer unannounced. It was the trip to the emergency room to treat her frostbite that put the real crimp in my day.

"Okay," I said, holding up my hands and backing away, "I'm leaving, and you can count on me not to say a thing. My lips are sealed."

He gave me a thumbs-up and I scurried toward the reservoir feeling like I was about to explode. Could I call 'em, or could I call 'em? I was *soooo* right this time! Vindication! Peter Blunt was wrong and I was right. Someone on our tour was a cold-blooded murderer! Yes!

I stopped dead in my tracks. But who?

"Get a picture of this, Dick," Helen instructed her husband as she hovered over a scruffy bush at the edge of the parking lot. "Does this thing look like it should be extinct?"

"There's a rodent over here!" Lucille Rassmuson yelled. "I think it's one of Marion's rats."

Dick Stolee walked the perimeter of the lot, training his camcorder on dirt, rocks, and an occasional candy wrapper.

"The view is supposed to be more scenic overlooking the reservoir," I said as I passed him.

"Not interested in scenic. I'm hunting for fossils. Hieroglyphs. Extinct crap like that. I'm gonna prove your gramma's not the only one with an eagle eye."

As I neared the dam, I noticed Jake sitting on a rock near a copse of pine trees, head down and knees parted, scouring the ground with his fingertips. Probably in search of another poisonous pest with which to terrorize people. If Henry caught him, I supposed Jake would claim he was collecting rocks, not spiders, so Henry better butt out before Jake sued the company for harassment.

Man, I'd be so happy if the police hauled Jake away, but what were the odds? If Claire died from a spider bite, how would the police know to connect that with Jake? The only people who knew about Jake's escaped redback were Jake, Lola and me, and none of us had talked to the authorities.

Unless —

"Emily!" Conrad hurried over to me. "The University of Melbourne is sending a team of zoologists to Ballarat today to search for your grandmother's rat kangaroo. Isn't that exciting? They told me to call them tonight so they can report their findings. They were delirious with anticipation. Naturally, I won't accept any of the credit should they find the creature. The glory belongs to your grandmother. But I can hardly wait to see what wondrous discoveries she captures today with her camera."

I gave him a narrow look as he rushed off. Damn. Could anyone who seemed as genuine as Conrad be capable of murder? Would the authorities be hauling him off instead of Jake? Was it even fair to assume that because he might have played fast and loose with Nana's plant that he was guilty of murder?

Where was Ellie? I needed to pump her for more information.

Cameras were clicking like crazy as I descended a short flight of stairs and stepped onto a concrete walkway that was narrow as a primitive rope bridge. The dam was semicircular, like half of an enormous satellite dish, with the walkway perched on the edge. To my left lay the reservoir, its water level so high that waves sloshing against the concrete splattered my feet. To my right, the massive curved wall that held back the water disappeared into the valley below. I peered over the railing, thinking it was a very long way down.

"Have you found the surprise yet, dear?"

Nana's boots clacked on the concrete like Fred Astaire's tap shoes. "Me and Tilly think we got it all figured out. The place is haunted."

I eyed the Polaroid developing in her hand. "Did you take a picture of a ghost?"

"Nope. Listen."

I cocked an ear. Background chatter. Film whirring. Birds cooing. Moaning.

Moaning?

"You hear it? Sounds like them noises we heard in the castle in Ireland."

I spun in a full circle, checking out the sky, the treetops, the guests hanging over the railings. "Where's it coming from?"

"Dunno. Sounds like it's real close though, don't it? Kinda like it's comin' from you or me."

And not only moaning. Heavy breathing. *Excited* heavy breathing. Soft, sucking sounds. Panting. A little slurping. It was like listening to the audio portion of an X-rated video.

My face grew hot. "Do you know what this sounds like?" I said in an embarrassed undertone.

"George," said Nana.

I suppressed a smile. "Gee, I'm surprised you didn't say Grampa Sippel."

"Your grampa used to forget what he was doin' and fall asleep halfway through." She regarded me sternly. "Don't tell your mother. She breaks out in a rash every time she thinks about me and your grampa doin' it."

Farther down the walkway, Guy Madelyn leaned against the railing with a silly grin on his face, listening. Osmond stopped beside me and tapped his hearing aids. "My batteries must be low. I keep thinking I hear people having sex."

"Any of you blokes figured it out yit?" Henry asked from the top of the stairs.

"The dam was built on an Aboriginal burial ground and is haunted by ancient wandering spirits?" Tilly ventured.

"It has a leak?" said Margi Swanson.

Henry shook his head. "If you'd hiked the hundred and forty meters to the opposite ind of the walkway, you'd have discovered that whatever you say at that ind can be heard at this ind as clearly as if the speaker were standing beside you. They call it the Whispering Wall — an acoustic miracle of sorts. Something to do with sound waves traveling long distances."

"A parabola effect," exclaimed Tilly.

"Quite right. Give a listen now."

Birds cooing. Water sloshing. Insects buzzing.

Hey, what happened to the moaning, panting, and slurping?

"Doesn't seem to be anyone over there at the moment," Henry lamented.

"Someone was there a minute ago," Nana piped up. "And they wasn't alone."

"They were making kissy-face noises," said Alice Tjarks. "We all heard it."

Like a circus audience instructed to observe the spectacle in the center ring, we riveted our attention on the far end of the curved walkway, raising our collective eyebrows when Lola and Heath strolled into view. Uh-oh. This wasn't good.

"Noises won't cut it," said Henry, nudging us aside as he maneuvered around us. "Let me trot over there so you can experience the whole package."

It was at that moment that I noticed Jake standing at the top of the stairs. I didn't know how long he'd been there, or how much he'd heard, but he was there now, and he wasn't smiling.

Nope. This wasn't good at all.

CHAPTER 12

"You'll notice that this vineyard has no system of irrigation," our winery expert pointed out as we gathered at the edge of a field of ripening grapes. Wire trellises, thick, gnarly vines, and black soil stretched for acres before us, as impressive as any Iowa cornfield. "Australia is the driest continent on earth, and South Australia, where the Barossa is located, is the driest state in Australia, so we dry-grow our grapes. This means that in order to find water, the vines must push their roots deep into the earth. This produces fruit of superior quality, with dipth, color, and flavor that you often find missing with irrigated vines."

I was hanging out at the back of the group, where I could observe Jake Silverthorn without being too obvious. He'd been eerily quiet with Lola after the incident at the dam, but I could see anger simmering in his eyes and knew his sullenness could explode into violence at any moment. I had to be on high alert to herd my group in the opposite direction if he finally did pop. Jake probably wouldn't take kindly to the group's newfound enthusiasm for picture taking, especially if they took close-ups of him slapping his wife around, or breaking a camera over someone's head. Guys like Jake didn't appreciate the concept of the Kodak moment.

"These vines were planted in the early eighteen-forties and are still growing on roots that came from European and South African vines. This gives the Barossa the distinction of being home to some of the oldest Shiraz, Grenache, and Mourvedre vines in the world. If you'll follow me, I'll show you the oldest vine in the vineyard."

"Excuse me, Emily." Ellie Carver worried her bottom lip as she glanced at a group of sheds whose stucco-and-stone walls had the look of candied fruit poking through the buttercream frosting on a Christmas stollen. "Connie's back there, poking through the old equipment, so you mustn't let on that I've spoken to you. He'd be cross if he thought I went behind his back, but you look like a savvy traveler, and I need to know. If Connie were to make changes to our return tickets home, would we have to pay a penalty or fee?"

"More than likely. Airlines usually make you pay through the nose if you alter your plans, especially for overseas flights."

"Oh, dear. I was afraid of that."

Warning bells jangled in my head. "I hope he's not thinking of leaving the tour early, Ellie." Like, before the police arrived. "We have a lot of continent left to see."

"It's worse than that. He wants to stay longer. I heard him making inquiries over the phone this morning. He told me it won't cost us anything to change the tickets, but I don't believe him. How can we afford to stay longer when every credit card we own is maxed out? I'll tell you one thing, he'd better not ask the children to foot the bill." Her voice trembled as she fought back tears. "Why is he lying? What is he so afraid to tell me?"

I could come up with a theory, but I didn't think she'd want to hear it. "Has he told you why he wants to extend your trip?"

"He said he didn't want to tell me because it would spoil the surprise, but he'll be the one who'll be surprised if the bill collectors come knocking on the door for lack of payment." Her jaw locked with granite hardness. "After all I've done to pay our bills on time for the last fifty years, if he ruins my credit rating, I'll leave him!"

"Um, I'm no expert on marriage, Ellie, but wouldn't it be a good idea if you and Conrad talked about your financial concerns before you walked out the door?"

"Talk?" She regarded me quizzically. "Connie and I don't talk, Emily, at least not about anything important. How do you think we've managed to stay married all these years? Do you want to know the secret of a successful marriage?" She tapped my forearm with her forefinger. "Never discuss critical issues. It makes living together a whole lot easier."

Excuse me? Avoid talking about workaholism? Retirement plans? Whose family gets us for which holiday? Was she crazy? "Have you heard of Dr. Phil?"

"Oh, your generation thinks a successful marriage means hammering every issue to death. Hogwash. The couples who do the most hammering are usually the ones who end up in divorce court. Marriage is an institution, and no institution is perfect. You simply have to accept the limitations."

I blinked surprise. "Really?"

"Take it from me, Emily, if you're head over heels about someone, forget all the silly issues and marry him. Everything else will get resolved eventually; you just have to remember always to be respectful and kind to each other."

"Really?"

She flipped me an "Aw, go on" gesture. "Young people. You always make things so difficult."

I was so blown away by her advice that I almost forgot the critical issue I'd wanted to talk to her about. "Not to change the subject, Ellie, but could I pick your brain for a minute? Do you remember when we were in the Port Campbell visitor center the other day, and Henry announced that the bus had broken down?"

"Of course I remember. Connie went back outside to explore and left me with a roomful of strangers. I always play second fiddle to his explorations. But that's Connie. He can never sit still. He always has to be exploring or fidgeting with something he's not supposed to. He'd much rather be off on his own than socializing. But he's taken a liking to you, Emily. If you get him alone, maybe he'll open up to you about the airline ticket business."

And if the police had any say in the matter, maybe he wouldn't be with us long enough to open up to anyone.

As the group headed back toward the main salesroom, we fell in at the rear behind

Diana and Roger, who were going at each other like spin doctors after a political debate.

"She doesn't want to drink your crummy shakes because they taste like the stuff people take for diarrhea," Diana sniped.

"Have you ever tried our shakes?" Roger fired back. "I should mail you a carton. They might change your appearance so much, you might even be able to lose the clown makeup. Why do you wear all that garbage anyway? Are you trying to hide something that you don't want potential customers to see? Did the animal rights activists scare Infinity into testing their products on their own scientists instead of laboratory mice? Did the industry's most perfect product turn you into Frankenstein's monster?"

Oh, my God. It wasn't just me. Other people were thinking the same thing.

"Who do you think has more credibility here?" Diana asked in an even tone. "A woman who wears foundation with an SPF of forty-five to protect her skin from sun damage, or a man with four former wives who all died under suspicious circumstances? What do they call you at GenerX? Dr. Bluebeard?"

Roger grabbed her arm. "That's not funny."

"It wasn't meant to be. Now let go my arm before I drive your privates up through your nose. Would you like a demonstration? We even have an audience." She nodded toward Ellie and me.

Roger released her arm and looked at me apologetically. "It's not like she makes it out to be. I loved all my wives; I've just had trouble keeping them alive."

I wondered if having a little food in the house might have helped.

"Freak accidents," he explained as he removed his GPS from its holster. He punched a button a few times and flashed us the numbers on the screen. "These are the coordinates for Venice, Italy. My first wife drowned when she fell out of our water taxi into the Grand Canal." He hit the button again. "This is St. Michael's Mount. My second wife drowned when the incoming tide swept her off the causeway when we were walking back to the mainland." He flashed new coordinates at us. "This is Alcatraz. Our boat was driven onto the rocks while we were sailing and my third wife fell overboard and drowned." He punched the button a final time. "This is the hot tub on my back deck."

"I hope your fourth wife was bright enough to grab a life jacket," said Ellie.

"She didn't need one. She was an Olympic caliber swimmer. She died when she fell through the hole I cut in the deck for the hot tub."

"Allegedly fell," said Diana. "Her family claimed you pushed her. Who knows where you'd be today if you hadn't hired some high-priced lawyer to get you off the hook."

Roger bristled like an angry porcupine. "Don't take this personally, Toots, but you're starting to piss me off. My past is none of your damn business."

"I can make it my business if the details are splashed all over the internet for the whole world to see. Your hometown paper has wonderful archival material. I expect Heath will be thrilled to entrust his mother into the hands of a man who has such a stellar track record with the gentler sex, don't you?"

"I didn't push her!" he yelled in a desperate tone. "The hot tub was supposed to be a surprise! She came back from her mother's early and fell into the hole in the dark."

"Sure she did," Diana taunted.

"Is that one of those picture phones?" Ellie asked as she scrutinized Roger's GPS. "Would you mind if I have a look? Connie could use something like that."

Roger shoved the unit at her while he continued to rail at Diana. "If you read the outcome of the trial, you'd know that I was acquitted of all charges!"

Diana spiraled her forefinger in the air in an unenthusiastic whoopie.

"How do you dial this thing?" Ellie asked me. "There's no keypad."

"You can't talk to anyone on it," I said, eyeing it with excitement. "It's a Global Positioning System."

"Is that like an iPod? The grandkids all have iPods . . . and hearing problems."

"It doesn't play music."

"Where's the shutter?"

"It's not a camera."

"It can't take pictures; it doesn't play music, and it won't let you talk to someone? Shoot, what good is it?"

"It helps you find your way if you're lost."

"What's wrong with using a compass?"

I shrugged. "Nothing, except it's not as cool as something that's ridiculously expensive, eats batteries, and labels you as a trendsetter."

She handed the unit to me. "Would you mind giving this back to our friend when he stops yelling? I'm going to catch up with the group."

Of course I'd give it back to him, *after* I checked out the waypoint he'd shown me at Sovereign Hill — if I could find it again. I pressed the click stick to change the screen, and when nothing happened, I pressed a button above the power switch. The main menu appeared, with the word "Waypoints" at the top. Now we were cooking.

"Stay out of my face, Diana," Roger threatened, "or you're going to be one sorry scientist."

She laughed dismissively. "What are you going to do? Invite me to go on a boat ride with you?"

I found the up and down buttons, wiggled the click stick, and accessed another menu. Highlighting the appropriate waypoint, I glanced at a new screen that showed the digits zero-one-four within a little flag. Ta da! But there were a gazillion numbers marking longitude and latitude. How was I supposed to remember all of them? I didn't even memorize phone numbers anymore. I used speed dial!

"I'd love to see what happens to you around water," Roger mocked. "My best guess is that your face dissolves. Am I right?"

"You're a dickhead, Roger. You're not going to win Nora over. I'll see to it personally — that's a promise."

"Don't make promises you can't keep, Toots. Hey, where'd the old broad go with my GPS?"

I powered off the unit and waved it at him. "Here you go. She wasn't impressed. She said she'd rather have a compass."

He regarded the blank screen. "Did you turn it off?"

"Yup. Didn't want to drain your batteries."

"How'd you know which button to press?"

"Lucky guess."

He eyed me suspiciously. "You better not have screwed anything up. No one touches my GPS. If that witch hadn't distracted me —" He threw an ugly look after Diana as she hiked back toward the main building.

"You two have become pretty fierce competitors, hunh?" I asked.

"She'll never be in my league. She's a rank amateur. What she doesn't know is, when she least suspects it, I'm going to crush her." He cracked his knuckles in seeming anticipation and smiled. "Metaphorically, of course."

I hoped his metaphorical definition of the word "crush" didn't include any activity that would impair Diana's ability to walk, talk, or breathe. He might be short, but he was so bulked up with muscle, he might as well have OVERSIZE LOAD tattooed on his forehead. If he fell on top of her, we'd need a crane to lift him off.

I blanched at the image. I hope he hadn't just confessed to meditating about premeditated murder. If Diana ended up dead, where would that leave me, other than being the sole witness who could squeal on him? *Oh, God.* "Uhh, I'm going to jog up to the main building and join the others before all the wine is gone." I edged away from him. "See you at the tasting counter."

"Never touch the stuff. Too many toxins. But you go ahead. We've all gotta die of something."

He grinned when he said it.

"White wines aren't actually white. They range from green, to yillow, to brown, with more color indicating more flavor. Rid wines range from pale rid to a deep brown rid and usually become lighter in color as they age."

Our wine expert stood behind a long counter in a room whose stone walls and exposed wood beams smacked of an English hunting lodge, minus the big-game heads mounted over the mantel. Boxed sets of the winery's premier labels sat on display tables along the walls, while sparkling stemware crowded the countertop, waiting to be filled.

"Proper tasting is a six-step prociss," our hostess continued. "See, swirl, sniff, sip, swish, and spit." She decanted a small amount of a straw-colored wine into a glass. "I'll go over these steps with you briefly, then we'll git right to it. You can till a great deal about a wine simply by looking at it, or 'seeing' it."

I tuned her out as I jotted down the coordinates I'd seen on Roger's GPS.

"If those are potential wedding dates," Duncan said over my shoulder, "I'm available, and I know for a fact that Miceli happens to be busy, so why don't you pencil me in?"

I closed my little notebook and dropped it back in my shoulder bag. "How do you know Etienne is busy?"

"He's retired, Em. Trust me, he already has an appointment with his sofa and big-screen TV on those dates. Miceli is a nice guy, but don't you think you're a little young to hang up the dancing shoes? Marry me, Em." He intertwined his fingers with mine and drew me close. "We can travel to every corner of the world together. We can see it all; do it all. I love you. How many languages would you like me to translate that into for you?"

"Nixt, we swirl the wine to release the bouquet, then we sniff deeply," our hostess announced, demonstrating the procedure.

I lowered my voice to a whisper as I surveyed the crowded room. "I'm not sure this is the place to be discussing love and marriage, Duncan."

"Where is the place? Tell me. We can ditch Miceli and —" His expression soured as he glanced beyond me. "Damn."

I followed his gaze to find Etienne threading his way through the crowd toward us.

"Remimber that your taste buds are on the front *and* back of your tongue," said our hostess, "so once you've sipped, swish the wine around to awaken your sinses. If you draw in a little air at the same time, you'll enhance the flavor even more."

"Emily, darling," whispered Etienne as he brushed his thumb down my cheek, "why is there a balloon hanging from your grandmother's ear?"

"Shoot, the hairpins must have fallen out. Where is she? I'll need to fix it." I went up on tiptoe. "And it's not a balloon, it's a glove — or it used to be, before I cut off four of the fingers."

"Of course." Etienne nodded his understanding. "A glove makes much more sense than a balloon."

"Have you talked to her about earmuffs?" asked Duncan.

Our hostess's voice grew louder. "After you've swished, I suggist you spit out your wine in any of the barrels provided throughout the room. If you prefer not to spit, it's perfectly acciptable to swallow after you *gurgle* it a little at the back of your mouth to release more flavor. See, swirl, sniff, sip, swish, and spit. Are you riddy to begin? Billy up to the bar, mates. I'll pour samples of our nineteen-ninety-eight chardonnay for each of you."

A crushing wave of humanity pressed forward, arms extended and fingers grabbing. It reminded me of a recent customer appreciation day at Fareway Foods when the hot giveaway item had been pork-flavored minimarshmallows.

"Wine anyone?" asked Duncan.

I gazed at the mayhem. "I value my life too much."

"Not as much as I value it," said Etienne, lifting my hand to his mouth and placing a soft kiss on my inner wrist that tingled all the way to my shoulder.

Eh!

"I don't mean to pry, Imily," Henry said as he joined us, "but why is your grand-mother wearing a condom on her ear?"

"Whin you sniff this chardonnay," our hostess yelled above the clinking, slurping, and spitting, "you'll note it has a stunning nose with a palate of ripe, tropical fruit, coconut, milon, and spicy oak. Does anyone ilse want a sample?"

"That's my cue," said Duncan. "Samples all around?"

"Not for me." Henry held up his hand. "The company frowns on their drivers git-ting hammered, especially whin they're on the job."

Which reminded me in a roundabout sort of way — "Are either of you familiar with global positioning systems?"

"Those new personal units are pretty ex-pinsive," said Henry, "but they make great toys for the hard-to-buy-for bloke. I have one on my Amazon wish list."

"My department was in the process of installing them in our police cars when I left," said Etienne.

"If I had latitude and longitude for an unknown location, but didn't have a GPS unit, do you know where I could look that would tell me where the location was?"

"A gazetteer," said Henry. "It would at least git you in the right ballpark."

"Google Earth," said Etienne. "Type in your coordinates, and you can zoom in on a dime you dropped in your driveway." He narrowed his blue eyes at me. "Why is it that you always put the fear of God in me when you ask questions like that, *bella?*"

"Ask and you shall receive," said Duncan, handing Etienne and me glasses half-filled with straw-colored wine. "I'd like to offer a toast." He raised his glass.

"Enjoy," said Henry as he left us.

Duncan clinked his glass against ours and gave Etienne a meaningful look. "What do you say, Miceli? May the best man win?"

"Farabutto," spat Etienne.

"Imbroglione," hissed Duncan.

I rolled my eyes. Not again. I knocked back my chardonnay and toasted them with my empty glass. "You two keep up the friendly dialogue. I'm going back for a re-fill."

I skirted the perimeter until I found a path through the crowd, then inched my way toward the counter, where our hostess was brandishing a new bottle in the air. "This is our nineteen-ninety-siven Riesling with a lovely nose of limes, marmalade, and apri-cots."

I spied Heath and Nora at the far end of the counter, wineglasses extended for a hit of the Riesling, while Roger and Diana brandished their stemware erratically and yapped at them like schnauzers. Huh, that was odd. What was Roger doing waving a glass around? Had he decided to drink the wine despite all the toxins he'd been fussing about? Jake lurked beside the group, looking ridiculously sinister as he cradled his wineglass against his chest. His proximity to Heath boded trouble, so I was glad Henry was close by so he could break up —

"CAN YOU BREATHE, DICK?" Helen Teig thumped her husband between his shoulder blades.

"Is he okay?" I asked anxiously.

"Yeah, he accidentally combined 'swish' and 'swallow' and got 'choke.'"

"The savory palate of the Riesling is a blend of spice and honey," our hostess informed us as she filled empty glasses.

"The lady said to *swirl* the wine, Dick," Grace Stolee scolded. "*Swirl,* not slosh. The idea is to release the aroma — not run through a spin cycle! You'll never get that stain out."

I heard a sound like a toy motorboat and glanced across my shoulder to find Osmond

Chelsvig with his head thrown back, acting as if he had a mouth full of Listerine. I made a slight detour toward him.

"Osmond?"

He gulped down what was in his mouth and smiled at me. "This tastes much better than my regular mouthwash."

"Why are you gargling?"

"That's what the lady said to do. Gargle before swallowing."

I shook my head. "Watch my lips. *Gurrr*gle. Gurgle before swallowing." I tapped my earlobe. "Check your batteries, okay?"

I placed my glass on the counter and tried to avoid getting crushed as I waited for it to be filled.

"Emily, dear! Yoo-hoo!" Nana plowed through the crowd with Tilly, Margi, and Bernice in tow. "Wasn't that chardonnay somethin'? I couldn't taste no coconut, though."

"That's because you have to sip *before* you spit," Bernice said dully.

Nana shrugged impishly. "I got my steps outta order."

"Bernice should talk," Margi balked. "She went directly from see to swallow. I don't know what happened to swirl, sniff, sip, and swish."

I cuddled up to Nana and gave her a hug. "Did no one bother to tell you that your hairpins came loose? Henry asked why you're wearing a condom in your ear."

"No kiddin'? What size?"

I pinned the remnants of the glove back under her hair while the other ladies placed their glasses on the counter.

"Have any of you seen Connie?" Ellie asked, looking like a lost soul as she bumped into us. "One minute he's spitting into a barrel, and the next minute he's gone."

Tilly scanned the room. That's one of the advantages of being six feet tall in your stocking feet. "There he is. Look for Jake Silverthorn's hat, and you'll be right on target."

"Party time!" said Bernice, grabbing a newly filled glass off the counter.

"Wait a minute," said Margi. "That's my glass."

"Is not."

"Is so. I put mine next to the one that's smeared with lipstick."

"That would be mine," I said, snatching it up.

"I'm keeping this glass," vowed Bernice.

"Well, I'm not drinking after you," said Margi. "I want a new one. S'cuse me! Can I get a clean glass over here?"

"I don't mean to confuse the issue," said Tilly, "but I could have sworn I put *my* glass next to the one with the lipstick print."

At birthday parties you played musical chairs; at wine-tasting parties it was musical glasses.

The sound of shattering glass echoed through the room, followed by a *boom* that vibrated the floorboards.

"What was that?" asked Nana.

"Call an ambulance!" a man shouted.

Our hostess slammed her bottle of Reisling onto the counter in disgust. "That's it! I've had it with you flaming tour groups. The idea is to *taste* the wine, not drink yoursilves into a bloody coma!"

CHAPTER 13

Osmond read from his tally sheet as we huddled next to the building where paramedics had been administering to Nora Acres. "Five people think she collapsed from the heat. One person thinks it was a heart attack. One person thinks she fainted from thirst. I reckon that'd be Lucille. Three people say she collapsed from old age, and one person says she's faking it to draw attention to herself." We all stared at Bernice.

"What? You've never heard of Munchausen's Syndrome? Don't you people ever watch *ER?*"

"She wasn't faking it," Tilly chided. "Did you see the poor woman when they took her away? She looked as if she were on her deathbed."

And if it was possible, Heath had looked even worse.

A local ambulance had arrived in record time and whisked them away. I hoped their efforts to stabilize Nora had been successful.

"How old a woman you s'pose she is?" asked Nana.

"A hundred and ten," said Bernice.

"They probably shouldn't let folks that old sign up for these trips," said Osmond, who was a birthday short of ninety. "I've heard that once you reach a hundred, things really start falling apart."

"That young man with her should have known better," Helen affirmed. "You think he's a relative?"

"That's her son," I said, not surprised by the drop-mouth expressions that stared back at me.

"No way," said Dick Teig. "Great-grandson, maybe."

"Do you suppose she had him late in life?" asked Alice.

"Yeah, like when she was eighty," said Dick.

"It's her son," I repeated. "He told me himself."

Henry walked our way, lips moving and finger waving in the air as he counted heads. "That's everyone. You can reboard the bus in about tin minutes. Sorry for the excitement, but I hope you won't let it affict the rist of your day. There's plinty more wine

245

for you to taste at the other vineyards, kangaroo with plum sauce to dine on for lunch, and you can relax knowing that Mrs. Acres is receiving the bist midical care that South Australia has to offer. I'm sure she'll be up and about in no time and anxious to rejoin us."

"How old a woman do you think she is?" Dick Stolee called out.

Henry unfolded a paper from his breast pocket and scanned the text. "She was born in forty-three, so that would make her — what? Fifty-siven going on fifty-eight?"

Gasps of disbelief. "No way is she only fifty-seven," argued Bernice.

"Says so right here on her midical form. She was born on St. Patrick's Day in nineteen-forty-three."

"Maybe she's got that disease what makes people look real old," said Nana. "What's it called?"

"Wrinkles," said Grace.

Uff da! Nora Acres was younger than my mom? I guess that's what happened when you lived in a place with too much sun and not enough drugstores selling sunblock with high SPF.

A digital tone rang out from Henry's hip. He walked out of earshot to answer it.

"If she's fifty-seven, I'll eat my —" Bernice gave herself a once-over in search of digestible clothing.

"Why don't you eat Dick's shirt?" suggested Grace. "It's made in China, and you like Chinese."

Henry walked back to us, a hitch in his normally fluid gait. "That's a call I wasn't expicting." He inhaled deeply, his cell phone still cradled in his palm. "I'm afraid I painted too rosy a picture about Mrs. Acres's recovery. That was Heath. His mother died on the way to hospital."

"What was it?" asked Dick Teig. "Heart attack?"

"I bet it was heatstroke," said Margi. "If people get too hot, their insides can cook like peas in one of those boiling pouches, and that can do them in real quick. The old and infirm are especially vulnerable."

"She wasn't old," objected Tilly. "She was only fifty-seven!"

"If she was fifty-seven, I'll eat —" Bernice looked around. "You got anything better than Dick's shirt?"

While the group debated the cause of Nora Acres's death, I slipped back into the tasting room, which was eerily quiet minus the sipping and spitting. The staff had cleared away the dirty stemware and swept

Nora's shattered glass off the floor, so the room sparkled once more with pre-tour group tidiness. You'd never know someone had just died here.

Okay, maybe not technically, but she might as well have died here. And if she had, I imagined things would be very different right now. The medical examiner might be snooping around, looking for evidence that might cast Nora's death in a suspicious light. He might have called in the crime scene unit, who would have gathered the pieces of her broken glass into an evidence bag, taken photos, and subjected us to lengthy interviews about where we were when the incident happened and what we'd seen.

I peered out the window, where I could see people straggling back to the bus, and wondered if any of the guests who'd been in her vicinity would have owned up to what had been going on. Heath wanting to cuckold Jake. Roger wanting to best Diana. Heath wanting to blow off Roger and Diana. Jake wanting to punish Heath. Diana wanting to destroy Roger. Roger and Diana wanting to break Heath. And Nora stuck in the middle of it all. Had she been aware of all the undercurrents? Or had her mind been so detached from reality that someone could have come at her with the business end of a corkscrew and she would have missed the intent?

Poor Nora. She'd seemed such a sad, lost soul. She'd probably never hurt a thing in her life, other than Jake's leaping spider. Why was it that people who were quiet and unassuming ended up dead while the obnoxious ones always managed to survive? It didn't seem fair. God obviously knew what He was doing, but on occasion, I wish He'd err on the side of the obnoxious ones.

But He was God. God didn't make mistakes. Only people made mistakes.

Turning to leave, I glanced at the shelves of sparkling stemware behind the counter and felt my pulse quicken as an absurd thought hit me.

Only people made mistakes.

Damn. What if —

Whoa! Was it possible that —

Holy crap. If what I was thinking proved true, Claire Bellows's killer had struck again, but he might have killed the wrong person.

"You don't think it was a heart attack?" asked Nana, when we were back at the hotel. "What about a ruptured gallbladder, or kidney stones? I don't think you die from stones, though. You just wish you could."

We'd finished our day of wine tasting, despite what had happened to Nora. Henry had suggested we return to Adelaide, but the seventy-and-over crowd had voted to continue with the schedule. Few people had bonded with Nora. The majority didn't even know what she looked like. So the loudest voices had convinced Henry to press on. As one man had articulated so eloquently, "I paid an arm and a leg for this tour, so I damned well better see what the brochure promised. I'm sorry about the old girl dying, but life goes on, and so should the tour."

I slid open our patio door to let in the cool evening air. "I think Nora was poisoned. We've seen this kind of thing before. You know how easy it is."

"Why would anyone want to poison Mrs. Acres?" asked Tilly.

"I don't think anyone wanted to." I sat down on the sofa while the ladies yanked off their boots. "I think the poison was intended for someone else. You saw all the confusion with the glasses in the tasting room. I'll bet you anything Nora drank from the wrong glass and died because of it."

Tilly leaned back in her chair, rubbing her

feet. "So if Nora wasn't the killer's target, who was?"

"I'll give you my short list: either Heath, Roger, Jake, or Diana. And did I tell you that Conrad changed his plane reservations? He's going to be staying on after the tour ends."

"Long enough to return to Port Campbell and look for your grandmother's plant?" asked Tilly.

"Ellie didn't say how long they'd be staying. She was more upset about where the money was going to come from to foot the bill."

"Are you thinkin' the same person what killed Claire Bellows killed Nora?" asked Nana.

"That's my current theory. Why, do you think it sounds stupid?"

"Nope, but there's somethin' I don't get, dear. Makes sense to me that Roger, Diana, or Conrad might a killed Claire 'cause a the plant business. Even makes sense why they'd wanna kill each other. But what's got me stumped is why Jake or Heath woulda killed Claire when they got no connection to her."

"Perhaps they didn't need a connection," said Tilly. "Have you considered the possibility that we might be dealing with a sociopath who kills for no reason at all?"

Nana gave that careful thought. "Where would you write 'Sociopath' on them medical forms we filled out? Under 'Pre-existing Conditions' or 'Other?' "

Unh-oh. I felt an acid indigestion moment coming on. "Umm, I never mentioned this before because I didn't want to scare you, but Jake could have had a hand in Claire's death. He didn't do anything deliberately, but there's a chance he might have killed her." I dropped my voice to a raspy whisper. "Accidentally."

"With poison?" asked Nana.

The words shot from my mouth like speeding bullets. "When he let his redback spider escape on the bus the other day." I held my breath, waiting for their reaction.

Nana looked at Tilly. Tilly looked at Nana. They both looked at me, Nana's eyes rounding to the size of half-dollars. "He let one a them poison spiders loose?"

"Accidentally."

"And he didn't tell no one?"

"He told Lola. That's who told me."

"Are you thinking the spider could have hidden in Claire's hair or clothing and bitten her right before she died?" asked Tilly.

"It's possible, isn't it?"

"Any chance the critter could still be on

the bus?" Nana asked, dry-mouthed.

"Uhhhhh, I'm guessing if it's still on the bus, it's dead. Someone probably stepped on it long ago. I mean, we didn't notice anyone twitching abnormally, discharging all their body fluids, and dying a grisly death while we were on the bus, did we?"

"What about Nora?" asked Tilly.

Nora? Shoot, I was so sure she'd been poisoned, I never considered she might have died from a spider bite. "Did anyone notice Nora twitching?"

"Could be the twitchin' didn't kick in 'til she was on the ambulance," said Nana as she examined the bottom of her boots for squished spiders.

"Or it could be that there's no twitching, fluid discharge, or grisly death involved at all," Tilly speculated. "Emily said that Jake is a fear monger. How do we know he was telling us the truth about a person's re-action to a redback bite?"

Nana sucked noisily on her dentures. "I'll find out." She stuffed her feet back into her boots, marched to the desk, and powered up her laptop.

Knock, knock, knock.

"You do your search," I said to Nana as I stood up. "I'll get that."

"I can't come in, but I have news for your

grandmother," Conrad said when I opened the door. "The team of zoologists the university sent to Sovereign Hill are beating the bushes in search of the rat kangaroo, but they've asked if you could fax your grandmother's photo to them at this number." He handed me a slip of paper. "I know what they should be looking for, but I'm not sure *they* know what they should be looking for. They might be embarrassed that a creature they'd misplaced for sixty-five years might have been living right under their noses, and it took a Yank to find it."

I arched a brow at the number. "What about the angiosperm photo? Should I fax that to the university's botany department? That might give them a better idea of what they're looking for, too."

"No, no." He took an awkward step back. "Sadly, the botany team has given up their search, so it would do you no good. Just the rat kangaroo, please. I must get back now. Ellie isn't feeling so well. I think it was the last Shiraz. Much too peppery for her."

I hoped it was the Shiraz and not something more sinister. I wasn't sure how much I trusted Conrad anymore.

I returned to the room and hovered over Nana's shoulder. "Conrad would like us to fax your photo of the rat kangaroo to the university zoologists at Sovereign Hill. Seems that after sixty-five years, no one is quite sure what the little guy looks like. Here's the number. How's it going?"

"Says here the initial redback bite isn't painful and sometimes you don't see no puncture marks. Pain sets in after about five minutes and some common symptoms are localized swellin', sweatin', muscular weakness, paralysis, stiffness, loss of coordination, and tremors."

"Claire was sweating when she was in the visitor center," I recalled. "And she was complaining about stiffness."

"Nora obviously lost coordination when she collapsed," added Tilly.

"Here's the kicker," said Nana. " 'Redback venom is slow-actin' and serious illness shouldn't develop for at least three hours.' It don't say nothin' about anyone dyin'. It says the symptoms can sometimes clear within a week." She snorted in disgust. "We been had. You was right, Emily. All Jake was hankerin' to do was scare us."

"And make fun of our reaction." Tilly looked down at her boots. "Do you suppose that little boutique in Melbourne accepts returns on slightly used sale items?"

I squinted at the tiny writing on the

screen. "Does it say anything about the venom being more toxic on people whose immune systems have been compromised, or who might have preexisting medical conditions?"

"I don't see nothin'. I bet he even lied about them other critters he was tellin' us about. Taipan. Funnel web." Nana cleared her screen and Googled 'taipan.'

"Wait a minute. Before you do that, would you check out something for me?" I ran for my shoulder bag and dug out my memo pad. "Can you call up 'Google Earth' and type in these numbers? It's Roger's waypoint on his GPS. I got it when he was arguing with Diana. I just hope I remembered the numbers correctly."

"Google Earth," said Nana as her fingers flew over the keyboard. "Is this somethin' new?"

"Etienne told me about it. I guess it can give you satellite images of just about anywhere on the planet. So if these numbers produce an image of the exact spot where Claire died, Roger Piccolo might have some explaining to do."

"To whom?" asked Tilly.

"To anyone who might show up to ask questions about the ever-increasing number of deaths on this tour!" I shuddered to think how many more people might die from apparent natural causes before the authorities arrived.

"Looks like I gotta download a program before I can access the site," said Nana. "You want I should do that, dear?"

"Go for it."

We stared at the window that appeared on the screen. "Could be a slow download through the modem," Nana predicted. She checked her watch. "This'd be a good time to hit the earring store and get Conrad taken care of. You s'pose they'd fax that photo for me downstairs at reception, Emily?"

"It's worth a try, but pin a note to your jersey: Remove the photo from the fax machine when you're done."

Nana gave the keyboard a maternal pat. "I hope no one was plannin' to make a phone call on account a the line's gonna be tied up for a while."

"There's one phone call we could make that would make all this fuss unnecessary," said Tilly. "Call Peter Blunt. See if he'll give you the result of Claire's autopsy report."

Peter? Damn, things had gotten so complicated, I'd forgotten all about Peter. I gave my forehead a whack with my fist. "I should have thought of that before. What is *wrong* with me? Okay, I'll just —" I regarded the download bar on the computer. "I'll run up to the guys' suite and use their phone. That'll be easier."

"You want we should wait on you for dinner, dear? Tilly and me are gonna take a cab to some famous seafood place."

"Go on without me." I grabbed my shoulder bag and headed out the door. "I'll wing it."

Tap, tap, tap.

Etienne answered the door wearing a towel slung low around his hips and nothing else. His hair was ruffled into a dark, wet tangle. His chest sparkled with errant water droplets. His skin gave off a delicious aroma of citrus, and wind, and sunshine. I sniffed appreciatively. "Oh, God, what is that? It smells wonderful."

He hooked his hand around the back of my neck and pulled me against him. "The hotel's shampoo/body wash." He tilted my chin and pressed a soft, lingering kiss on my lips. "I'll share. It works up into an incredibly erotic lather."

Eh! I kissed him back and swallowed half his tongue. He kicked the door shut and wrapped me in his arms. I flattened my palms against his naked spine. His skin was warm and moist. His body hard. His mouth deliciously hot.

"Amore, amore," he rasped.

I felt suddenly unbalanced. The arches of my feet tingled. Light danced behind my eyelids. I was either having an orgasm or a stroke. My hearing grew muffled. My fingers went numb. My bones turned to san—

My shoulder bag crashed to the floor.

"Figlio di puttana!" Etienne hopped backward, holding his foot.

"I'm sorry! It slipped!"

He fell against the wall, mustering a smile as he rubbed his foot. "No harm, *bella.* I don't use my left foot that much anyway."

"I'm sorry. Really. Are you okay?" I smoothed my hand over his ankle.

"I'm sure I'll be fine once the bones mend."

"Nooo. Seriously, do you think you broke something?"

"Every bone in my foot." He wiggled his toes. "Do you know the best treatment for a man who has broken every bone in his foot?"

"Air cast?"

"Bed rest." He gave my lips a hungry look. "With round-the-clock nursing care."

Oh, my God. I hadn't played nurse since I was nine, and I'd never played with a patient who had movable or expanding body parts. *Hoochimama!* I glanced down the narrow hall toward the living room. "What about Duncan?"

He cupped his hands around my face. "He's swimming laps. Something about working his frustration off. But I have a better method." He drew my bottom lip into his mouth, and as he kissed me, stutter-stepped me around the corner into the first bedroom. He backed me onto the edge of the bed and followed me down onto the mattress. *"Fammi l'amore, bella."*

"What?"

"Make love to me."

"Right now?"

"I'm dressed for the occasion."

"Yeah, but —"

"But what?" He made a slow, sensuous foray into my ear with his tongue.

"Yeah, but —" *Oh, God.* "Okay."

"What?"

"I said, okay."

He boosted himself onto an elbow. "You're sure? You're absolutely sure? You don't need more time to —"

I pulled his head down to mine. "Shut up

and kiss me."

His mouth came down hard on mine. His breathing quickened. His hands were everywhere. Off came my top. Off came my walking shorts. I hoped I didn't have holes in my underwear. This was it. This was really it!

He boosted himself up again, his breath ragged. "I need — We need — You know. In my shaving kit." He crawled off the bed.

I reached for his towel and gave it a playful yank. "You won't be needing this anymore, will you?"

He turned to face me.

JESUS, MARY, AND JOSEPH! HOLY MOTHER OF GOD!

Scalding warmth swept up my throat. Struck dumb, I stared in wonder.

"I hope this means you're not disappointed. Don't move. I'll only be a second."

I fell back into the pillows. Disappointed? *Jesus, Mary, and Joseph. Holy Mother of God.* I stared at the ceiling, eyes wide and mouth agape.

The hall door clicked open. "Hey, Miceli, you left your purse in the hall. You want it?"

Duncan? *Eh!* I shot under the covers like Alice down the rabbit hole. I heard footsteps, then —

"Say, Em, a guy at the pool told me about a great restaurant where they do a killer roast squab with parsley ravioli in truffle-scented sauce. Sound good to you? I could be ready to go in twenty minutes. Will that give you enough time to get ready?"

I snaked my hand out through the covers and flashed a thumbs-up.

"Good. I'm psyched. Where's Miceli?"

I aimed my finger at the inner wall.

"Bathroom? Hey, Miceli!" He pounded once on the wall. "Make it quick! I've gotta shower! And, Em, this restaurant apparently makes a passionfruit tart that'll knock your socks off."

I poked my head out just enough to send Duncan a withering glare.

"What? You're not a big fan of passion-fruit?" He braced his shoulder against the doorjamb and smiled innocently. "I'm not interrupting anything, am I?"

CHAPTER 14

At 7:16 the next morning, I was still waiting for the computer to finish downloading the Google Earth database.

"Sorry it's takin' so long, dear," Nana apologized when she got back from breakfast, "but maybe it'll be done by the time we get back this evenin'. And to think that when modems first come out, we thought they was so fast."

"What if tonight isn't soon enough?" I fretted. "What happens if the killer strikes again before we have our answer? Wouldn't we have a much better time today if we knew there *was* no killer? Or if the killer had been taken into custody?" Hmm. "How was breakfast? Anything noteworthy to report? Runny eggs? Limp bacon? Unexpected police activity?"

"The group was blissfully subdued this morning," said Tilly. "Jake and Lola sat by themselves, staring out the window. Diana and Roger were at opposite ends of the room, and Conrad and Ellie ate with Henry. Your grandmother and I spent a relaxing hour drinking tea and reading the Adelaide paper."

So the police *still* hadn't arrived? *Uff da.* What was the hold up?

"The obituary section took my breath away," said Nana. "It went on for pages."

I regarded her oddly. "Why are you reading the obituaries in a place where you don't know anyone?"

She shrugged. "Habit."

"Were you able to learn anything when you called Peter Blunt last night?" asked Tilly.

"I got sidetracked last night," I confessed guiltily, "so I, uh, never made the call."

Nana beamed at me. " 'Bout time you seen some action, dear."

"Nooo! I didn't see any action. I was about to see some, then Duncan showed up, so I spent the rest of the night sipping wine and eating parsley ravioli while the guys threw epithets at each other in Italian."

"Are you sure they were cursing?" asked Tilly. "They seem to have become such good friends."

"It wasn't so much the words, as how they

said them. On a brighter note, the parsley ravioli was surprisingly good."

Nana tapped her watch. "If you wanna try Peter, I seen public phones downstairs. Maybe you can call before we board the bus. But we better move it 'cause we only got twenty-eight minutes to catch the elevator and make it out the front door."

After spending ten minutes analyzing how to make a long-distance call on a pay phone and another five minutes gathering change, I got Peter Blunt's voice mail and left a message for him to call me at the hotel at his earliest possible convenience. "It's a matter of life or death." Which was probably a slight exaggeration, but I figured it might grab his attention.

As soon as I took my seat on the bus, Henry veered into morning traffic. "Mornin', folks. Wilcome to day five of your Great Aussie Advinture. Today we'll be taking a thirty-minute flight to Kangaroo Island, which is a hundred and twenty-three kilometers off the coast. At Kingscote we'll split into two groups since tour buses on the island accommodate fewer passengers, but no worries. You'll all be seein' the same sights."

"Have you heard anything from Heath Acres?" Lola Silverthorn called out.

Wow. The woman didn't know when to leave well enough alone.

"Thanks for asking. He rang me up last night. They haven't released his mum's body yit, but whin they do, he'll be taking her back to Coober Pedy for burial."

"Do they know what killed her?" asked Dick Teig.

"No word yit, but he'll probably know by the ind of the day. And speaking of that, I bought a sympathy card that I'll sind around for all of you to sign, if you like. Make sure it gits back to me sometime today, and I'll post it to Coober Pedy."

Aw, that was so thoughtful. I dug out my memo pad and wrote a note to myself. Things to pack for next trip — sympathy cards. Maybe if I prepared for the worst, nothing bad would happen. It was worth a try. Nothing else seemed to work.

Two snazzy Mercedes-Benz buses awaited us at the Kingscote airport. "Doesn't matter which bus you git on," Henry announced as he herded us toward the parking lot. "But once you decide, stay with the same group the entire day so you don't foul up my hid count."

My group charged toward the nearest bus like racehorses out of the gate, Nana and

Bernice in a footrace at the head of the pack, elbows flying and boots clacking.

"Marion! Marion!" shouted Conrad.

Nana arrived first and did a little jump-around to celebrate. In fact, she looked fast enough to challenge Bernice in the five-yard dash at this year's Senior Olympics. Conrad caught up to the group, staggering against the bus as he gasped for air.

"Hey, back of the line," Dick Stolee admonished.

"I'm not *in* line," Conrad choked out. "Marion, I have exciting news from the university search team."

"They found the rat?"

"Not yet, but the photo you took *is* the desert rat kangaroo, so they're pulling out all stops to track it down. They'll want to interview you when it happens. You'll make headlines all across Australia. You'll be the celebrity du jour!"

"You s'pose they'll take pictures?"

"Of course, they will. You'll be a media darling!"

"I better find me a beauty parlor."

"I'll keep you informed. They're going to call Henry with any news. Has anything this noteworthy ever happened to you before?"

"Well, I found a hundred-million-year-old

plant earlier in the week."

He dismissed that with a wave of his hand. "Besides that."

"I won seven million dollars once."

Conrad's mouth puckered like a drawstring pulled too tight. "Oh."

When we got the okay, we crowded onto the bus, gushing over the luxuriously cushy seats and fancy TV monitors. I claimed a window seat at the back, and Nana sat beside me. "I'll move if one a your young men wants to sit here, dear."

I glanced out the window to find them climbing onto the other bus. "Looks like they'll be sitting with each other today."

"Probably brushin' up on new cusswords. If you overuse the old ones, they lose their effect."

Guy Madelyn strolled down the aisle, taking candid shots of everyone. "I'm sorry, Marion," he said when he reached us, "but I couldn't help overhear your conversation with Conrad. I hope you won't let his promise of pie in the sky influence your decision about coming to work for me. Has he fessed up about Australia's track record with other significant discoveries? I hope you realize they have a habit of losing everything they find."

"Like what?" she asked.

"Gold reefs in the central desert. Ancient fossils. The topography is so monotonously similar that people make discoveries one day and lose them the next. That rat kangaroo I heard Conrad talking about? Don't get your hopes up. Remember, here today, gone tomorrow. I'm offering you a sure thing, Marion. Give it some serious thought."

He snapped our picture and moved on, leaving Nana in an uncharacteristically pensive mood. I squeezed her hand. "Will you be terribly disappointed if they never find your rat kangaroo?"

"Nah. But I was kinda lookin' forward to havin' my hair done."

After introducing us to our driver — a typically young and handsome Australian named Trevor — Henry took a quick head count, then hurried down the aisle and handed me an envelope and pen. "Could I trouble you to be in charge of the card, Imily? That way, I know I'll git it back."

I agreed to be keeper of the card, though I worried a little about how to carry it around all day without dog-earing the corners. As we left the airport and headed south, I wrote a little note to Heath, signed my name, and handed the card to Nana.

"I'd like to offer you a frindly wilcome to

Kangaroo Island," Trevor said pleasantly, "the third largest island off the coast of Australia. We're isolated from the mainland and haven't sold our souls to devilopers, so our landscape and wildlife are the same now as they've always been. The last hundred pairs of scarlet fan-tailed glossy black cockatoos on the planet live on Kangaroo Island. Tin percint of the world's sea lions waddle onto Seal Bay. We don't offer night-life or glitz, but we have an abundance of salt air, clear water, and the kind of solitude you'll niveh find in Sydney or Milbourne."

The scenery was unremarkable. Meadows and trees. A few fences. We could have been driving down a road anywhere in the Mid-west. When we turned east, it got a little more exciting because the pavement ended, forcing us to continue down a rutted dirt road that bounced us around worse than the Star Wars ride at MGM Studios. Mead-ows and trees still abounded, but looking out the window at them was like watching a movie with a jumpy video track.

"Our first stop this morning will be Emu Ridge Eucalyptus and Craft Gallery. Sixty years ago the island supported forty euca-lyptus oil distilleries. Today, Emu is the only one lift. They dimonstrate the extraction prociss every half hour, but if that's not your cup a tea, you can shop the gallery for souvenirs and crafts. I ricommind the Ligurian honey, collected from hives first imported from the Italian province of Liguria back in eighteen-eighty-one. All the bees on the island are pure Ligurian and descinded from that original strain."

We pulled into the parking lot of a rustic compound of squat bungalows with red roofs and whitewashed siding. Perched atop a building that identified itself as MACGILLIVRAY POST OFFICE 1953 was an emu weather vane that kept watch over derelict machinery in various stages of decay, mangy undergrowth, and a huge cauldron whose contents steamed like witch's brew.

"We're here for forty-five minutes," announced Trevor. "The comfort station's around back."

I decided that watching eucalyptus leaves being pressed didn't interest me, so I hit the gallery, amazed at how much merchandise could be shoehorned into a compact space. Hats, cloth bags, books, cards, dream catchers, paintings, magnets, T-shirts, honey, and all things eucalyptus, from candles and soap to shelf liners and lotion. I felt as if I'd stepped into a mini Mall of America.

"Listen to me, Marion, this will be the

best decision you ever make. Trust me. It was too bad about Nora, but I believe things happen for a reason. Maybe Fate intended that *you* be the face of Infinity Inc., not Nora Acres."

I looked over my shoulder to find Diana Squires directly in Nana's face. Rolling my eyes at her persistence, I grabbed a jar of the famed Ligurian honey and marched over to them.

"I'm sorry for interrupting your conversation, but Mom would love this." I handed the jar to Nana. "I think you should buy it for her. And look, there's no line at the cash register at the moment, so this is a good time to check out."

Nana flashed me a grateful smile. "If there's no waitin', maybe I oughta buy two." She shuffled off.

Diana crossed her arms, displeasure in her eyes. "You obviously don't have your grandmother's best interests at heart. Why are you holding her back? What are you afraid of? That she might start looking better than you?"

"Oh, please." I whipped out the sympathy card. "While I have you here, can I get you to sign this?"

She scribbled her name and handed it back. "I hope you realize you're looking a gift horse in the mouth."

"Gift horses can have a lot of nasty side effects."

"Infinity manufactures the safest products in today's market. Ask anyone."

"I could ask Nora Acres, but unfortunately, she's no longer with us."

Diana blinked erratically, as if her eyelids were collapsing beneath the weight of her liner. "Are you implying that an Infinity product may have been responsible for Nora's death? Heath refused to let her sample any of our product! Who knows, maybe if he'd loosened up a little, she'd still be alive. When a woman is as old as she was, I think it's criminally negligent to deny her treatment that could reverse the aging process."

"She was only fifty-seven."

Diana's bottom lip sagged open, either from shock or an excess of gloss. "Get out of here. *I'm* fifty-seven. She was decades older than I am. Her face. Her hands."

"Fifty-seven."

"Holy shit, she must have led one hell of a hard life."

"But a pretty quick death. You were there when it happened. Did you notice anything unusual?"

"Other than her dropping her glass and passing out? What is this? A roundabout way of asking me if I slipped her a deadly dose of face powder?"

I heard the click of a camera shutter. "Nice profile shot," said Guy, as he checked his display screen.

"I told you to stop taking my picture!" Diana shouted. "What part of 'Don't take my picture' can't you understand?"

"I'm sorry, I —"

"Erase it." She grabbed his camera. He slapped her hand.

"Get your paws off my equipment."

"Erase it!"

He punched a button. "There. It's gone."

"Good. And so help me, if you ever try taking my picture again, I'll smash your freaking camera and have you arrested. You got that? Now stay away from me."

She stormed out of the shop. I raised my eyebrows. "Do you suppose this means she'll be a no-show for the group photo at the end of the trip?"

Guy laughed good-naturedly. "I wouldn't have kept the profile shot anyway. Her face came out blurry. All her shots have come out blurry. She has an annoying habit of moving just when I press the shutter. I've had to erase all the shots I've taken of her, not that I'd give her the satisfaction of telling her. It's way too much fun ticking her off."

"That is *such* a guy thing. Why do men enjoy ticking women off so much?"

"We don't do it to all women, just the ones who overreact. Must be a control thing. You're so levelheaded, I bet no man has ever succeeded in ticking you off."

I smiled stiffly, thinking that *two* were getting dangerously close. I held my hand out for Guy's camera. "Would you like your picture taken against a backdrop of authentic Aussie bush products?"

He twitched his mouth indecisively. "I'll let you in on a little secret, Emily. The world-famous photographer is even less photogenic than Diana Squires. Honest. In most of our family portraits I end up looking like roadkill in a mock turtleneck."

"I bet my Dick takes a worse picture than you," Helen Teig claimed as she browsed nearby. "You should see his passport photo. DICK! GET OVER HERE!" She cupped her hand to her mouth. "He looks like public enemy number one."

"You should see mine," I said, digging it out of my shoulder bag and flipping it open. "How bad is *this?*"

Helen regarded it dismissively. "That's

actually quite nice, considering what your hair normally looks like."

"You want to see bad?" Guy fished his neck wallet out of his polo shirt and handed Helen his passport. "I look like a character out of *Deliverance*. All I'm missing is the banjo."

"You're right," Helen agreed. "This is much worse than Emily's."

"It can't be worse than mine!" I objected. "I have to show two forms of photo ID when I pass through Customs. The last time I renewed my driver's license, the woman who took my picture suffered a nervous breakdown." Helen flashed me Guy's photo, causing me to gasp. "Euw, that's *much* worse than mine."

Dick stomped toward us. "What in tarnation is so all-fired important that —"

"Show Emily your passport photo," she said, poking his stomach.

"Are we supposed to show passports here?" asked Osmond, as he came up behind us.

Dick wrestled his shirt out of his pants to access his waist wallet.

"Why is Dick undressing?" asked Margi.

"Everyone get your passports out!" said Osmond. "This is a checkpoint."

Hissing. Groans. Foot shuffling.

Alice tapped me on the shoulder. "Excuse me, Emily, are we being strip-searched?"

"I don't have the stomach to watch Dick get naked," whined Bernice. "YOU GOT ANY FITTING ROOMS IN THIS PLACE?"

"Who's supposed to get these?" yelled Lucille Rassmuson, waving her passport in the air.

"Emily wants 'em," said Dick.

I staggered against the display counter as passports came at me from every direction. "Hold it! I don't want —"

"G'day, folks," a voice blared over a loudspeaker. "Our oil-distilling dimonstration begins in one minute by the big vat outside. One minute. Git there early for the bist views."

The group cleared the area in a half second, hitting the door like stampeding cattle. "Come back here!" I bellowed. "You forgot your passports!"

"Give 'em back later," Dick Stolee called out as he pushed through the exit.

Great. This was just great. I regarded the armload of passports I'd just accumulated. What was I supposed to do with them in the meantime?

Guy focused his camera on me and

clicked. "This one should be priceless. You can call it, 'Ever-cheerful tour escort just doing her job.' " He nodded toward the passports. "Do you have mine in there someplace or does the lady with the disappearing eyebrows still have it?"

I sighed. "I have no idea."

"Not a problem. If you have any trouble sorting them out, mine will be the one with the scary photo. Now, if you'll excuse me, I might need to take a few shots of this eucalyptus-distilling process. What are the chances Diana will be out there?" He gave me a devilish wink. "One can hope."

I shook my head as I watched him leave. *Men.*

Laden with two bags full of Aussie souvenirs, I exited the shop twenty minutes later. The live demonstration had ended, so guests were scattered around the compound, either lined up at the comfort station, where I spied Etienne and Duncan, or taking pictures of each other in front of the rusted machinery. Henry leaned against our bus, nodding to me when I approached. "You've done some damage, Imily."

"It's what I do best." Well, one of the things I do best.

When his phone started chiming, he

apologized and picked up. "This is Hinry."

Since Emily Post had written her book of etiquette before cell phones were invented, I found myself in a gray area, unsure what would be more rude — eavesdropping on his conversation or climbing aboard the bus.

"Drug overdose? Bloody hill."

That clinched it. I was eavesdropping.

"Could your mum have mistakenly gotten into something she shouldn't have? Did she have any midications with her that she didn't list on her midical form?"

Oh, my God. He was talking to Heath.

"All right. Lit me known as soon as you hear." He rang off, looking at me, stunned. "That was Heath. Preliminary postmortem tists on his mum indicate she might have died from a drug overdose."

"Did he say what kind of drug?"

"The lab people have to run more tists before they can determine that, but here's the tricky part. Nora wasn't taking drugs. As odd as her behavior was, she wasn't being treated for any kind of mintal illness or condition. Heath said she didn't even take aspirin."

"So, in all probability, the drug was given to her by someone else?"

Henry nodded in slow motion. "Bloody hill. Someone murdered the old girl."

I *knew* it! I was right! Someone had poisoned her wine yesterday. But which one of my suspects had slipped her the stuff? And for God's sake, why? One thing was for sure: there was so much tension between the guests right now, I was terrified the body count was going to rise. "I realize the phone call you received at the dam yesterday never happened, Henry, but have you had any word from the authorities about when they're going to show up? I mean, how long does it take to drive across town to cuff someone?"

"Lit's find out." He punched a number into his phone. "Carol, this is Hinry. What can you till me about the blokes who are seving that arrist warrant?" He listened attentively, nodding and frowning as the woman talked. "Ah, brilliant. Any mintion who they're going to nab or why? I see. Thanks. I'll keep you posted."

"What did she say?" I blurted.

He struggled to suppress a smile. "Carol is six foot five with a nick like a bulldog and chist hair up to his jaw. Carol's a bloke."

"At least his parents didn't name him Sue."

"The old Johnny Cash song!" Henry enthused. "The whole country's taken a fancy to all your modern American music artists. Johnny Cash, Dill Shannon, Doris Day."

Oh, God. "What about the authorities?"

"According to Carol, they should be on the island alriddy, so we need to sit tight and wait for thim to show up."

"They're coming all the way to Kangaroo Island to make the arrest? Why didn't they do it in Adelaide?"

He regarded me thoughtfully before pressing redial on his phone. "This is Hinry again. Why didn't the police make the arrest in Adelaide?" He paused, rolling his eyes. "Easy on, it's a fair question. You don't have to — I was only — Flaming hill." He disconnected and gave me a sour look. "He said he invited the authorities to the office for tea and interrogation, but they declined his invitation."

"Excuse me?"

"I'll translate. He doesn't know any more than what he's already told me." He threw a cautious look around us. "I'd appreciate it if you could keep your group out of the thick of things when the police arrive, Imily. I don't want anyone ilse gitting hurt."

I gave him a thumbs-up. Good thinking to isolate the group from the perpetrator. You

281

just never knew what a cornered rat might do.

CHAPTER 15

Our footgear sent up a deafening clatter as we walked the boardwalk leading down to the beach at Seal Bay Conservation Park. "I apologize for the wind," said the park ranger in charge of our group, his hand anchoring his wide-brimmed hat, "but there's nothing between here and Antarctica to stop it."

The ocean roared before us, angrily white-capped and aquamarine in the sun. Waves pounded the sand where scores of sea lions basked like garden slugs. "The colony here numbehs about five hundred, but on average, you'll see no more than a hundred snoozing on the beach at any one time. Whin the weather's poor, they hid for higher ground and snuggle under the scrub on the dunes."

The dunes swept east and west, rolling toward high, rocky headlands that were stark as an Irish moor.

"Whin we're on the beach, I'll ask you to

git no closer than four meters to the animals. If they feel thritened, they'll give chase, and I can guarantee you don't want to be singled out by a five-hundred-kilo bull."

"How much is five hundred kilos?" asked Lucille Rassmuson.

The ranger smiled. "Enough to roll you flatter than piecrust. Be careful on the stairs now. They're fairly steep. Hold on to the railings."

A logjam formed at the top of the stairs as guests with bad knees and replacement hips waited their turn to grab the handrails. Roger Piccolo appeared at my side, looking impatient with the holdup. "All this could be avoided if the AARPers would lose the diet colas and knock back a few health shakes. Have I mentioned that our products actually regenerate joint cartilage?"

We'd already had this conversation. I whipped out the sympathy card. "Would you like to sign this while you're standing here?"

"What the hell. The old crone didn't do me any favors, but you have to admire her kid for being so devoted to her. He looked worse than she did after she collapsed." He signed the card and handed it back. "He'll probably feel guilty for the rest of his life about signing her up for this tour, but hey, when you're as old as she was, the old Pearly Gates loom large as the next travel destination."

"Did you know she was only fifty-seven?"

"Who told you that?"

"Henry. It was on her medical form."

He muttered an epithet that expressed his doubt in one explosive syllable. "Show me her birth certificate with the gold seal of authenticity. That's the only way you'll ever convince me."

"I'm not sure she had an authentic birth certificate. I think a lot of her personal records were lost when she emigrated. Heath told me she was a war orphan. I guess war affects even the people who aren't involved in the fighting."

"If they ever find her real birth certificate, they'll discover she was ancient. You want my theory? She died from massive deterioration of all her major organs."

If he was the guilty party who'd dispensed the drug overdose, he had to be hoping that's what the medical examiner found. Diseased organs probably couldn't bear the same level of scrutiny as healthy ones, which could very well let him off the hook.

I invited more guests to sign my card while we waited. Conrad had a microscopic signature, as if he were trying to keep his name a secret, while Ellie's was the size of John Hancock's. I'm sure it said something about their personalities, but not being a handwriting expert, I didn't have a clue what. Lola dotted the "i" in Silverthorn with an enormous heart, and Jake shoved the card back at me and suggested I buzz off. "He was aiming to shag my wife! Git the bloody hill away from me."

Nana and Tilly strolled up to me, all smiles. "If you gotta visit the potty, dear, use the one in the souvenir shop. The Aussies have a real gift for designin' pretty potties." She lowered her voice. "They could give the Italians a few pointers."

I grabbed their arms and pulled them aside. "I didn't want to say anything on the bus, but I have news about Nora. Henry received a call from Heath. There's evidence she may have died from a drug overdose."

Nana gasped in shock. "She was one a them addicts? I'll be. Just like on that egg commercial on the TV."

"What egg commercial?" asked Tilly.

"The one what shows a fella talkin' about your brain then fryin' up a couple a eggs. If you hit the mute button, you can't tell if he's advertisin' breakfast at Perkins or nonstick cookin' spray." She regarded me seriously. "Was it heroin or coke?"

"Neither! She wasn't a drug addict. She didn't even do aspirin."

"So what did she overdose on if not recreational or hard drugs?" asked Tilly.

"They don't know yet, but — too much of anything can kill you, right?"

Tilly nodded. "Too much water. Too much prescription medication. Too many over-the-counter painkillers and herbal remedies."

"Too much sex," said Nana.

I gave her the evil eye. "I wouldn't know. Anyway, everything is going to be coming to a head very shortly, so if you see anything weird happening, keep your distance. Pass the word along to the rest of the gang, okay?"

"How am I s'posed to know if it's weird?" asked Nana.

"I'll help," Tilly assured as she urged Nana forward. "Recognizing deviant human behavior has been my stock in trade for a half century."

When the crowd thinned I descended the stairs, awestruck by the beach's savage beauty, charmed by the clusters of furry creatures who lazed belly-up in the sun, a little annoyed by the sand that was blasting me in the face. If Iowa had a shoreline that faced Antarctica, I guess I might have realized that hurricane winds plus beach sand equals microderm abrasion. But the good news was, it was free of charge!

While the ranger guided the group down the beach, I plopped onto the sand, kicked off my sandals, assumed the lotus position, and angled my face into the wind.

"What are you doing, *bella?*" Amusement filled Etienne's voice as he sat down behind me, wishboning his arms and legs around my body.

"Exfoliating."

"And the purpose of that is?"

"To make my skin soft and supple."

He smoothed his hands down my bare arms. "It's working."

"Where did you leave your shadow?" My voice was breathy as he nuzzled my ear.

"He's browsing in the gift shop. I think Lazarus is a closet shopaholic. You know what that means, don't you?"

"He has an American Express card with no credit limit?"

"He travels heavy. No plane will ever be able to transport the two of you at the same time, which, of course, bodes well for me."

"Try to be nice."

"I'd rather try something else." He drew

my earlobe into his mouth, causing every bone in my body to liquefy. I fell out of lotus position and wilted against him, uttering a little moan. This wasn't doing much for my complexion, but my hormones were having a field day.

"Would this be a good time to discuss your retirement plans?" I heard myself say in my erotic delirium.

"*Bella, bella,* wouldn't you rather hear how much I love you? Or how turned on I am right now? Or what indecent plans I have for these beautifully long legs of yours?"

That was the other thing about men. They always changed the subject when you mentioned something they didn't want to talk about. "How indecent?"

"Obscenely so." He laughed as he rained kisses on my neck. *"Ti amo, bella. Sposiamoci."*

I sighed my frustration. "What does that mean?"

"Marry me, Emily."

"I'd seriously consider it if we could talk about —"

"Shhh. I've arranged a package deal. Would you like to hear the details?"

I tried to look nonchalant as a ranger traipsed past us with another small group of tourists. "I'm listening."

"What do you love most about your job?"

"Being curled up on the beach with you."

"Besides that."

"My paycheck. Did I tell you Mr. Erickson gave me a three percent raise last year? That's pretty kick-ass in this economy."

"How would you react if someone offered you twice your current salary to do exactly what you're doing now?"

"What?" I nearly snapped my head out of joint as I twisted around.

"I've purchased a tour company, *bella.* Deluxe accommodations for the senior traveler at discount prices. I'm gearing up for your American baby boomers. When they retire and start traveling en masse, I'm going to dazzle them with travel packages they won't be able to pass up. Exclusive hotels. Exotic destinations. Gourmet cuisine."

It took a moment for his words to register. "You bought a tour company?"

"I did, indeed. All that's missing is a catchy name . . . and you. Come work for me, Emily. I'm going to need a small army of people to fill positions like yours, and I'd like to begin by hiring you."

"At double my salary? Are you kidding?"

"Double isn't enough? You drive a hard bargain. All right, triple."

"No, I'm not questioning your generosity! I'm just amazed that you decided to do something so unpredictable. This is so unlike you."

"You inspired me." He nuzzled my neck. "You've shown me that with a little vision and a great deal of enthusiasm, anything is possible."

Bless his little heart. He was evolving. That was so sweet!

"The Swiss are much too enamored of predictability," he continued, "so I'm cutting loose, taking a walk on the wild side, going where no Swisser has ever gone before. It's clear to me now, Emily. The world is our —" He paused. "Our —"

"Oyster." We needed to have a serious talk about this new dictionary of his.

"Oyster. Of course. I was going to say clam, but I was sure the word had more than one syllable. So what do you say, *bella?* Have I convinced you?"

"I'm . . . I'm speechless. What you're offering me is so incredible, Etienne, but how can I abandon my seniors? I'd feel so disloyal. Who'd chaperone them around the world if I left the bank? I adore my job; I've gotten good at what I do. Mr. Erickson praises me for being organized and cheerful, and I've become so patient dealing with people that I'm not even tempted by sharp objects when I'm around Bernice and the Dicks anymore. I'd love to come work for you, but how can I turn my back on Mr. Erickson when he was so kind to offer me the position in the first place? I know you're offering me an opportunity of a lifetime, but what am I supposed to do about —"

"Emily," he said, sounding distracted, "did the park ranger warn guests about standing too close to the sea lions?"

"He sure did. Why?"

"Some of your group seem not to have heard."

I glanced toward the ferocious Southern Ocean to find sea lions dipping and bobbing in the surf before catching waves that launched them onto the beach like fired torpedoes. Bernice paced at the water's edge, trudging left and right in her stiletto boots, shooting closeups as they landed. "The ranger said to stand no closer than four meters. What's that in feet?"

"About twelve."

I stood up and let fly my signature whistle. "Bernice!" I whistled again and cupped my hands around my mouth. "BERNIIIIIICE!"

She turned around, looking annoyed at

the interruption.

"Get out of there!"

She angled her hand behind her ear and shrugged at me.

"It's twelve feet, not four! Move!" I made frantic sweeping gestures in the air. She waved back.

"You're yelling into the wind," said Etienne. "She can't hear you."

"URRRK URRRK URRRK." A mammoth bull drew her attention as he rolled onto his belly and waddled straight at her, muscles rippling and flippers kicking up sand. With the ocean at her back and the bull blocking her front, she stood paralyzed for a moment before reverting to the only survival technique she knew.

"HELLLLLLP!"

"Oh, for crying out — RUN!" I screamed. Then to Etienne, "Grab a ranger! We're going to need him!"

"URRRRK URRRK URRRK."

Bernice let out a shriek and ran like hell. I slogged through the sand after her, intercepting her as a rogue wave crashed onto shore and upended both of us, tossing us around like empty Coke bottles. Water shot up my nose. Sand skinned my knees. Struggling beneath an avalanche of sea foam, I flailed desperately for Bernice, hitting a bony limb and grabbing hold so she wouldn't get dragged out to sea.

"URRRRK URRRK URRRK."

Swiping at the hair that tentacled my face, I looked toward the sound. The damn thing was still coming. I shook Bernice's limb. "Are you alive?"

She wheezed deeply. "My —" *Blub.*

"Good." I hauled her to her feet and seized her hand. "Don't stop running until we reach those rocks."

I sloshed through waves and wet sand, pulling Bernice behind me. By the time we reached the headland, the bull had tired of the chase, preferring instead to swagger around a harem of cows, wowing them with his manly grunts. Bernice sagged onto a rock, shivering, her teeth clacking like castanets. I doubled over, wincing as I held my side.

"That's it, Bernice!" I gasped for air. "You're not taking any more trips with me —"

"You can't do that! It's d-discriminatory. Ageism! Ageism!"

"— until you learn the metric system."

"Oh." She glanced back down the beach. "That wave t-took my camera. The b-best camera I ever owned! Digital. All the b-bells and whistles. Every picture I've shot of this t-trip was on that camera. How am I sup-posed to c-compete with your grandmother if every freaking p-picture I've taken is gone! I need that photography job m-more than she does. She's got her m-millions. Now it's my turn! It's not f-fair. Everything she touches turns to gold. Everything I touch turns to c-crap."

My *Escort's Manual* stresses that in times of crisis, the creative escort will always provide options to a distraught guest. "I have a disposable in my shoulder bag. Say the word. It's yours."

She regarded me dourly. "All the p-people on this island, and I get stuck with P-Pollyanna." She wrestled her boot off her foot. "It was all that p-park ranger's fault. Four meters. How am I supposed to know how m-much that is? Who uses the m-metric system anyway?"

"The entire world — excluding US citi-zens and a few headhunters in New Guinea whose system of weights and measures revolves around the human skull. We're definitely in the minority here, Bernice."

"Yeah, well, it's not my fault that the r-rest of the world is wrong." She peeked inside her boot, then tilted it sideways, pouring out seawater as if from a teapot. Her face crumpled with disappointment so obvious, I felt a little tug on my heartstrings.

"I'm sorry about your boots."

"Guess I won't be wearing these again anytime s-soon." She yanked off the other one and dropped it to the ground. "If the job th-thing didn't work out, I thought I could make my photographic c-comeback in these boots. Get a few magazine g-gigs like in the old days. Branch out with geriatric calendars and s-some online stuff. I could have gone far." She kicked the nearest one with her bare toe. "Now l-look at them. Ruined and useless. Just like m-me."

Uh-oh. She was taking this really badly. It was almost as if she were mourning the death of a family pet. I wasn't trained to handle clinical depression, but my *Escort's Manual* did suggest shopping as a possible remedy for occasional blue moods among female and gay guests.

"Maybe that boutique where you bought them has a branch in Adelaide. Let's check the phone book when we get back. You might be able to buy another pair exactly like them. I'll hire a cab and take you there personally."

She heaved her shoulders in a pathetic sigh.

"You could take them home with you and have them bronzed. Mom did that to my baby shoes. Nana was going to do it to Grampa Sippel's L. L. Bean hat with the earflaps, but she buried him in it instead."

She shook her head glumly. "I'll just take 'em home and s-sell 'em on eBay."

"Sell them? You're going to *sell* them? How can you sell them? Look at them. They're ruined!"

"You are *sooo* out of touch. How do you m-manage to get along in life? You ever heard the saying, 'One m-man's trash is another man's t-treasure'?"

I gave her a hard look. "Don't you think that's a little unethical?"

"Have you heard, 'Sticks and stones may break my bones, but names will never hurt me?' "

"Are you ladies all right?" a park ranger called, as he and Etienne trudged toward us.

I flashed him a tentative thumbs-up. Bernice flashed him a boot.

"What am I supposed to do for sh-shoes now? I can't walk around barefoot. And l-look at me. I'm so c-cold, my knees are knocking together. That water was freezing. I p-probably have hypothermia. I could die at any m-moment!"

Etienne pulled off his shirt and wrapped it around Bernice's shoulders. "Is that better, Mrs. Zwerg?"

She eyed his naked torso and batted her soggy lashes. "Actually, I've heard that body heat is the b-best cure for hypothermia."

He pressed her hands together and rubbed them like a Boy Scout kindling fire. "How's that?"

"Not exactly what I had in m-mind, hon, but it'll do for now."

I choked back a laugh. Yup. He was destined to be a big hit in the travel industry.

"I'm sorry I didn't arrive quickeh," the ranger apologized, as I sluiced water off my goose bumps. "Had some official police business that couldn't wait, but it looks to be oveh now."

I froze in place. "Police business? You mean, the police were here? Just now?"

"All the way from Milbourne."

"Did they arrest someone?"

"Don't know. Whin the lady cried for hilp, I had to abandon thim." He slanted a long look toward the boardwalk. "That's thim leaving agin."

I craned my neck to see, but glimpsed nothing more than a couple of heads that disappeared beyond the vanishing point.

"One of the blokes had his handcuffs out and looked like he intinded to use thim, so I'm thinking whin you hid back to Adelaide tonight, you'll be minus one tour gist."

Yeah, but which one?

CHAPTER 16

"Diana? Really?" My voice echoed inside the restroom stall as I stuffed my wet tank top and walking shorts into a plastic bag.

"I was shootin' a picture a Tilly when I seen two men slap cuffs on her and escort her back up the beach," said Nana. "I was pretty sure that must be the weird thing you warned us about, until Bernice started screamin', then I was torn."

"That wasn't weird," Tilly scoffed. "That was typical."

"It was real odd, dear. Diana didn't put up no fuss at all. Almost seemed like she was expectin' someone to drag her off."

I broke out the Seal Bay T-shirt and running shorts I'd just purchased in the gift shop. "Diana," I repeated. "I *knew* it was Diana." Or Roger. Or Conrad. Or Jake. "The police must have discovered evidence that connected her with Claire Bellows's death. I just wish I knew what. Henry told me yesterday that the police were coming, but he made me swear to keep it under my hat."

"Do you think Diana was the person who took Marion's other two Polaroids at Port Campbell?" asked Tilly.

"Took Nana's Polaroids. Murdered Claire. Performed a cover-up with the angiosperms. Slipped Nora an overdose of drugs. For being on holiday, Diana Squires has been one busy botanist."

"You s'pose Henry's gonna explain to everyone why Diana's went away?"

"He'd better! He owes us some details." I stepped out of the stall and struck a supermodel pose. "Ta da! Dry again, except for my underwear."

"I got extra, dear." Nana opened her pocketbook and unfurled a pair of bloomers the size of a hot-air balloon. "They're real good ones. Fruit a the Loom. You wanna borrow 'em?"

"Mmm, you might want to offer them to Bernice. I think they're more her style."

"She won't want 'em. She says she's gonna stay in her wet clothes."

"Why? I told her the bank would foot the bill if she wanted to buy some dry clothing."

"If she's dry, she'd have nothing to complain about," said Tilly, "which would mean the Apocalypse is here."

"She talked Henry into lettin' her switch buses, though," said Nana. "She's sayin' she has to sit next to your young man so he can keep her warm. I don't wanna be an alarmist, dear, but you better watch out for her. I seen on *Access Hollywood* where December/May flings are all the rage, and with her bunions gone, she can wear them hot shoes that drive men wild."

I smiled indulgently. "I'm not worried." I glanced in the wall mirror and screamed at the spike-haired freak who stared back. *Ehh!* That couldn't be me.

I ran to the sink and yanked on my hair.

It *was* me! Okay, now I was worried. "I can't go out looking like this!"

"Hollywood celebrities do all the time," said Tilly. "They think they're glam."

"Hollywood celebrities don't look like *Bride of Chucky!*"

Nana held up her bloomers. "I bet you could twist these into a real nice turban, dear. I got safety pins."

A knock on the outer door. "Ladies, I have to ask you to shake a leg. The buses are about to leave."

Panic filled Nana's eyes. She tossed me

her bloomers and hit the door a half step ahead of Tilly. "See you out there, dear."

I looked in the mirror again, realized the hopelessness of the situation, then turned on the water full force and stuck my head under the faucet. When your short, sassy, Italian hairdo was having an off day, there was only one solution: improvise.

The buses were still loading when I ran out to the parking lot. Henry flagged me down and took me aside. "The excitement's over, Imily. Thanks for keeping mum. I'll make an announcement about Diana, but I'm going to wait until we're all togither at the airport this evening so everyone will git the news at the same time. You wouldn't believe how put out some blokes git whin they think they haven't received news first."

"What did the police tell you about her?"

"Nothing, other than she'd be traveling back to the mainland with thim, and they'd arrange for her bags to be picked up at the hotel."

"That's it? They didn't tell you what she's being charged with?"

"Are they supposed to? I thought they were being very informative tilling me what they did."

"You didn't hear them say something like,

'Book her, Dano, murder one?' "

"Murder! Diana killed someone?"

"I think she killed two someones. Claire Bellows and Nora Acres."

"Codswallop." He blinked numbly. "I've been in this business for eighteen years, and niveh once had dealings with the police. Bloody hill, if she's a killer, they should have grabbed her a hill of a lot sooner!"

"I guess it took them a while to travel from Melbourne."

"Milbourne?" He released his cell phone. "This is Hinry. You could have *told* me the police were traveling from Milbourne. I had a killer on my hands! What if —"

Click.

He stared at the phone. "A killer on my tour. This really takes the air out of my tires."

I patted his arm. "It always does the first time."

When a bus horn tooted, Henry straightened his cap and escorted me briskly across the lot. "There's been some shuffling of passengers between buses because of that Zwerg woman, so I'm afraid you might have lost your seat on the first bus. Lit me chick."

Nana pressed her nose against her window and waved as I waited. Henry returned in moments. "They're full up. Looks like you'll have to ride bus number two with me."

"I'm easy." With Diana Squires in custody and the other guests no longer in jeopardy, I didn't care where I sat or with whom.

Duncan nabbed me as I climbed the stairs. "Gotcha now." He took my hand. "The backseat has our name on it."

"But —"

Etienne occupied the front seat with Bernice, who was snugged into a silver survival blanket like a stick of gum in its wrapper, her head resting on his shoulder.

"Harold and I weren't married many years before he passed on, so I'm practically a virgin," she said. "And in the best shape of my life. Did I happen to mention that I'm an Olympic sprinter?"

The muscle in Etienne's jaw twitched as I passed. Poor guy. He was too new at this to know about the benefits of earplugs.

We arrived at the back and sat down behind Jake and Lola, which would have creeped me out an hour ago, but with our killer in custody, Jake and his bugs no longer seemed so scary. Nothing in the *world* seemed scary anymore!

I exhaled a relieved breath, feeling as if a tremendous weight had been lifted off my shoulders. The situation had resolved itself almost too quietly. I guess I'd gotten too used to fire alarms, police sirens, guns, mace, and chokeholds. Having someone else take down the bad guy felt a little anticlimactic, but I welcomed the change. Now maybe I could relax and enjoy the rest of the trip.

I settled back and stretched my legs. *Ahhhhh.* No more worries. None. Not a single one.

"I was under the impression the only creatures allowed to swim at Seal Bay were the sea lions," said Duncan. "So what's with the wet hair?"

I gave it a ruffle. "Do you like it?"

He trailed his fingers through my wet locks and gave me a look that burned halfway through my skull. "It's hot." His voice dipped to a husky whisper. "You're sexy when you're wet."

Okay, I might still have one small worry.

"I hope you enjoyed Seal Bay," the driver announced. "Our nixt stop will be Stokes Bay on the north shore, where there's a spictacular beach and a ripper café where you can pick up lunch. Won't be so windy there. It's a fifty-five-minute drive, much of it on unsealed roads, so the going could git a bit bumpy. We'll drive through a nice patch of gums near the Cygnet Riveh, but the landscape won't git dramatic until we reach the coast. The bist part of the island is around the idges. If you have quistions at any time, just call 'im out."

As we rolled out of the parking lot, Duncan removed a sack from the overhead rack and dropped it on my lap.

"What's this?"

"Open it."

I stuck my hand inside and pulled out a furry toy sea lion pup with huge eyes and a droopy, ill-tied bow around its neck. "Oh, Duncan, he's adorable! Thank you. Does he have a name?"

"I'm not sure. It might say on the tag."

I found the manufacturer's tag tucked behind the ribbon, dangling beside a diamond ring whose stone was the size of a gumball. "Oh, my God, Duncan." Uh-oh. *Big* worry. "It's beautiful. I mean, it's incredible. I — I don't know what to say."

"How about, 'Yes, Duncan, I'll marry you.' "

I angled the stone toward the window, dazzled when it splintered with a million points of light. "Wow."

"I hope it's big enough. I considered a three-carat stone, but I thought your hand was too small to carry off three carats, so I settled on two. If you'd prefer three, I can exchange it. I don't want you to feel short-changed."

He was so excited, so boyishly enthusiastic. How was I supposed to deal with this? "Does Etienne know about the ring?"

"I don't broadcast my every move to Miceli."

"I thought you two were best buddies."

"We are." He twisted two fingers together. "Like this."

"You can't stand the sight of each other, can you?"

"I despise the man."

"So *why* are you on this trip together?"

"I thought you might have figured that out." He looked at me with the kind of yearning the world's greatest actors couldn't fake. "I want you; he wants you. You know what they say: 'Keep your friends close and your enemies closer.' I don't want to lose you, pretty, and I'm not about to let Miceli get the upper hand. I love you too much."

Oh, geez. What *was* it with me and my feast-or-famine love life? Was it normal for thirty-year-olds to have problems like this?

My heart raced. My palms grew sweaty. Of course it wasn't normal! If it was normal, *Cosmo* would have had a quiz about it, along with lists of the ten most exciting places in a two-car garage to make love and twelve erotic uses for athletes foot powder.

"Don't fall for it," Lola advised over her seat back. "They say anything to git you in the sack, then they turn into aliens. 'Specially the good-looking ones."

Duncan leaned forward. "Excuse me, but no one invited you to take part in this conversation."

"Piss off. I'm not talking to you. I'm talking to your girlfrind."

"Put a sock in it, would ya?" Jake snarled at her.

"*You* put a sock in it!" She whacked his shoulder. "Don't be tilling me to shut up whin I'm handing out important advice. If someone had given *me* the lowdown on you blokes, maybe I wouldn't have got stuck with you!"

"I've got a flash for you, Mrs. Silverthorn. No one but me would put up with you. Everyone knows what you are. Trash. You driss like trash. You talk like trash."

"And who are you? Mr. Prince Charles freaking Windsor?"

"No! I'm apparently the local trash collector!"

Heads turned. Eyebrows lifted. Just what every tour needed: two dead bodies and a fistfight in 9A and B.

"How long have the two of you been married?" I asked as a stopgap measure.

"Too long," spat Jake.

"Bloody ratbag! You think it's been a picnic for me living with you and all your creepy crawlies? My big sisteh reels in a dintist. My baby sisteh nabs a pilot. Who do I git? The king of pist control! Tin years of bloody —"

"Eleven."

"Tin!"

"Eleven!" he yelled. "Oops, my mistake. Stupid people can't count that high! Not enough fingahs!"

"You — !"

"How about a little traveling music?" our driver interrupted.

"ROLL OUT THE BARRE-LL . . ." I slapped my hands over my ears as the tune exploded through the speaker system. *"WE'LL HAVE A BARRE-LL OF FUN . . ."*

Lola grabbed a fistful of Jake's tank top. "You hear that, you miserable bahstid?" She broke into a sudden smile. "That's our song!"

We climbed off the bus at Stokes Bay dazed and punchy. I sighed with exhaustion. "Who would have guessed that *She'll be Comin' 'Round the Mountain* had so many stanzas?"

"It wasn't meant to be sung in rounds," said Duncan. "I think Henry got it confused with *Row, Row, Row Your Boat.* Damn, I could use a cold beer, or" — he smiled with roguish charm — "we could make it champagne if you'd say yes."

Champagne wouldn't cut it. I needed Valium. "I'm not being coy, Duncan. Honest. But *please* give me a little time to think. I feel all scattered."

"How's that for timing? I make my big play for the girl during the planet's loudest shouting match and singalong. Just call me Mr. Romance."

"It could have been worse."

"I realize that. You could have said no." He eyed me with sober resignation. "I'll give you all the time you need, Em, and if you decide the ring belongs on your finger, it'll be right here waiting for you." He patted the deep front pocket of his shorts. "All you have to do is say the word."

"Thanks," I said, meaning it sincerely.

He winked. "No worries." He scanned our surroundings, easing the emotion of the moment. "So this is our spectacular beach, is it?"

The shore was cobblestoned with rocks the size of melons, smoothed and polished by the surf and strewn in a rough mosaic between surly headlands. Duncan let out a low whistle. "This place has 'broken leg' written all over it. I hope no one's planning to take a dip. Was the other beach this rugged?"

"You didn't see the other beach?"

"I was a bit preoccupied embellishing your sea lion."

"You were in the gift shop the whole time?"

He ticked off points on his fingers. "First, the clerk had to find ribbon. Then we argued about how to tie it into a pom-pom. You know what the biggest problem was?"

"He wouldn't listen to your suggestions?"

"He wasn't gay."

Yeah, no way could two straight guys ever figure out how to fluff a bow.

"And when those two detectives arrived with Diana Squires in handcuffs, I got too intrigued to leave. Who knew, huh?"

I pushed gravel around with the toe of my sandal. "I, uh, I suspected her all along."

"You're kidding me. How'd you know she was a thief?"

My foot came to a grinding halt. "Excuse me?"

"I heard the officer tell her she was being arrested for theft."

"Theft? They were supposed to arrest her for murder!"

He studied my face. "Oh, no. You've been doing it again."

"Doing what?"

"Imagining that everyone who leaves the earth is doing so by unnatural means. Listen to me, Emily: not everyone who dies has been murdered. Did the coroner give you any reason to believe the Bellows woman was a victim of foul play?"

"No, but I have a call in to him. Coroners can miss things at a crime scene, especially if they don't realize it *is* a crime scene."

"So you think Diana killed Claire?"

I worried my bottom lip. "I did until the police arrested her for theft. I don't get it."

He gave my nose a playful tweak. "When we get back to the hotel, I'm treating you to a full body massage. No wonder you're feeling scattered. You're pulling double duty as Nancy Drew. Let the police do the investigating, Em. You need to get the relaxation juices flowing, and there's nothing better than deep muscle massage to do it. Warm oil. Body heat. Fluffy towels. It'll be better than a spa. What do you say?"

I pulled the sympathy card from my

shoulder bag and smiled. "Have you signed this yet?"

CHAPTER 17

Theft? What had she stolen? The angiosperms? Nana's photos?

As hungry guests hustled toward a weathered hut called The Rockpool Café and staked claims on nearby picnic tables, I lagged behind, trying to sort out the puzzle.

She couldn't have been hauled off for stealing Nana's Polaroids. I mean, we hadn't even filed a police report! And how could she be arrested for digging up a plant no one could prove existed? Detectives wouldn't cross state lines to drag her back to Melbourne for that, would they? And why the Melbourne authorities? If she committed a crime in Port Campbell, wouldn't the local authorities be responsible for transporting her back?

Why wasn't this making any sense?

I surveyed the grounds, keeping an eye peeled for Jake, Conrad, and Roger. This wasn't good. If Diana hadn't killed Claire and Nora, someone else had, and that someone was still running around free as a bird.

My stomach sank to my knees. Now what?

"If you don't git in the queue, you'll niveh git served," Henry cautioned on his way by. "Don't be fooled by the ramshackle looks of the place. The Rockpool has the bist seafood on the entire island — whiting, yabbies, crays. My favorite is the crays."

"Crayfish?"

"Caught locally."

"Shelled or unshelled?"

"Unshilled. That's the only way to eat a crustacean."

Not to a Midwesterner. We didn't even like our peanuts in shells because of the time we wasted fighting to get them out. "Um, my group could have a problem with the crayfish."

"Allergies?"

"Patience."

"You'd bist warn thim then. Whin the café caters to tour groups, they cast the orders in stone."

I found most of them gathered around a picnic table, shooting pictures of each other beside a seabird who'd landed on the barbecue grill. "Are you sure it's a rare species?"

asked Helen Teig as she focused her camera on Dick.

"Helen, will you take the picture already?"

"I don't want to waste any more film if it's not a sure thing! Emily, what kind of bird is that?"

I eyed the majestic bird with the white breast and gray wings. "Seagull."

"You hear that, Dick? It's a seagull. Seagulls aren't rare!"

"They are in Iowa," said Margi.

"Can I see a show of hands? How many of you have ordered your food already?" Everyone's hand went up.

"Our bus arrived three minutes ahead of yours, so we beat everyone else out to be first in line," crowed Lucille.

Oh, yeah, big surprise there. "So what did you order?"

"CRAYFISH!" they yelled in synchrony.

"It's caught locally," said Dick Stolee.

"And the person who took our order said it's the best thing on the menu," added Alice. She clutched a slip of paper as she checked her watch. "They should call our numbers any minute now."

"They serve it with feta cheese and island-grown olives," said Osmond.

"Does anyone want my feta cheese?" asked Margi. "Feta doesn't sound like something I'm going to like."

"Show of hands again," I said. "How many of you have had crayfish before?"

No hands went up.

Uh-oh.

"What a dump," Bernice whined as she waltzed over to us on Etienne's arm. "They call this beach spectacular? Maybe to another rock. All I have to say is, the crayfish better be good."

She'd ordered the crayfish. I hung my head. There was no God. There was no God.

"This isn't the good beach, luv," Henry announced as he passed out packets of disposable hand wipes. "The swim beach is on the other side of those rocks." He nodded toward a headland of boulders to our east. "The tide's low, so it'll still be accissible if you don't spind too much time eating."

I saw the uncertainty in people's faces as they exchanged looks with each other. Talking tides to Iowans was like talking snowshoes to Pygmies.

"Forget that tide business," groused Bernice. "We don't have tides in Iowa. You know why?"

"I know, I know." Margi shot her hand into the air.

"Because tides are stupid!"

Margi looked confused. "I thought it was because we don't have a coastline."

"What's so special about the beach?" asked Etienne as he seated Bernice at the table.

"It's a little piece of paradise," said Henry. "A criscent beach at the foot of limestone cliffs. Sand like sugar. And there's a rock-inclosed pool that proticts the kiddies from the rips and occasional shark. It's a favorite with the locals, especially whin the surf in the southern beaches gits too wild."

"Does it have toilet facilities?" asked Osmond.

"There's nothing but sand and water, and you're asked to leave nothing behind but footprints."

I could feel their excitement start to build. Dick Stolee surveyed the mountain of boulders with a critical eye. "How in tarnation do we get over there? Drive?"

"Tunnel. Goes clear through to the other side. It used to go only halfway, but after World War II a couple of farmers decided to finish the job, so they dynamited their way through."

The Dicks let out high-spirited whoops, obviously tantalized by the idea of exploding rocks. "We need to see that," Dick Teig enthused. "Which way to the tunnel?"

"You're not going through any tunnel," Helen piped up. "What if it collapses? You'd die under all that rubble, and you can just imagine the talk at the local hospital when they see that hole in your boxers. I will *not* be subjected to that kind of embarrassment."

"You're not going either," Grace Stolee carped at her husband. "It sounds far too dangerous."

"The hell it does!" Dick Teig thundered. "I've got news for you, girls. We didn't come all the way to Australia to be dictated to by a couple of OVERbearing, OVERprotective, OVERwrought fraidy cats!"

I held my breath, hoping he'd know enough to stop before he hit overweight and over-the-hill. That could get really ugly.

"Yah!" chimed Dick Stolee.

"You're not our mothers, so quit acting like them!"

"Yah!" said Dick Stolee

"Dick and me are gonna explore that tunnel, Helen, and if I hear one more word from you, so help me, I'll —"

Helen fisted her hands on her hips and glared at him. "You'll what?"

Osmond raised his hand. "Would it be all right if I go with you?"

"Me, too," said Margi. "I've never been in

a rock tunnel before, but I rode across a covered bridge once."

"NUMBEH FIFTEEN," a voice announced over a loudspeaker. "PICK UP YOUR ORDEH. NUMBEH FIFTEEN."

Alice dashed to the café while the Dicks and their wives continued their verbal tug-of-war. Is this what happened to marriages that lasted for decades? Did they become little more than power struggles between people who were starting to look alike?

"I'm going!" huffed Dick Teig.

"Go ahead!" Helen yelled. "But don't bother coming back!"

"Don't start, Helen!"

"Or else what?"

Oh, God. I let fly a whistle that produced group winces and instant silence from everyone except Osmond, who slapped his hands over his double hearing aids. "Let me know when she's done," he complained. "I can't handle the feedback."

"Okay, guys," I said in a no-nonsense voice, "we're getting nowhere fast. Let Henry finish telling you about the tunnel before you grab your Indiana Jones hats." Grudging nods. Twitching. Pursed lips.

"It's not the easiest path to navigate," Henry continued. "The ground's uneven

321

with some unexpictedly steep dips, and there's a couple of places where the space narrows to liss than a meter across. If you're claustrophobic, I wouldn't try it, but if you're careful, and watch your footing, and start out before the tide changes, everything should be apples."

"That clinches it," said Dick Teig. "I'm going."

"You are not!" Helen shouted.

"NUMBEHS SIXTEEN AND SIVENTEEN, YOUR ORDEHS ARE RIDDY. NUMBEHS SIXTEEN AND SIVENTEEN. PLEASE PICK UP YOUR ORDEHS."

"This discussion isn't over, Helen," said Dick as he stormed toward the café.

"Yah," said Dick Stolee, wagging his finger at Grace as he followed behind Dick. "What he said."

Henry turned away from the group and said to me in an undertone, "There could be a serious problem with the two hifty blokes, Imily."

"Don't pay any attention to them. They're always having disagreements with their wives. It's part of their schtick."

"I mean with the tunnel. I can't quite remimber how narrow the passage gits, if you catch my drift. You might want to chick it out before they git into something they can't git out of."

Oh, this was nice. Get the Dicks all hypered into a frenzy, then pull the rug out from beneath them. "Where's the entrance?"

He gestured toward the far end of the rockribbed headland. "It's about thirty-five meters thataway. There's a couple of markers that'll git you close, then you just have to keep your eyes peeled."

Alice returned with a platter of salad greens, chunks of white cheese, olives, lemon wedges, fancy pineapple slices, and a spiny crustacean that looked like a cross between a Maine lobster and Arnold Schwarzeneger's *Predator.* "Euwww." Bernice pulled a face. "If you're planning to eat that thing, I don't wanna watch."

Lucille regarded it, aghast. "Please tell me that's not the crayfish special."

"Why is it in a shell?" asked Helen. "Aren't crayfish like catfish? Catfish don't have shells."

"It has eyes," Grace whispered in disgust. "There's no way I'm eating eyeballs for lunch."

"If that's crayfish, I'm changing my order." Bernice stood up.

"I don't understand," Helen muttered in

confusion. "Whitefish don't have shells. Bluefish don't have shells."

I motioned Bernice to sit back down. "You can't change your order. It's too difficult to make substitutions when they're serving large tour groups."

Alice rapped a knuckle on the creature's shell. "Are we supposed to eat the whole thing? I'm not sure my dental insurance will cover emergency crowns overseas."

"The crayfish in Sardinia is exquisite," said Etienne as he lifted Alice's crayfish off its platter. "I imagine this is just as good. You attack it like so." He snapped it backward at a joint between body and tail, exposing a succulent hunk of white meat. "You then take your wooden pick and gently pry the meat out of the tail, into your drawn butter, and into your mouth. Don't think of it as an annoyance, ladies. Think of it as an adventure."

It was a funny thing about women. When a black-haired, blue-eyed European with one percent body fat and a dreamy accent said something, they tended to listen.

"Will you help me when my food arrives?" asked Lucille.

"Me, too?" asked Margi.

"It would be my pleasure." He executed a little aristocratic bow that left them with goofy smiles, fluttery eyes, and a breathless craving for Kangaroo Island shellfish. I shook my head, feeling a sudden deficiency in my people skills.

Maybe I needed to work on my accent.

"Talk about lowdown tricks," Dick Teig sputtered as he dropped his tray on the table. "Look what they're expecting us to eat. The creature from *Twenty Thousand Leagues Under the Sea.* You can do what you want, Helen, but I'm not eating anything with antennae growing out its nose."

"Sit down, Dick," Helen urged sweetly, "and shut up. It looks delicious. Absolutely delicious."

"Okay then," I said, as the tension eased, "while Etienne gives you a hand with the crayfish, I'm going to check out the tunnel. If it doesn't look too treacherous, maybe we can all hike through to the beach."

Cheers. Whoops. One dissenting snort. "I'm not going," Bernice sniped, "and there's nothing you can do to make me."

Wasn't it neat how we sometimes lucked out in life without even trying?

I crossed the picnic area and navigated the shoreline's rocky flanks with extreme caution, stepping over shallow tide pools, slipping on green algae, and crunching the occasional seashell beneath my sandals. Spying a simple marker with an arrow emblazoned on it, I scanned the headland for an entryway and spotted a vertical break in the boulders.

The passage twisted and turned like a maze tunneling to the center of the earth. There was an eerie prehistoric feel to the landscape, as if raptors still scavenged for food around every corner, and woolly mammoths came here to die. I followed the trail around the jagged rocks, scraping my shoulder bag at every turn and wishing I'd left it behind. I had so much stuff crammed inside, it had ballooned to the size of a whole other person. But I was encouraged by the accessibility of the trail, until I reached a spot where I had to turn sideways to squeeze between opposing rock walls.

Uh-oh. I sucked in my tummy and wiggled through. If either of the Dicks tried this, he'd become a human wedge until a rescue team freed him. Henry had sure called that right. But the poor Dicks were going to be so disappointed, they'd probably be impossible for the rest of the day, unless —

My mood brightening with a sudden thought, I quickened my pace to reach the end of the tunnel. *Unless Henry's little piece of paradise turned out to be nothing to write home about.*

It was glorious. A deserted, horseshoe-shaped cove, hugged by craggy cliffs and washed by sparkling turquoise water that glazed the sand with froth. A breakwater of low rocks formed a protective pool around half the beach, while beyond the barrier, the ocean swelled with booming rollers that didn't look at all user-friendly.

Wow. This place was amazing. A few palm trees, some forbidden fruit, and it really would be paradise. But I couldn't tell that to the Dicks. I needed to play it down so they wouldn't think they were missing anything.

In other words, I needed to lie.

I kicked off my sandals to walk barefoot on the beach, hopping on tiptoes when I realized the sand wasn't just sugary. It was hot! "Ouch. Ouch." I ran toward the water and sank my toes into the cool tidal sand, tottering off-balance when the ground oozed from beneath my feet on an ebbing wave.

"Turn around and do something sassy!" a voice called from behind me.

Guy Madelyn sat on the beach in the shade of a boulder that may have broken off from the cliff a million years ago. He brandished his camera in the air. "The light doesn't get more perfect than this, Emily. You want to give it another shot?"

"No! This is the worst hair day of my life!" Well, other than the day in Italy when it caught fire.

"Your hair looks fine. Hold that pose." He checked his display screen. "Hey, I think we finally hit pay dirt." He stood up and crossed the beach to me. "What do you think of this?"

My complexion glowed in the light. My hair looked casually windblown. My smile held mystery. My eyes sparkled with a "come hither" look. Good God, I looked sensational. "Wow."

"Nice, huh? See? I told you all you had to do was relax."

"Do you have a price list for your wedding photo packages?"

"On my website. Search Guy Madelyn, and that should get you there. Does this mean you've narrowed your field of eligible suitors to one?"

Did it? Had my heart made the decision without informing my brain? Did I know subconsciously? Had I always known?

Yeah, I think I had.

I smiled at the revelation. "I know the one."

"Great. We do honeymoon packages, too. Have you discussed your wedding trip yet? Islands are the big thing. How about a destination wedding? You and a handful of friends and family could fly to Tahiti, or Bora Bora, or Moorea, and the most critical detail you'd have to worry about is making plans early enough to insure that everyone who doesn't have a passport has plenty of time to apply for one."

"Speaking of passports, I still have yours." I swung my bag off my shoulder and poked through the jumbled contents, yanking out Nana's bloomers and my plastic bag of wet clothing. "Somewhere. I need to get rid of some of this stuff. I think I've reached critical mass."

"Would you like me to hold those for you?"

"That would be great. And while I have you here, would you sign the group card for Heath? I think your signature is the only one that's missing, other than Jake's. He had issues with the sympathy thing." I dug out a pen. "Do you have enough hands?"

"No problem. I juggle more equipment than this when I'm on a job." He shoved the clothing under his arm, then went down on one knee to sign the card. I grabbed a handful of passports, flipping them open one by one. *Osmond Chelsvig. Margi Swanson.*

"If your passport was pink, I could find it in a second."

"Sorry. Same old navy blue as the States."

Alice Tjarks. Lucille Rassmuson. Lucille was wearing her brooch with her late husband's face on it. Wow, his cigar had come out *really* well. *Dick Teig. Guy Madelyn.* "Found it!" I angled the page away from the sun's glare to regard his photo once again. "For a good-looking guy, you really do take a horrendous picture. This doesn't look anything like you." I eyed the dates on the right. "You were a St. Patrick's Day baby! Oh, my God, you're not going to believe this, but you and Nora Acres were born on the very same day: March 17, 1943. Small world, huh?"

"Anytime you get a group together, two or three people will always share the same birthday. It's a statistically proven fact."

The next line gave me pause. "You were born in England?"

"Yeah, my dad worked as a newspaper correspondent for a few years during the war. High risk, low pay. He and my mom didn't stay long after I was born."

"That's such a coincidence." I looked at

him as if for the first time and frowned in disbelief. "Did you know Nora was born in England?"

"Really? I thought she was Australian through and through." He stood up and handed me the card. "Trade you."

I handed over his passport. "She was orphaned in England and transported to Australia for adoption. I guess that happened to a lot of children after the war." I searched his face, unable to reconcile what I was thinking. "She lived a pretty hard life in the Outback. Maybe if she'd lived in Canada, she'd have had something to show for her fifty-seven years other than wrinkles. I can't believe you're fifty-seven. You look at least a decade or two younger."

"I'll take that as a compliment." He shook out Nana's bloomers. "Don't take this the wrong way, but you struck me as more of a Victoria's Secret kind of gal."

I snatched the undies from him and glanced around the deserted beach. "I bet you wouldn't be so cheeky if there were children around. Where are the kiddies, anyway? I thought this place was supposed to be their favorite haunt."

"I expect they're in school. Australian schoolchildren don't take long summer breaks. That's an American peculiarity."

I scrutinized his features as I jammed the plastic bag and bloomers back into my shoulder bag. Was it my imagination, or did he resemble Heath through the eyes and mouth? My notion was completely absurd, and yet — "Did your parents take a lot of pictures when you were a baby?"

"I beg your pardon?"

"Do you have an album with a lock of your hair, and a christening photo, and all the statistics people mark down for newborns? You know. Baby's first year?"

"Is that a polite way of asking if I'm adopted?"

My heart pumped double time. "Are you?"

"No, I'm not adopted! And if I don't have a baby album, it's because parents in the forties didn't bother with things like that, especially during wartime."

"A lot of parents never told their children the truth."

"Sorry, Emily, but you're way out of line. If you're trying to prove that Nora Acres and I had some connection because we have the same birthday, you're going to end up looking very foolish."

Spoken like a man without an ounce of female intuition. "Do you remember the photo Nora showed you in Port Campbell?"

"Vaguely. What I remember most was that it was about to disintegrate."

"It showed Nora posing with her sister, Beverley, and their mother. The twins were in pinafores and had Shirley Temple banana curls."

Guy lifted his brows. "And?"

"Okay, you might think I'm really grasping at straws, but what if the reason you never had a baby album was because your parents never saw you as a baby? What if Nora's photo is actually a picture of her mother . . . and another child who was born in England on March 17, 1943?"

He struggled to keep a straight face even as laughter exploded from his chest. "You think the other child is me? Why would I be posing with Nora Acres? Better yet, do I look like a Beverley to you?"

"No! But you were born in England. The English have been known to stick their male offspring with girls' names — Evelyn, Marian, Carol, *Beverley.*"

"Are they also guilty of dressing little boys in pinafores?"

"I've seen some of my grandmother's family photos where you couldn't distinguish the girls from the boys because they were all in dresses and pipe curls. People did that back then. Little boys didn't get into trou-

333

sers or have their hair cut until they went off to school."

"And they all ended up in therapy."

"Seriously, I think I'm onto something. The twins were placed in different orphanages during the war and never saw each other again, so the only link Nora had to her past was that photo. She assumed the other child in the photo was her sister, but what if it wasn't? What if it was her brother? What if the children weren't identical twins? What if they were fraternal twins?"

"I'm not adopted!"

"Oh, my God, Guy! You may have found a sister you never knew you had! Don't you believe in serendipity?"

"I believe in good fortune happening by accident. I *don't* believe in pipe dreams. Now, will you drop it?"

"But think what this could mean to Heath! You could provide the closure he and his mother had been looking for for so many years, and that would be so meaningful to him. You look like him, you know. I didn't see it before because I wasn't looking for it, but you have the same full lips, the same blue eyes. You even have the same physique! You could have DNA testing done to eliminate all doubt. You have to talk to him, Guy. This is so amazing! You come to Australia to meet the relatives, and you end up with one more than you expected. A nephew! We need to speak to Henry. Heath is supposed to call him later, and when he does, maybe you can —"

"I told you to drop it!"

"But don't you want —"

"NO! I *don't* want! Kee-REIST, what the hell is wrong with you? You couldn't leave well enough alone. You had to keep picking and picking. And that's a damn shame, because I liked you, Emily. I really did."

Liked? Uh-oh. Past tense wasn't a good sign. "I'm sorry, Guy. I've been acting like an unfeeling, insensitive clod. I just get so excited when I start connecting the dots. This has to be a huge shock, and I haven't allowed you any time for it to sink in. Why don't we go back to the café and —"

"What a lousy way to learn you're not who you think you are."

Guilt lodged like a hairball in my throat. "I'm sorry," I rasped, hoping a whirlpool would appear at my feet and swallow me whole.

"They could have told me when they were alive, but no, I had to find out after they were dead."

I placed my hand on Guy's forearm.

"They probably had a very good reason for not telling you."

"It was all lies. There was no newspaper job in London. It was one giant cover-up to keep the truth from me. But I couldn't understand why. The newspaper clippings, the old family records, why would they want to hide those from me? Madelyn was one of the most respected names in Australian history. You'd think they would have been proud of that. But that's exactly why they had to keep it from me: because if I started asking questions, their world would collapse like a house of cards."

I could hear him talk; I just wish I understood what he was saying. "Um, I'm a little confused. Would you mind backing up to the part about newspaper clippings and old family records?"

He regarded me with eyes so distant, I wasn't sure he could actually see me. "I found them in the attic after my dad died — after the nephrologist told me that in addition to my being diabetic, my blood type was incompatible with my dad's, which meant, he couldn't have fathered me. I found everything — travel documents, passports. My parents left Canada right before the war for Australia. I found clippings about the *Meridia* and photos of my dad with his Aussie relatives. News articles about a ship that carried English orphans to New South Wales in nineteen-forty-six. A record of adoption for an English male child named Beverley Gooch by Nicole and Guy Madelyn. *My* adoption papers. I was apparently born in England, but my parents adopted me in Australia, then whisked me back home to Canada even before the ink had dried. I guess my dad didn't want the Aussie relatives finding out that Guy Junior, no longer known as Beverley, wasn't the genuine article. What a blow to the ego, eh? A man so inept, he can't get his own wife pregnant, so he needs to settle for someone else's kid."

"It's not settling! Adopting a child has to be a wonderfully rewarding experience. Your dad couldn't have thought that."

"Then why the lies? Why the isolation? I'll tell you why. Because he was so ashamed, he couldn't face telling them the truth! So he cut off all ties to them so he wouldn't have to. I knew something was wrong. My dad always gave off these tense, angry vibes that would earn you a good smack if you crossed him on certain days. He was so cold and secretive. And that was the other thing. I wasn't blind. I wanted to know why I didn't look like either of my parents, and you wouldn't believe the double talk my dad dished out to explain it. I think that's the reason I went into photography. I wanted to find a face that looked like mine."

"And now you've found one!" I enthused. "Heath! Did you get pictures of him? Could you see the resemblance?"

Something dark and disturbing flickered in his eyes. "I didn't need to see him." He removed his wallet from his back pocket and slid a photo out from its plastic sheath. "I knew the moment I saw this."

He handed me a photo of a young woman with bobbed hair who was cuddling two toddlers in frilled pinafores and pipe curls. "This is Nora's picture. What are you doing with it?"

"It was in the same box as my adoption papers. When my mother delivered us to the orphanage, she apparently left a photo with each of us, only mine didn't include any names. I didn't know who the three people were until Nora showed me her photo, then it became fairly obvious. The three of us had been a family at one time. It was a photo of my biological family."

"So from that first day at Port Campbell, you knew Nora was a relative?"

"I knew she was a relative. *You* made the

nightmare complete by telling me she was my twin. What a great way to ruin a gold mine tour."

"You knew, and you didn't say anything?"

He reacted as if he'd been slapped. "What? Give up the celebrity of being a Madelyn to admit I was brother to a pathetic old crone whose biggest thrill in life had been to visit a Big Banana and a Big Oyster?"

"Yeah, but she was your sister! Did it really matter what her taste was in tourist attractions?"

"She was an embarrassment! Can you imagine the looks on my kids' faces if I introduced them to the aunt they never knew? You think they'd want to introduce her to their friends? Maybe she could have entertained them by killing insects with her bare hands! How do you think that would have gone over?"

"She wasn't a freak," I said quietly.

"The only reason you can say that is because she wasn't related to you! In the neighborhood where I live, with the high-class people I run with, she'd be a freak."

I inhaled a calming breath, but it didn't do much good. "I'm not sure why I ever thought you were such a nice man. You're nothing but a . . . a world-class snob! And for your information? Nora had more class than you could ever *think* of having. Here's your picture back."

He seized my wrist. "Like I said, Emily, I liked you, so I'm sorry it's come to this."

"What — !" I wrenched back on my arm. "What do you think you're doing?"

"Getting rid of leaks. Sorry, baby doll, you know too much."

"About your family history? Who cares about your stupid charade?" Which is when I realized that Guy Madelyn cared. He cared very much. "Oh, my God. *You* killed her. You killed Nora!"

"You saw the shape she was in. She was way overdue. I just gave nature a little nudge before her fool son could track me down on any of the new internet adoption sites. You told me yourself he was getting close. So it was either take care of the problem now or risk having her show up on my front door-stoop. And that last part wasn't an option."

"You bastard! You drugged her wine at the vineyard." Which must have required some fancy sleight of hand considering he hadn't been anywhere near her at the wine tasting.

"You know about the overdose?" He clucked his disgust. "Autopsies are a real pain in the ass. However, in a tour group this size, I can't be the only person taking insulin tablets. And since I have no connection to Nora, what possible motive could I have had to kill her?"

"You spiked her wine with insulin? You killed your only sister by sending her into insulin shock?"

"You're not hearing me. I didn't *want* her as a sister. And I didn't touch her wine. I dropped the crushed tablets into her cucumber raita at the Indian restaurant the other night. It mixed up incredibly well in that thick yogurt base. I doubt she ever tasted it."

"But she didn't take ill until the next day! Do you know how many hours you made that poor woman suffer?"

"She didn't look as if she was suffering too badly."

"Not suffering badly? She died!" I yelled, driving my foot into his kneecap.

"OW! You — !" He yanked me against his chest and grabbed my hair, jarring every bone in my body and all thirty-two teeth. My bag fell off my shoulder. The photo blew away.

"Is that how you killed Claire?" I yelled into his face. "Did you send her into insulin shock, too?"

"Claire Bellows? Why would I kill her? I

didn't even know her."

"You didn't know Nora, either!"

"And thankfully, it's going to remain that way. Look, Emily, I'm sorry to have to do this, but one of us needs to make an exit, and it's not going to be me."

He tramped into the surf, pulling me by the hair behind him. My mind raced. Adrenaline shot through me. Oh, my God. He was going to drown me in the kiddie pool!

"HELLLLLLLLLLP!" I shrieked. Hey, it always worked for Bernice. "HELP ME! SOMEBODY HELLLLLLLP!"

"Jeesuz Mighty." He clamped his hand over my mouth and jerked me off my feet, crushing me against him.

"*MMMMMMMMMHHHHHHPPPPPP!*" I pounded his forearms and flailed at his legs, my limbs whipping around like eggbeaters.

He waded deeper into the surf, dragging me with him. *Oh, God!*

I bared my teeth and bit down hard on his finger.

"*Aaarhh!*"

"I'm glad Nora never found out you were her brother!" I screamed, when his hand flew off my mouth. "She didn't have to live with the disappointment!"

He plunged my head under the water.

Foam. Bubbles. Muffled quiet. *Nooo!*

I pulled my legs up beneath me and kicked out like a mule, jackknifing my feet into his groin.

His grip faltered. I rocketed out of the water and gasped for air. "HELLLL —"

WHOOSH.

He plunged my head deeper, holding me down with two hands. I batted the water. Struggled to hold my breath. Kicked helplessly while seawater stung my eyes. I screamed in my throat, but I knew it was a sound no one would ever hear. Panic overwhelmed me. Pain seared my chest. Images flashed through my mind. Beloved faces. Welcoming arms. And the one face I loved more than all the rest, but would never see again. We'd wasted so much time! If only I could do it over again. If only we'd —

My lungs burst like a popped balloon, causing my breath to escape in a riot of bubbles. I clawed at the seabed as water poured into every orifice, scalding my throat, filling my nos—

Fresh air hit me in the face as I was hauled to the surface amid fevered shouts and cries. Chaos surrounded me. Splashing. Thrashing. Kicking. Punching.

"You've got it all wrong!" Guy bellowed

at Etienne and Duncan. "I was trying to save her!"

Etienne drove his fist into Guy's face with a crunch of bone and cartilage. Duncan followed up with a blow to the midsection that sent him backflopping like a beached flounder. Etienne seized his shirt-front, spat something in Italian, and tossed him back at Duncan. "You got him?"

"I got him."

I paddled and splashed my way into Etienne's arms.

"Are you all right, *bella*?"

I burrowed against him, wheezing and gasping, my legs wobbly beneath me. "I thought I'd never see you again," I sobbed.

He kissed the top of my head, calming me with his quiet touch. "Emily, Emily. Heath called with the results of Nora's autopsy. She died from an insulin overdose, and according to Henry's medical forms, only one person on the tour is taking insulin."

"Guy Madelyn." I watched Duncan strong-arming him toward shore.

"But he was nowhere in sight. Henry suggested he might have hiked over to this beach, which is where you were heading, so that's when all hell broke loose. I'm probably only a half-step ahead of your grandmother and her crew." He hugged me tighter. "Let's get you to shore. You're shivering."

As we splashed through the surf toward dry land, I noticed that the deserted beach was deserted no longer. People were popping out of the tunnel with their cameras already clicking. Nana, Tilly, Alice, Osmond, and Margi rushed forward, hovering over me as I sank onto the hot sand.

"We was so worried about you," Nana fretted.

"Everyone dropped their crayfish to come rescue you," said Tilly.

Margi nodded breathlessly. "We would have got here sooner, but it's pretty slow-going through the tunnel, especially with certain people hogging the passing lane."

"Someone needs to go back to tell Henry to call the local police," I rasped, my throat still stinging and my nose burning all the way to my brain.

"We're on it," said Nana, grabbing Tilly and taking off like a shot.

"You fellas really knocked the stuffing out of old Guy," said Osmond, looking farther down the beach. "Would you look at the size of his bottom lip? Woo-hee." His camcorder chimed as he powered it up. "This is going to be so good. Real blood!"

"Does he need a nurse?" asked Margi,

chasing down the beach after him.

"Maybe I can get a group shot," said Alice. "Any chance we can locate a shark for local color?"

Etienne went down on one knee, cupping my face in his hands and smiling gently. "Are all you Americans this resilient?"

"Not all." My eyes filled with tears as I smiled back. "It helps to be from Iowa."

"It's gonna be a while before we can get to Henry!" Nana yelled from the direction of the tunnel. "It's on account a the Dicks. They're stuck!"

CHAPTER 18

After breakfast the next morning we were scheduled to drive southeast for a morning of shopping in the German settlement of Hahndorf, but in light of the harrowing day we'd spent on Kangaroo Island, Henry canceled the tour and gave us a free day in Adelaide to get our feet under us again. He suggested the real diehards in the group could entertain themselves by hopping the Glenelg tram to the seashore or visiting the East End Market, but if we wanted something more relaxing, he recommended the rooftop pool and a pitcher of maragaritas. Nana was so relieved I hadn't drowned, she announced an open house and prepool appetizers in our suite, so by ten o'clock, our living room was crawling with people eating smoked salmon on mini bagels and knocking back fresh-squeezed orange juice.

"This fresh-squeezed is a pain," griped Bernice. "I'll be spittin' out pulp all day.

Who's got floss?"

We'd moved Nana's laptop to make room for the food, and I was happy not to have to look at it anymore. The Google Earth download had been useless. The program finally transferred, but when we typed in Roger's coordinates, the image it relayed showed Port Campbell National Park as it had appeared three months ago! Remote areas of distant continents apparently got *no* respect when it came to live satellite feeds.

"I'm offering a toast," Henry said, raising his juice glass. "May the nixt lig of our tour be nothing like the first lig."

A resounding, "Hear, hear!" echoed through the room.

Conrad gave Nana a sheepish look as he clinked glasses with her. "I've received terrible news this morning, Marion. The disappointment might be too much for you, so you might want to sit down."

She glanced around the room. "No place *to* sit. How 'bout I just lean." She braced her hip against the desk. "Okay, shoot."

"I talked to the zoological team looking for the desert rat kangaroo a short time ago, and they affirmed my worst fear. They can find neither the creature nor any evidence of its habitat at Sovereign Hill. Wherever he was when you photographed him, he's not there any longer."

"So I'm not gonna be famous?"

"I'm sorry, Marion. I'm afraid not."

"Good thing I didn't waste no money on a cut and blow-dry, then."

"Tell her the rest of the story," Ellie insisted. "Tell her what you're going to do about it."

Conrad's mustache wiggled at the edges. "It's because of you that I'm staying in Australia, Marion, if I can iron out the paperwork. I've been offered a position by Melbourne's Museum of Victoria to help classify the backlog of unnamed plant specimens they've collected through the years. They can use someone with my professional stature and knowledge on staff, and with luck, perhaps I'll find another sample of the angiosperm we lost at Port Campbell. I still believe your plant is out there, Marion. I'll never give up."

"Don't lose no sleep over it."

Ellie cuddled up to her husband, their differences apparently forgotten. "And the best part is, free housing and a nice income. And from now on, *I'm* handling the finances."

Nana slipped her a business card.

"What's this?"

"My email address. Drop me a line if you need investment advice. I got the inside scoop on what's hot."

"Have you learned any more information about Diana Squires?" Duncan called out to Henry.

"Ah! That's right. I haven't gotten you up to speed. Some of you may have noticed that Ms. Squires was taken away by the authorities yesterday. I talked to the main office this morning and from what they've learned, she's been arristed for stealing everything that wasn't nailed down from her hotel room in Milbourne. Towels. Sheets. Ashtrays. Blankets. Even the phone."

"What's so bad about that?" asked Bernice. "Everyone steals things from hotel rooms. It's expected."

"Not anymore," argued Henry. "At least, not in Milbourne. The hotels have agreed to priss charges aginst violators to stop the financial bleeding. The loss of property is tremendous, so they've declared war."

"How'd she fit all those extras in her luggage?" Dick Teig threw out.

"She didn't pack thim," Henry said, laughing. "She mailed thim! All the way to America. It cost her more to mail the box than the merchandise was worth."

I glanced at Duncan, whose crimson neck

probably indicated how he felt about his unintended part in helping her mail the contraband.

"But that wasn't the worst of it," Henry continued. "David Jones Department Store wants her for shoplifting, as does the gift shop at the wildlife park in Ballarat. They have surveillance video of her in the act, but they couldn't idintify her because her face was blurred in every frame. The authorities are theorizing that her makeup contains a compound that blocks a camera's ability to capture clear visual images. Kind of like lid with an X-ray. Quite the ruse. I bit you can't buy that at the Estee Lauder counter. I thought she was trying to cover up acne scars with the heavy makeup, but what she was really trying to cover up was a life of crime."

The backpack made sense now. No wonder she'd bought the expandable model. Over a two-week period, she was expecting to fit a lot in there besides lipstick and blush.

"What about Guy?" asked Tilly. "What's happened to him?"

"He spint the night on Kangaroo Island, but he'll be brought back to Adelaide today for procissing. His arrist is going to make quite the splash here in South Australia."

Guy said he liked splash, but I imagined

this wasn't the kind he had in mind.

"These are yours." Bernice shoved a couple of photos at Nana.

"My Polaroids! I thought they was gone forever. Well, I'll be. I knew if I kept prayin' to St. Anthony, they'd show up. Where'd you find 'em?"

"I didn't find them exactly; I borrowed them."

"See, dear?" Nana held them up to me. "This one's a little anthill that was right off the parking lot, and this here's one a the ants. Never seen an ant what looked like that before. See how the body's almost transparent?" She snapped her gaze back to Bernice. "What do you mean, 'borrowed?'"

"That photographer was making such a fuss over your pictures, I thought I'd borrow a couple. I figured I'd study what you did right so I could get the same effect in my pictures and maybe land me a job like you were being offered. I knew you wouldn't mind. In fact, I thought you'd be flattered."

"You *stole* Nana's photos?" I accused.

Bernice rolled her eyes. "You are *such* an alarmist. I told you. I borrowed them, and now I'm giving them back. Damned if I could figure out what was so special about them. Dirt. Rocks. Ants. You know what I think? I think your fancy-schmancy photographer was full of crap."

I looked from Bernice to Nana, suddenly enlightened. "So if Bernice took two of your pictures —"

"— Claire probably took the other one," said Nana.

"And if she was the only person to recognize the angiosperms when the photos were being passed around —" said Tilly.

"Then no one would have any reason for wanting to kill her!" I exclaimed.

Bernice squinted at the three of us. "You people are Looney Tunes."

When the desk phone rang, I scooted down the hall and picked up in the bedroom.

"Imily? This is Peter Blunt in Warrnambool. I apologize for taking so long to answer your call, but we've been swamped. If you were calling about Ms. Bellows's autopsy, I have the results."

"Let me guess. It wasn't foul play, right? We just figured it out, and I have to tell you, I'm *so* relieved. You wouldn't believe what we've been through, trying to piece together why anyone would want to kill her."

A pause. "Didn't I mintion there was no evidence of foul play at the scene?"

"You mentioned it, but were you a hundred percent sure? You seemed a little iffy to me."

"I wasn't being iffy. I was flirting with you."

"Oh."

"Claire Bellows died as a result of deep vein thrombosis. Have you heard of it?"

"I've heard the term, but I'm not sure I know what it is."

"It's a blood clot in a deep vein in the leg. In Claire's case it formed above the knee, then broke off and traveled to her lungs. It can happen to folks during long-distance travel, especially if they don't exercise their legs or stay hydrated. We're will aware of the problem here since there *are* no short flights from Australia to anywhere ilse in the world, so we're always preaching comprission stockings."

"Excuse me?"

"Graduated comprission socks. They're tighter at the foot than the calf, which hilps with circulation. Just about every store sills them. They're a bit pricey, but we ricommind them to anyone who boards a plane, especially people over forty who are carrying a bit of weight."

"But Claire wasn't over forty!"

"Goes to show you. You just never know."

I hung up the phone, overwhelmed by a sense of dread.

"Problems?" asked Duncan, stepping into the bedroom and closing the door behind him.

"You bet."

"Anything I can help with?"

"Can you persuade eleven money-conscious Iowans to spring for compression stockings?"

He grinned. "You're on your own with that one. I couldn't convince your two Dicks to fork out five cents for toothpicks at the café yesterday." He kissed my hand and sat me on the bed. "You have a good group, Em. I'm going to miss them."

"I'm sorry?"

He tucked a strand of hair behind my ear. "I told you in Italy that Lazarus men have a reputation to uphold. We pursue relentlessly until we get the girl. Remember? But we're not entirely stupid. Some of us can actually tell when it's time to throw in the towel."

I felt a little hitch in my throat. "You're giving up?"

"Not because I don't love you, Em, because I still do. There's a part of me that'll always love you. But I know the way you look at Miceli, and I know the way you look at me, and it's not the same. Something gets lost in translation when you look at me."

"Oh, Duncan, that's not tru—"

"Yeah, it is true. But that's okay. It was a fair fight, and the best man won — but you tell Miceli that if he's not good to you, he'll answer to me." He kissed my forehead, and whispered, "Be happy, pretty," before taking my hand and escorting me out of the room.

"You know the one thing I'm *not* going to miss about your tours?" he asked when we reached the suite's main door.

I forced a smile. "The body count?"

"Always being last in line. No one ever gets ahead of your group. What's up with that anyway? Let me know when the engagement becomes official. The first magnum of champagne is on me."

"Who was on the phone, dear?" Nana asked when I rejoined the group in the living room.

"Peter Blunt," I said, suppressing a pang of wistfulness. "He had the results of Claire Bellows's autopsy."

Silence descended. All eyes turned to me.

"I still bet she died of thirst," said Lucille.

"She died from deep vein thrombosis. That's what can happen when you sit in a cramped airplane seat for fifteen hours and don't exercise your legs. A blood clot can form and travel to your lungs. And it often happens to people who are over forty and have lost their youthful figures."

Awareness registered on everyone's face. Eyes shifted nervously. Mouths twitched in alarm.

"I told you we should travel first-class," Helen Teig said as she thwacked Dick. "There's more legroom there."

"Do I look like I'm made of money, Helen?"

"A lot of good your bankroll will do if you're dead!"

Lucille brightened. "Of course, if he did die, Helen and I could room together and I wouldn't have to pay the extra charge for a single room anymore."

"The Aussies apparently wear compression stockings when they travel," I continued. "They promote circulation so clots won't form. Peter said you can buy them anywhere."

"Are they expensive?" asked Dick Stolee.

I went in for the kill. "They're a lot cheaper than a first-class air ticket."

Juice got chugged. Plates got dumped on every hard surface. A little pushing and shoving, a slight bottleneck at the door, and they were gone.

I checked the second hand of my watch.

Twenty seconds. Not bad. I smiled at the people who remained in the room. "Gee, that went well."

"Me and Tilly are going, too," said Nana. "You want we should pick you up a pair?"

"Sure, if there are any left."

Henry set down his plate and glass and peeked at the Polaroids Nana had dropped on the desk. "Did you shoot these, Marion?"

"Yup."

He leaned over for a closer look. "Do you mind if I ask where?"

"At that Twelve Apostles place."

He stared some more. "I'll be damned. Do you know what you have here?"

"An anthill."

"No, it's much more than that. I know a thing or two about insicts, and what you've found here looks like a rare species of ant that hasn't been seen since the eighteen-eighties!"

Nana arched an eyebrow. "Sure, sure."

"Really! Marion, this is a significant discovery."

"Right."

"We need to call someone. The state university. The government. You could become famous!"

"Uh-huh." Nana grabbed her pocketbook. "You ready, Til'?"

"You can't ignore this, Marion! You need to do something about it."

Nana picked up the photos, ripped them into shreds, and threw them in the wastebasket. "How's that?"

A horrified peep escaped Henry. Nana grabbed Tilly and headed out the door. "See you later, dear."

Henry stared helplessly at the wastebasket before scooping it off the floor. "Would you mind if I took this back to my room, Imily? I might be able to tape the pieces back togither."

"Knock yourself out."

Etienne leaned against the frame of the patio door and toasted me with his juice glass. "Another successful gathering, *bella*."

"You think?" I collapsed on the sofa. He sat down beside me and gathered me in his arms.

"You gave me the worst fright of my life yesterday, Emily. Please, don't ever do that again."

"If you thought *you* were frightened, you should have been in my shoes."

"I thought you'd drowned. When I grabbed Madelyn, I wanted to tear him apart with my bare hands." He twined his fingers with mine. "I wanted to kill him. If he had harmed you in any way, I would have."

I turned his hand over, wincing at his bruised knuckles before feathering a kiss on each one. "Your timing was impeccable."

"I'm Swiss. How does one live around so many clocks and stay unaffected?"

I felt that familiar hitch in my throat again. "Thank you for being there when I needed you most."

He kissed me gently. *"Ti amo, bella,"* he whispered against my lips. *"Ti voglio anima e cuore. Voglio restare con te per l'eternita."*

I sighed. "What does that mean?"

He reached into his pants pocket and presented me with a small drawstringed pouch that was stamped with gold lettering.

"Rees and Benjamin?" I said, perplexed. Untying the strings, I upended the contents and quietly let out my breath, for there in my palm lay an elegant gold band in a lacy filigree pattern, quite the most beautiful ring I'd ever seen. "The ring from Sovereign Hill." My eyes welled with tears. "Oh, Etienne. How did you know?"

"I went back and asked the clerk what you'd been looking at. She showed this to me and said it fit you as if it had been made to order." He slid it on my finger. *"Spo-*

siamoci, Emily." He brought the ring to his lips and kissed it. "Will you marry me?"

Unlike so many of life's challenging questions, there was only one answer to this one. "Okay!"

ABOUT THE AUTHOR

Maddy Hunter has endured disastrous vacations on three continents in the past five years. Despite this, she aspires to visit all seven continents in the future. *G'Day to Die* is the fifth novel in her critically acclaimed, bestselling *Passport to Peril* mystery series featuring Emily Andrew — *Alpine for You* (an Agatha Award nominee for Best First Mystery), *Top O' the Mournin'*, *Pasta Imperfect,* and *Hula Done It?* are available from Pocket Books. Maddy lives with her husband in Madison, Wisconsin.

Visit her Web site: www.maddyhunter.com.